THE BEACH HOUSE

BOOK 3

VICKY JONES
CLAIRE HACKNEY

HACKNEY & JONES

CONTENTS

ABOUT VICKY JONES

Vicky Jones was born in Essex, England. She is an author and singer-songwriter, with numerous examples of her work on iTunes and YouTube. At 20 years old she entered the Royal Navy. After leaving the Navy realizing she was drifting through life with no sense of direction, she wrote a bucket list of 300 things to achieve which took her traveling, facing her fears and going for her dreams. At the time of printing, she is two-thirds of the way through her bucket list.

One item on her list was to write a song for a cause. Her anti-bullying track called "House of Cards" is now on iTunes to download.

Writing a novel was on her bucket list, and through a chance writing competition at her local writing group, the idea for *Meet Me At 10* was born. Vicky hopes she can change hearts and minds due to some of the gritty themes of the book.

Vicky is a keen traveler, stemming from her days traveling the world in the Royal Navy, and has visited around 50 countries so far. She has also graduated from The Open University after studying part time for her degree in psychology and criminology—another bucket list tick! She is currently writing a book about her bucket list adventures, entitled 'Project Me, Project You', alongside planning and writing more fiction books and book marketing guides for self-published authors.

She now lives in Cheshire, splitting her time between there and visiting her family and friends back in Essex.

For more information on upcoming book releases, to tell us what you think of the books, or just to say hi, visit the sites below:

facebook.com/VickyJonesWriter

twitter.com/vickyjones7

instagram.com/vickytjones

youtube.com/hackneyandjones

ABOUT CLAIRE HACKNEY

Claire Hackney is a former English Literature, Drama and Media Studies teacher who, after attending a local writing group with Vicky and writing several of her own short stories over the years, has now decided to focus her career on full-time novel writing.

She is an avid historian and has thoroughly enjoyed researching different aspects of the 1950s for the 'Shona Jackson' trilogy of novels.

Claire is very much looking forward getting started on the many future writing projects she and Vicky have in the pipeline, including the up-coming 'D.I Rachel Morrison' thriller series and several standalone novels.

For more information on upcoming book releases, to tell us what you think of the books, or just to say hi, visit the sites below:

facebook.com/ClaireHackneyAuthor

twitter.com/clairehac

instagram.com/clairehackneyauthor

youtube.com/hackneyandjones

JOIN IN!

We'd love to invite you to join in with our ongoing adventures. In our newsletter, you will receive regular behind-the-scenes updates, beta reading opportunities, giveaways and much, much more!

Simply visit the site below and enter your email address so we know where to send your newsletter:

www.hackneyandjones.com

ALSO BY VICKY JONES AND CLAIRE HACKNEY

Shona: Book 1

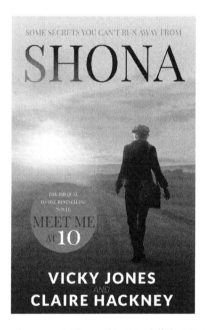

Everyone has a secret. Hers could get her killed... Mississippi, 1956. Shona Jackson knows two things—how to repair car engines and that her dark childhood secret must stay buried. On the run from Louisiana, she finds shelter in the home of a kindly old lady and a job as a mechanic. But a woman working a man's job can't avoid notice in a small town. And attention is dangerous, especially when it comes from one woman in particular...

ALSO BY VICKY JONES AND CLAIRE HACKNEY

Meet Me At 10: Book 2

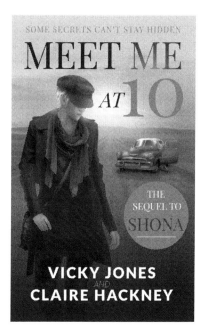

Four lives inextricably linked. Will tragic events part them forever? Shona Jackson is on the run again, forced to flee Mississippi and the town she'd called home. Arriving in Alabama, to continue her journey to safety, she convinces Jeffrey Ellis, the wealthy co-owner of a machinery plant, to give her a job. But when Chloe Bruce returns from college and is introduced to the workforce, there are devastating consequences for all those involved.

ALSO BY VICKY JONES AND CLAIRE HACKNEY

The Burying Place: Book 1

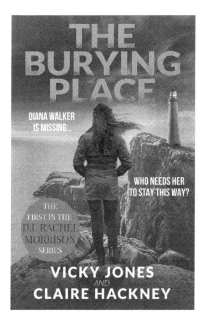

One high-profile case. No leads. No witnesses... And no body.
Amanda Walker's mother is missing. Detective Inspector
Rachel Morrison has no leads on the case and time is running
out. Amanda appeals to the public, but when no one comes
forward, she chooses to immerse herself within a murderous
underground group she believes is responsible for her mother's
disappearance. But will the group believe Amanda's cover
story? Or is time running out for her as well?

ALSO BY VICKY JONES

Bucket List Book I: Project Me, Project You

"Writing this book changed my life. Reading it could change yours." Back in 2011, suffering depression after leaving the Royal Navy, author and songwriter Vicky Jones embarked upon a life-changing bucket list, including 300 things to tick off over the course of the next decade of her life. This is the story of how this list came about, how it has helped her combat her depression, and how it can help you too.

THE BEACH HOUSE

PART 1: AUGUST 1958

Chapter 1

"Is it them?" Shona said. She whipped her neck around to look out of the back window and then back to look at Chloe whose knuckles were now white from her increased grip on the steering wheel.

"I think so," Chloe replied, her right foot pressing down on the gas pedal. Trying to keep composed, she kept her eyes fixed on the road, glancing up to her rearview mirror every few seconds. "I'd know that truck anywhere."

The dark green Ford pickup that had been following them for the last five miles on their way to the Mississippi border with Arkansas began to speed up.

"But that's impossible. They're murderers. The sheriff can't have let them out. And even if he had, would they *really* come all this way from Alabama?" Shona could feel her heart thumping as she wrapped her arms around the back of her seat and stared through the back window.

"We're the reason they lost their garage," Chloe replied, shaking her head with frustration. "But those Bullens have done so many favors for folks, I'd be surprised if strings *hadn't* been pulled. They've been in and out of jail so many times they're bound to know people." Chloe rammed the gas pedal in as far as it would go, causing the engine to roar even louder. "Come on, goddamn you!"

Shona looked down at her map. Locating Route 82, she ran her fingertip along the line. "This road goes on for thirty miles before a turnoff. We'll run out of gas before then if we're going at this pace. I knew we should have filled up when we last stopped." She looked back down at her map and frowned. "We've got what looks like a really long bridge to get across too. It's just up ahead. Less than a mile by my reckoning. There's nowhere to turn off until we get over it."

"A bridge?" Chloe said and gripped the wheel even tighter. She glanced up into the rearview mirror and licked her lips. "They're getting closer. Shona, I don't want to drive over a bridge. What if they try and ram us? We'll end up in the river." Her voice was shaking. Shona looked from side to side, through all of the windows, to see if there was any option for them to get off the road quickly, but neither side of the highway had any offshoots. It was featureless, save for a few trees and shrubs. Up ahead, she saw the steel jaws of a long gray cantilever bridge about to consume them.

"I got an idea," Shona said. "As soon as we hit the bridge, I want you to slow down."

"Slow down? Are you crazy?" Chloe replied, her brown eyes wide.

Shona's voice was eerily calm. "This engine is way more powerful than some pickup, but we're topped out right now. We need some lift." Shona nodded to the sign. "Here it is. The Benjamin G. Humphreys bridge. Chloe, do you trust me?"

"Of course I do."

"Then take your foot off the gas. Then, when I say so, floor it."

Chloe did as she was told. The Chevrolet began to slow down and, in turn, the green pickup crept closer, eating up the distance between them. Shona kept her eyes glued to the side mirror, waiting for the right moment. With their hearts in their mouths, the car began to cross the bridge, creeping more into the middle of the lane, just in case.

"Shona?" Chloe asked, her foot resting against the gas pedal.

"Now!" Shona ordered. They both recoiled with the force of the accelerating car. Thirty became fifty in moments, and the green pickup had no chance of keeping up. "That's it. We're nearly across the bridge. Don't slow down."

The tires thudded against every road joint, until they reached the sign welcoming them to Arkansas and thanking them for driving carefully.

"Look, there," Shona said. "A rest stop. We can pull in there. It's bound to have people there. They won't dare try anything then."

"Thank God," said Chloe, breathing a sigh of relief as she saw the sloping roof of the rest stop and its giant red and yellow sign. "Is the truck still following?"

"Yeah," Shona replied. She let a few moments pass by, the writing on the sign now readable. "Almost there. One, two, three. Now."

Chloe left it until the last possible moment before stomping on the brake and swinging the Chevrolet Deluxe skidding into the parking lot. Gravel and dust was churned up all around them, choking them momentarily. They both looked back up to the highway, waiting to see if the pickup would turn into the rest stop parking lot too. Seconds felt like hours as both Chloe and Shona stared. And waited.

"Please. Please, just drive past," Shona prayed quietly.

Chloe's hands, drenched in cold sweat, flexed around the steering wheel. Just as it looked as if the truck was slowing down to exit the highway, the male passenger leaned out of the window and made a lewd gesture towards Chloe. Whooping, he threw a beer can towards the Deluxe as the driver sped off along the road, passed the turnoff and into the distance.

"It wasn't them," Chloe said, resting her head heavily against the steering wheel, jumping when Shona lay a hand on the back of her neck. "Just some dumb punks."

"It's OK. We did the right thing. If it had been them then..." Shona tailed off, remembering that night she was almost murdered by Earl and Ernest Bullen. "We're safe, baby, no one is gonna chase us anymore. We got a new life now to look forward to. A new start. You OK?" Shona stroked the black string of Chloe's pink pebble necklace with her thumb, until after a few seconds she lifted her face from the steering wheel. It was wet with tears, her eyes red from the dust.

"That night, thinking you were dead, was the most terrified I'd ever been in my whole life. Even more scared than when Kyle..." She swallowed hard. "Did what he did to me."

"I know. But it's all OK now. Look at us. We're together. Those bastards are in jail, and Kyle? Well, he'll never see the light of day again, not with all the stuff the police had been dying to pin on him. They emptied the filing cabinet. We don't have to worry about anything other than enjoying our life together, Chloe. Just me and you. Forever. I promise. We're free now."

Shona leaned in, dying to kiss Chloe and comfort her further, but the car that pulled up near them made them both spring back into their seats.

"Well, not completely free. But there's a motel around the back there. Why don't we stay here tonight?" Shona flashed Chloe a smile that meant only one thing. Returning it, Chloe leaned over and grabbed her purse from the back seat.

"Back in a minute. I'll check us in."

"No, let *me*. You paid the last time, remember?" Shona insisted.

Chloe saw that smile again and blushed. "How could I forget? Our first night together."

"That's right. Well, it's my turn to treat you. I still got some money of my own. I'll be right back." Shona hopped out of the car and into the motel reception. Minutes later, she reappeared, jangling the room key.

Leaving the bigger bags they had in the trunk, they took what they needed for the night and headed to the motel room on the ground floor of the tired old block. Inside, the décor was pretty standard, the faded yellow wallpaper peeling at the corners. The two single beds were both draped in honey-colored comforters, the pillows looking less than plush. Between the two beds was a nightstand on which stood a chipped ceramic lamp complete with stained shade. At the far end of the room was a tiny bathroom, the mold-encrusted shower curtain just about visible through the sliding door. The room wasn't anywhere near as opulent as the Fortua had been, but this time it didn't matter.

Within seconds of the door closing behind them, they threw their overnight bags on the floor. Unable to resist any longer, Shona pushed Chloe up against the wall next to the door and began planting hot kisses on her neck, exactly in the spot where she knew it made her groan. Running her hands through Shona's hair, gripping it tightly, Chloe lifted her head up to meet her lips with her own. The force of her kiss made Shona stagger back, finally landing on one of the beds, with Chloe on top of her still kissing her. In one fluid movement, Shona rolled over so she was now lying on top. Pulling her lips away for a second, she swept her hand over Chloe's cheek and smiled at her, her blue eyes shining.

"God, you're so beautiful," she murmured. "There was so much I wanted to do that night. So much of you I wanted to explore. But I was so nervous, I didn't really know what I was doing."

Chloe gazed back at her, her hands still holding the back of her head, fingers stroking her messy blonde hair. "Are you nervous now?"

"No. Not anymore," Shona whispered back.

"Then what are you waiting for? Make love to me. The way you want to, the way you've always wanted to."

Shona didn't need to be told twice.

Shona and Chloe checked out of the motel just before dawn. With the sound of the morning birdsong in the air, they packed up the car and set off on the highway towards their next destination. Chloe had unclipped and lowered the roof on the Deluxe, letting the wind blow through their hair as they sped along in the glorious heat of the late summer sun.

"So what are we telling people? About who we are?" Shona asked.

"Well, I did think we could tell people we were sisters." Chloe paused and glanced over to Shona, taking in her baby blonde hair and bright blue eyes. "But we look nothing like each other." She smiled.

"That might be our only option, though, in the circumstances." Shona smiled at Chloe's confused reaction, her eyes twinkling. "No one will buy the idea that we're just friends. I can't keep my hands off you."

"But you think it's OK for you to do that if you're my *sister*?" Chloe said as she raised an eyebrow.

Shona blushed. "Oh yeah. I guess I didn't think that one through, did I?"

Chloe laughed. "It's OK, I knew what you meant. But either way, we're gonna have to be careful in plain sight. Lucky for us there are a lot of war widows around, so no one will bat an eyelid if they see my sister living with me now.

They'll just think my *poor husband* is lying in bits somewhere on a battlefield. Never to be seen again." A smile formed at the corners of Chloe's mouth, her finally feeling free from Kyle's vicious clutches. "And we can't have none of that caper you got going on there," she joked, nodding down at Shona's wandering hand which was now brushing the inside of Chloe's thigh.

"Can you blame me? I got the most gorgeous girl in all the world next to me." Heeding Chloe's words, she lifted her hand away and lay back in her seat. "You smell that air? Every mile we drive we're getting closer to the ocean, I know it." She stared off into the horizon then breathed in a huge lungful of air, letting it out slowly.

Their journey took them through the plush greenery of Arkansas, the landscape noticeably changing to drier, dustier plains as they drove day and night, weaving their way onwards through Oklahoma, Texas, New Mexico, Arizona and finally across the border into California, via the bridge over the Colorado river.

"Welcome to California. The Land of Milk and Honey," Chloe said, a glimmer of excitement in her tired eyes. It was just after seven o'clock that Thursday morning and their long journey was almost at an end. With their final destination ever closer now, she turned onto the highway that led straight to the coast. In the fields on either side of the road were swathes of yellow poppies blowing gently in the light breeze, still going strong in the late summer warmth.

"Do you know where we're going?" Shona asked, looking at all the road signs they passed along the way.

Staring straight ahead, Chloe nodded, the tiniest smile at the corner of her mouth. "Yes. I know exactly the place," she replied.

Passing through Greenfield, then Salinas, the scent in the air seemed to change hour by hour as Shona lifted her nose

7

and sniffed. The ocean was close; she could sense it. She closed her eyes and leaned her head back as the car ate up the miles.

"I wanted to surprise you with something. It's not far now," Chloe said, looking sideways at Shona, who was staring out of the window for her first longed-for glimpse of the ocean she'd craved to be near for so long.

Twenty minutes later, Chloe took a turnoff that began to lead down to a sandy path and there, at the end of it perfectly nestled next to the ocean, was a sight that made Shona gasp.

"What have you done?" she said, her mouth hanging open, her eyes wide.

"I made a few enquiries before we left Mississippi. I, well... I wanted you to have something special to come to after everything you've been through. I know this was your dream so..."

Chloe stopped the car and Shona, her legs feeling like jelly, climbed out of the car.

"All I need to do is go and see the realtor before they close at five and pay the deposit." Chloe reached out for Shona's hand. "It's ours, Shona. It's our new home."

Shona was in shock and put both hands up to her mouth. The beach house was an exact replica of the one where she'd spent a week back in 1956 with Dorothy down in Gulfport. It was almost identical to the postcard she'd bought as a memento of that week. Save for a lick of blue paint on the window frames and a touch-up of the white weatherboarding, it was just perfect.

Shona turned to Chloe, tears in her eyes, unable to believe what she was seeing. "How did you know?"

Chloe reached into her purse and took out the postcard of the beach house that had originally belonged to Shona, with numerous pinholes in each corner.

"When I saw Dorothy that first time, when I wanted to find out more about you, she let me stay the night in your old room. I saw the postcard pinned above your bed that you'd left.

Dorothy explained what happened with that Lucy girl, that she gave you her copy of the postcard to take with you. I somehow just knew it was important to you. When I left the next morning, I asked Dorothy if I could keep your postcard and she said 'yes', if I promised that one day I would make your dream a reality. So here we are."

Shona walked towards the beach house in a daze.

Chloe walked up behind her and whispered in her ear, "It's still early enough to go get the keys. You wanna stay in your new home tonight?"

"*Our* new home," Shona corrected. "Chloe, I don't know what to say. How can I ever show you just what this means to me?"

"Just make every day count. That's all I want, Shona. Just you and me, for always. In our forever home. Now, let's go get those keys."

Chapter 2

Sunnybrook was the name of the town only a mile up the road from the beach house. Just after they passed the welcome sign, they drove around the first corner of the town square, which was flanked on each side by small local businesses and the usual array of stores. After the town's garage came the local family butcher's, the drugstore and a small boutique hair salon. There was also a shoe repair shop, a candy store and a little bakery. At the end of that row was one of the roads leading out of town. Chloe continued to explore the town's amenities, pulling around the corner to the next side of the square where a smart-looking bar was situated.

"Looks like a nice place. Friendly. Named after the owner, it would seem. Bertie's," Shona said, reading the sign above the door of the bar.

The seating area underneath two blue and white striped awnings was populated by a small group of women laughing and fooling around. The deck area was immaculately scrubbed and presented, and there were small shrubs in planters at each edge of the front and umbrellas fixed to each bench seat. At the corner of that side of the square was the post office and next to that was a gorgeous little flower shop.

Nice, Chloe thought, remembering how much Shona loved pink roses.

Next door to the flower shop was the diner, then the grocery store. On the third corner of the square was the police station with only one patrol car parked outside, and the town's gas station adjacent to it. As Chloe did a second loop of the square, Shona pointed at the one place that had piqued her interest more than the others, the garage.

"Hey, you reckon there might be the chance of a job there?" Shona asked, her eyes keen.

"I dunno, what does that sign say?" They drove closer until Chloe could read it clearly. "Auction. Next Week. Hmm...well, maybe when the new owners open up?"

"Yeah, I guess," Shona replied, a little downcast. "How about that bar?" She pointed over to Bertie's. "Maybe I could get some work in there? Be a bit different to what I'm used to but I learn quick, so..."

Chloe laughed and gave her a cheeky smile. She refocused her eyes on the road, a thought crossing her mind as she drove around the town square. Spotting the realtors' office next to the flower shop, she pulled up in the nearest parking spot.

"I won't be a minute."

About twenty minutes later she reappeared holding a brown envelope and a big set of keys. Shona jumped in her seat like an excited puppy.

"For real? It's ours?" Shona grinned.

"Our new home. Bought outright. Cost almost all of the money I brought with us from my savings, but I don't care. No one can take it away from us."

Shona looked shocked. "You had *that* much money? In cash? In the car all this time?"

"I went to the bank before we set off, remember? My father used to put money in my account all the time for me, and there was my salary too that I hardly spent any of while I was with

Kyle. I had no friends to go out with. Well, apart from those few times we met up. But strawberry shakes aren't that expensive." Chloe smiled at the memory of her meetings with Shona in Ed's diner. Her face then hardened. "It's the least my father owes me after what he did. Oh, I know I could have been all proud and said I didn't want a penny from him, but I ain't stupid. That money is the key to our future, and it's mine by rights anyway. I see it as the inheritance I'll never get. And I can do so much more good with it than my father ever did. It buys us our dream, Shona. I asked the realtor to arrange for it to be furnished too. Nothing major, just the basics like a bed, couch, tables. Enough to get us started." Chloe's defiant expression melted into worry. "You ain't mad at me, are you?" She bit her lip. "I just wanted it to be perfect for you."

Shona waited for a few seconds of contemplation, before her face lit up. "No, of course I'm not mad. I'm too excited to be proud right now too. You call it inheritance from your father, but you know what I call it? I call it compensation. Come on, what are we waiting for? Get us back there!" Shona shrieked until Chloe turned the key in the ignition and floored the gas pedal, sending them roaring off back along the road they came in on.

"You OK?" Shona asked, her excitement to get home marred by concern for Chloe's strange silence on the way back to the beach house.

"Yeah, I'm fine," Chloe replied, fidgeting in her seat. "Just had a funny feeling pass over me a few minutes ago. It's nothing, probably just butterflies." She smiled and pulled into the front yard of the house. Before the car had even fully stopped, Shona jumped out and raced up to the porch steps.

Chloe, however, exited the car much more tentatively. Her face creased in confusion as she looked back down at her seat. Oblivious, Shona began bouncing around the veranda that bordered the perimeter of their new home, listing off the tasks she couldn't wait to start doing to fix up the house. As she reached the porch steps again after a full circuit, she looked over to Chloe, whose face had turned pale. The smile fading on her own face, Shona walked over and saw what Chloe was staring down at.

A small patch of scarlet blood had stained the white leather driving seat.

"What's that?" Shona asked. Chloe remained silent, as if in a state of shock. "Are you OK?" Shona reached out for Chloe's hand, her touch waking Chloe out of her daze.

"Huh? Oh, yeah. I'm fine. At least I think I am." Chloe pulled at the back of her lemon yellow cotton skirt.

"Is it your time?"

Chloe shook her head. "No, it's not due yet. I felt a little discomfort down there, when I got back into the car before. I was just so excited to show you the keys that I guess I must have stretched my leg too far getting in my seat."

"You're still healing...from *that* night that Kyle..." Shona paused, her fists clenching as if by automatic response to the thought of what Kyle did to Chloe. She lay a gentle hand on Chloe's shoulder.

Chloe nodded. "Maybe."

"Or...do you think it was me, last night? Did I hurt you?" Shona's voice quivered as the thought crossed her mind.

"No, not at all," Chloe reassured. "I'm sure it was just me forgetting I have to be careful for a little while, with moving too sharply. Honestly, Shona, you are the gentlest, most considerate person I could ever wish to share my body with. It'll be fine, I promise."

"I swear, if I ever see that bastard again, I will kill him for what he did," Shona blurted out.

Seeing Chloe visibly shaken by the memory, Shona softened and wrapped her arms around her. She led Chloe to the porch swing and sat her down. "Don't worry, I'll be OK," Chloe said. "I'd better go clean myself up," she added, standing up and walking into the house to the bathroom.

"OK, baby, I'll take care of the car seat," Shona replied.

Half an hour later, they strolled down to see the beach for the first time. Nothing but the brightest blue ocean was up ahead, filling the space between the edge of the powdery white sand and the horizon. They sat down on the beach and both took in a huge lungful of sea air.

"This place is just perfect," Shona began. "I feel so free here. So safe."

Chapter 3

C hloe and Shona strolled down the beach, feeling the warm water lapping between their toes. They sat down on a blanket and stared out onto the horizon, catching a glimpse of a flock of seagulls diving for their lunch. The sunlight danced across the surface of the ocean.

"I love it here," Chloe said, exhaling. "I feel so great wearing these clothes too." She pulled at her loose skirt and cotton undershirt. "I don't have to wear those god-awful skin-tight skirts anymore. I couldn't breathe in those things. It feels so amazing to have the sand between my toes."

Shona laughed. "I didn't see any problem with those skin-tight skirts. From where I was standing you looked pretty amazing. That first day I saw you on that balcony, well. You didn't wanna know what I was thinking." Chloe swatted Shona playfully. "Yep, looking up at you on that balcony? I knew I was in trouble," Shona continued.

Chloe leaned back into Shona's lap, watching the calm water roll up and down on the shore, the crashing waves far off in the distance.

"Can I ask you something?" Shona said.

"Of course."

"Did you ever in your wildest dreams think you would one day settle down with a woman?"

Chloe sat up and gazed deep into Shona's blue eyes, surprised by the frankness of the question. "You're my soulmate, Shona. You had me intrigued every time I saw you in that canteen. I couldn't face being apart from you. It was like torture."

Shona pulled Chloe into an embrace and kissed her. "I wanna grow old with you, Chloe. I never wanna be without you, not now that I've found my soulmate too. I never thought I'd ever find peace and here it is. And it's all thanks to you."

Later that evening, Shona and Chloe sat talking over what name they should put on the house deeds. They knew they couldn't use Jackson or Bruce as that would be far too easy for someone to look up if they wanted to find them.

"What about Clark?" asked Chloe.

Shona grinned, tears in her eyes remembering Dorothy. "It's perfect. Shona and Chloe Clark. Sisters," Shona added with a wink.

Chloe leaned over to Shona. "No sisters do what we've been doing these last few nights in there." She lifted her eyes in the direction of their bedroom. Shona's cheeks reddened. Then her smile faded.

"Chloe, I read a news article a few weeks ago saying that all homosexual people were sick. Am I ill?"

"Well," Chloe began, "if you are, then I don't ever want you to get better." She leaned over the table and kissed her. "Now, do you want to fill this in or shall I?"

Shona grabbed the pen from Chloe's hand and wrote their names down on the house deeds in black bold ink.

After dinner, Shona and Chloe sat on the porch swing facing the ocean.

"Hey, I was thinking," Chloe began. "Maybe I should get a

different car? It's quite distinctive and I don't really wanna remember the reasons I got it," she added.

"Sure. Probably for the best in case anybody is still looking for us. You stand out like a sore thumb." Shona chuckled. "What will you get instead?"

"Oh, I don't know yet. Something more functional. That car ain't worth a damn on the sand out there."

"I know." Shona paused. "Beautiful beast, though. I remember the first time I saw it up close." She laughed and nudged Chloe with her shoulder, recalling her painful first introduction to the Chevrolet's shiny red hood.

"Yeah, I know. You ain't never let me forget *that* one, have you?" Chloe nudged her back.

"I still got the bump," Shona replied, rubbing the back of her head.

Chapter 4

"What you doing?" Chloe asked, finding Shona at the kitchen table hunched over a notepad.

"I found some nice writing paper in the drawer over there, thought I might write to Elbie. Tell him we made it outta Daynes after all. I was gonna give him our new address so he could come visit. Once we got that spare room all decorated nice like," Shona replied, her eyes glowing.

"That's a lovely idea. Make sure you say hi for me." Chloe paused and looked down at the letter Shona was writing. "I guess I should write to Mother. Let her know I'm OK. Even though she's an old dragon, she'll still be worried she hasn't heard anything. More so because she won't know what to tell the townsfolk."

"Are you sure? If you send it from here, she'll see the postmark and know where we are," Shona remarked.

"OK, maybe that was a bad idea, then." She turned to wander back to the living room.

"Hey, I got an idea. Why don't I ask Elbie if he minds sending the letter to your mom for you? I could put it in the envelope when I send this letter. That way the postmark will say Tennessee."

Chloe turned around, her eyes wide. "You think he would?"

"Of course he would, it's Elbie. You know how much he loves you."

Chloe's face melted into a relieved smile. She walked back over to the table and wrapped her arms around Shona.

"I was thinking, I might drive into town tomorrow morning and have another look around to see if anyone's hiring. I'm still gonna need a job, especially if that garage isn't open for business at the moment." Shona leaned against the frame of the bathroom door just before bedtime, aiming her voice through the thin strip of light that glowed through the edges. "I could get some work at the grocery store, maybe, or in the—" She stopped, hearing Chloe retching. "You OK in there?" Shona tapped on the door, then tried the handle. Just as it clicked open, the door pulled away from her and Chloe appeared, dabbing her face with a towel.

"I'm OK. I think," she said, running her hand through her hair.

"Something you ate, d'ya think?" Shona asked, stroking Chloe's arm.

"Maybe."

"Well, I reckon we should see how you are in the morning. Then, if you still feel bad, we should see about getting you in to see a doctor. Can't be too careful, not with that flu going around last year. Paper's said it killed thousands." Shona stopped talking after catching a sharp look fired her way. "Oh, I didn't mean that... I'm sure it's nothing as serious as..." Shona ran an embarrassed hand over the back of her head.

Chloe grinned. "Honey, stop digging yourself a hole there. I'm gon' go to bed. You coming?"

"Yeah, sure. I just gotta go lock up. You go, I'll bring you some peppermint tea."

"OK, thank you. Don't be long now," Chloe wrapped her shawl around her shoulders and disappeared into the bedroom.

∾

Chloe slipped her sunglasses on, dropped the roof of the car and sped off up the sandy drive to the road leading into town. In five minutes, she was there, stopping off at an ice cream stand halfway. With one hand on her ice cream cone and the other on the wheel, she sang loudly to the tune on her radio with the wind blowing through her shoulder length brown hair loosely wrapped around a piece of fabric. She didn't wear much makeup in the days since they'd left Daynes, but what she did wear accentuated her naturally stunning looks, large chocolate brown eyes and full red lips.

Driving past the large sign reading 'Welcome to Sunnybrook', Chloe let the relief flow through her. They really had been lucky to find a town that looked and felt every bit of its name. Flower baskets and green spaces greeted her as she drove along the road through the square, passing the garage that had piqued Shona's interest. Stopping momentarily outside it, Chloe pulled down her sunglasses as a thought crossed her mind. Pushing them back on her face, she set off again, passing a bakery which was emitting the most mouthwatering smells imaginable. Fresh baked bread, cakes and pies wafted on the sweet Californian morning air, making Chloe stop again and inhale.

After making a mental note to pop back there later to pick up Shona's favorite chicken pie for dinner, Chloe pulled back around the square and found a parking space outside the drugstore, which was next door to the doctor's office. She climbed out of the car, took another glance around the town square and the lovely green space contained in the middle of it, and walked into the doctor's office, the little bell connected to the door tinkling above her.

"Thank you, Doctor Thomas, you've really put my mind to rest now. I thought it was gon' be bad news," said a young woman holding a small boy's pudgy hand. "He has been so upset." She softened her gaze at the young, handsome doctor standing in front of her.

"My pleasure, Mrs. King. Nothing but a bad sprain. Try to keep Billy from using it too much for a coupla days," Doctor Thomas added, a twinkle in his soft brown eyes.

Mrs. King turned around, then yanked on her son's good arm. "Billy. For goodness' sake. You ask Doctor Thomas if you can have one before you go takin' one," she barked down at Billy who was trying to grab a sweet.

Billy looked up at Doctor Thomas with his large blue eyes. "Please, doctor. May I have one?" he asked, wiping his nose on the back of his hand.

Doctor Thomas laughed then reached down to pick up the boy. "Of course, sonny, you've been such a brave soldier today. If you'd been in my unit, back in '44, I'd be very proud of your conduct today." He let Billy reach the jar of candy canes, then placed him back down on the ground and saluted him. Billy saluted back, then munched on his candy cane.

"Say thank you, Billy," Mrs. King prompted.

"Thank you, Doctor Thomas," Billy mumbled, the candy cane in his mouth. "When I grow up, I wanna be a doctor just like Doctor Thomas," he said as he was walked out of the office, his mother blushing as she said her farewell.

As Doctor Thomas headed back into his room, his path was crossed by two women.

"So, Marion, when do you suppose you'll be able to get the money, then? This idea of yours sounds just amazing. And just what this town needs," the older of the two women said to the other as she walked back behind her post at the reception desk.

"I have the money. I'm just waiting for the auction next week. That old garage across the street will make the perfect daycare center. It has just the right dimensions and that beautiful lil' wildflower garden behind it. Just needs a little imagination to smarten that building up is all," Marion continued.

"Well, I think it's fabulous, don't you, Doctor Thomas?" the receptionist gushed, fluttering her eyes at him.

"Yes I do, Blanche. But you know what'd be even more fabulous?" He paused as both women gazed into his bright green eyes.

"What?" they both said in unison.

"If you, Marion, would take Mister Gordon through for his appointment and you, Blanche, would see to this nice young lady who's been standing at your desk for the last five minutes waiting for you to finish your conversation," he said with a wink. "Sorry to keep you waiting, Miss...?"

"*Mrs.* Clark. Chloe Clark. I'm new in town. I just came down to register myself and my...um... sister, Shona. Clark."

"Well, then, Mrs. Clark. While you're here, why don't I give you a little check over, blood pressure, general health and all that. Won't take a moment. Blanche, could you help Mrs. Clark fill in the basics on the form, then send her through to me, OK?"

"Sure thing, Doctor Thomas."

Chloe took the pen from the receptionist and filled out the registration card, handing it over to Blanche when she'd finished.

"Why thank you, Mrs. Clark. You can go straight through," Blanche said, smiling as she filed Chloe's card in her Rolodex.

Chloe nodded her thanks and walked over to Doctor Thomas's door.

"Come in," called the voice inside.

Chloe opened the door and was invited to sit by the doctor.

"Nothing to worry about today, Mrs. Clark. I'll just take a blood sample, tick a few boxes, make sure you're fighting fit, that's all." He reached across to his telephone. "Marion, could you come in here, please?"

Marion came in with a small dish and needle. She wrapped a thin rubber band around Chloe's arm and pulled it tight. "Won't hurt a bit, now hold still," Marion said, her voice not in the least bit reassuring.

"Ouch," Chloe said as the needle pricked her smooth, pale skin.

"Now, you hold still. I gotta take a bit more," Marion scolded.

Chloe looked over to Doctor Thomas who nodded to check she was OK. His eyes seemed to glow brighter the longer he looked at her.

"All done. Just press this cotton ball to your skin for a few minutes and you'll be fine."

"Thank you," Chloe whispered.

"We should have the results in a few days. Pop back then when you've settled in your new home," Doctor Thomas said as he walked Chloe out of his office. "And ask your sister to come in to register too when she has a minute. Shona, was it?"

Chloe nodded, then said her goodbyes and headed back out onto the street.

Marion stood by the reception desk sorting through patient notes. "Hmmm...well, who knew *he* was an alcoholic. And this guy? Well, I'd want that checked too if I was him." Picking another file out of the pile on the desk, Marion opened it and let out a low whistle. "I *knew* she was cheating on her husband. He can't have kids but she's three months gone. Well, I'll be damned..."

"Marion, can you please concentrate on your job, not the

lives of others in this town?" Doctor Thomas's stern voice sounded behind her.

Spinning around, Marion found herself face to face with her boss, who looked more disappointed in her than angry.

"Yes, Doctor Thomas. My apologies."

Chapter 5

Edie Foster sat in the corner of Bertie's bar reading from a large, heavy looking encyclopedia. Every few minutes she let out a low whistle as she came across an even more amazing fact.

"Woah. Well, I'll be a monkey's uncle. Hey Bertie, did you know two thirds of the world is actually water? That's insane. I mean, there are billions of people on this planet. How do we all even fit on a third?" She pulled off her cat-eye glasses and looked over to the bar area where the owner, Bertha, known as Bertie to everyone in the town, was counting the stock and filling out an order form. Bertie was in her mid-thirties, short and stocky, with slicked back black hair.

"Yeah, everyone knows that, you lemonhead." Bertie leaned a chubby tattooed arm on the bar, smiling when she saw Edie roll her eyes. "Now quit bashing my ears with all these facts, will ya?"

"OK," Edie replied.

"The others will be here in a minute so budge up outta my seat," Bertie barked, walking around the edge of the bar and motioning for Edie to move.

"Hey ladies...and Bertie," a voice rang out from the doorway. Two women entered the bar, one wearing a blue men's suit jacket and trousers, the other wearing black denim jeans, a plaid shirt and a wide-brimmed black hat, her lank dark hair hanging loose. "Still working on that duck butt there, Bert?" the suited woman pointed up at Bertie's hair.

"Ha ha, very funny, Dee," Bertie replied, mock-grinning to the woman in the blue suit. She raked a lock of hair out of her eyes and leaned her large body back into the booth. "Where you two been anyway? I said to be here by eleven. I gotta open up soon," Bertie's piercing blue eyes stared at the two latecomers.

"Hey, don't flip your lid. Blame Lula here. She's in one of her moods again. Took me ages to persuade her to get out of her pit." Dee nodded her head to the other woman who appeared to have pulled her hat down lower on her head.

"What's eating you today, Lula?" Bertie asked, her voice less harsh than it was towards Dee.

"Nothin'. Just feelin' annoyed today. Broke another string on my guitar," Lula mumbled, leaning her body back against the bar, one foot flat against the mahogany wood. She looked down at the floor as she nibbled on her fingernail.

"Well, I got some news that might get us all jazzed around here."

"Yeah?" Dee asked, sitting down in the booth opposite Bertie and Edie. Lula sauntered over and sat with a thud next to her.

"Yeah," Bertie continued. "You know that garage across the street? Well, I finally got the dough together to put in an offer at the auction next week. My sister came through with the loan I asked her for, so I can put that together with the money from this place the bank agreed to free up. So come next Monday I'll be there, front and center." Bertie's round face broke out into a huge grin. She wasn't attractive in the conventional sense of the word, but her smile now accentuated the light in her blue eyes.

Lula looked up from the edge of the table she was fiddling with. "That's great news, Bertie. So what kinda business you gonna run there?"

"Ooh, maybe you could open up a record shop or something?" Edie suggested.

"Or a place that sells guitar strings. I'm sick of havin' to go across to the next town every time I break one," Lula said, scrunching up her face.

"Or...I could reopen the garage," said Bertie. The women around the table nodded as if the suggestion was too obvious to even consider.

"Well, I guess that would be the most sensible thing to do," Edie remarked. She looked at her watch. "Shit, I'd better hit the road. My shift starts in an hour. I gotta get home to change." She reached over to where her polka dot jacket was lying and wrapped it around her. "Later, girls. Congratulations again, Bertie."

"I'll walk you out," Bertie offered.

As they reached the doorway, they saw two police officers standing on the sidewalk staring at the bar and muttering to each other.

"G'mornin', officers. How may I assist you on this fine morning?" asked Bertie, the sarcasm in her voice staying just on the right side of polite.

"Now, don't play the innocent with me..." the first police officer hesitated, "lady." He put his hands on his hips. "Deputy Lawrence and I know what kinda place this is and I have to say we don't care for it too much." The young officer stuck out his chin.

"What Danvers here means is we have eyes and ears all around this town and for too long you've been encouragin' the *wrong* type of clientele to this place." Deputy Lawrence chewed his gum, waiting for a response from Bertie. She said nothing.

"You and your kind ain't a good fit for this town. We're

gonna make it so you go out of business real soon," Officer Danvers added.

Bertie cleared her throat and considered every word she was about to speak. "Deputy Lawrence." She looked him in the eye, then looked at Danvers. "What is it you suppose goes on in here?" She folded her thick arms across her large chest. "I serve good beer, play good sounds and my apple pie is the talk of the town. Everyone who comes in here gets the same warm welcome, from families to couples just wanting a great night out." She smiled as she got to the important part of her well-rehearsed speech. "I pay my taxes on time, comply with all licensing regulations and never stay open past the curfew." She watched their faces harden, knowing she was right. "Boys, I'm a straight down-the-line businesswoman just trying to earn a crust. And you fellas are welcome here anytime. First draft's on the house."

Lawrence and Danvers grunted and walked back to their patrol car, leaving Edie to sidle up behind Bertie and grab her around the shoulders.

"Nicely done, Bert. Although you know as well as I do there ain't nothing *straight* about this place," she said out of the corner of her mouth before sauntering off.

Pursing her lips at Edie's cheeky comment, Bertie exhaled. She'd seen off the latest confrontation with the law, but they kept coming back. Looking over to the garage she was planning to buy, she smiled. "I'll show them knuckleheaded cops they can't keep me down," she whispered to herself.

Behind her, Lula and Dee appeared, looking concerned. "What did those germs want now?" Lula asked, wrinkling her nose as if she'd caught a stench of shit in the air.

"Oh, just the usual." Bertie looked past Dee's shoulder over to the garage and stopped smiling, noticing something she'd missed before.

"What?" Dee asked.

"The auction sign ain't there no more," Bertie replied, her eyes scanning the garage parking lot. "I got the number for the vendor. I'll give him a call see what's going on."

"OK, well, we'd better split too. I gotta drive this one into the next town for that damn guitar string. Otherwise I'll have to stare at that miserable face all day," Dee said, playfully jostling Lula, who scowled back at her.

"See you later tonight, yeah?" Bertie replied, her eyes still fixed on the vacant space left where the auction sign once was.

Chapter 6

It was late afternoon by the time Shona saw dust and sand blowing up on the horizon at the end of their tiny track leading to the main road. A heavy rumble filled the air but the sight she was expecting to see was puzzlingly different. Stepping outside, Shona hopped down the three steps from the veranda onto the front garden, hands on hips as a faded blue pickup truck trundled towards the beach house. Her eyes widened as she realized who was driving it. Speechless, she watched the driver hop out carefully and slam the rickety door shut, then again until it finally stayed put.

"What do you think? A peach, ain't she?" Chloe announced, wiping her sweaty brow and grinning. She walked over to Shona and linked arms with her. "Come on, I'll show you."

Chloe led Shona up to the truck and pointed out all of its features, including the hook and winch on its tail.

"OK...I'm confused. This is great an' all, but where's the Chevy?" Shona asked, her blue eyes wide.

"I sold it." Chloe stepped back from the truck and spread her arms out wide.

Shona stood motionless, trying to process what Chloe was telling her. "And you bought *this* hunk of junk instead?" Shona's jaw dropped. "Are you crazy? That car's worth ten, no, twenny of these."

Chloe stood smiling at Shona's animated reactions.

"Well, that settles it then. I'm gonna have to get a job as soon as possible. I didn't realize we were so low on money that you had to sell the car. I thought you were gonna swap it for something of the same value. Jeez, this place must have cost too much for you." Shona paced the sandy ground between the truck and the beach house, running her hand through her blonde hair.

"Come with me. I got a surprise for you," Chloe said, climbing back into the truck and starting the engine. It groaned and spluttered as the thick diesel chugged through the pipes.

"Where we going?"

"Just get in and quit bellyaching. It'll be worth it, I promise," Chloe replied, her brown eyes twinkling with excitement.

As they pulled out of the driveway and onto the road, Shona looked over to Chloe, her eyes moist. "I swear I'll find some work. It's my job to provide for *you*, for us and I won't stop until I find something. I don't wanna live off you forever. I got my pride. You didn't need to sell that car, honey; I just needed a bit more time."

By the time Shona had finished her speech, Chloe had already made it to town and had pulled up at the side of the road. She turned the engine off and looked at Shona. "I know, Shona, but I didn't want you to have just any old job working for someone who don't appreciate how good a worker you really are. So, I reckon it's about time you had something of your own."

Chloe looked past Shona's head out onto the sidewalk and nodded at the building they were parked outside. The familiar 'For Sale' board had been removed, as had the notice of the upcoming auction. "It's yours." Shona turned around and stared behind her at what Chloe was looking at. In shock, she fumbled for the truck's door handle and stepped onto the sidewalk.

"You bought the garage? For me?" she said, her eyes welling up with stunned tears.

Chloe jumped out behind her wanting nothing more than to wrap Shona's trembling body in her arms, but she had to be mindful of anyone watching them. She rested a limp hand on Shona's forearm. "Yes. Well, I bought the lease for now, but I know you'll make it work. And one day we can buy it outright. I wanted you to be in charge for once. You can do things your way now, hire the people you want to. And no one will *ever* say you can't 'work in a place like this' ever again." She squeezed Shona's arm gently.

"But how? How did you afford it? After buying the house, where did...?" As soon as she'd asked the question, and looked back at their new truck, the answer became clear to Shona.

"You think I'd accept any less for that Chevy than what it was worth? I drive a hard bargain, you know. Probably the only thing working for my father actually taught me. I used the money I had left from my savings and put it together with what I got for the car, then went over and put an offer to the vendor. I might have used my charm on the vendor of this place to get him to take it off the market a week before the auction. And damn, he even threw in the pickup for free." Chloe giggled.

Shona's face erupted into the most beautiful smile Chloe had ever seen. "I got my own garage? Like for real?"

Chloe leaned into whisper into Shona's ear. "For real, baby. I love you so much."

"I love you too," Shona whispered back, then walked over to the garage and ran her hand over each surface she came into contact with.

"What are you gonna call it?" Chloe called after her.

"Clark's Autos," Shona replied, not even pausing to think about it. "Had it on my mind since I worked at Wreckers. Swore to myself if I was ever lucky enough to get my own place I'd call it that. Plus it makes more sense than ever now, with our new surname."

"Perfect," Chloe replied, her heart bursting to see Shona grin back at her as she disappeared around the back of the garage to explore further.

Chapter 7

O ver on the freeway outside of Sunnybrook the next morning, a car was being flagged down by a patrol car. Sheriff Everett flashed his lights three times until the Buick he was following rolled to a stop. Everett climbed out of the car, fixed his hat and strode over to the Buick, his baton strapped to his utility belt hanging loosely by his side. He tapped gently on the Buick's driver's side window. The young man inside lowered the glass and smiled up at the sheriff.

"Gee Sheriff, I'm real sorry. Was I going much over the limit?" The young man was dressed in army-issue fatigues, his duffel bag slung in the back and a small jewelry box perched on the passenger seat.

"You do know it's fifty back there, son?" the middle-aged sheriff scolded, his right eyebrow raised. He took another look around the contents of the young soldier's car.

"What was I doing?" he asked, both hands still clamped to the top of the steering wheel.

"Eighty-five. You escaping the old lady or something?" The sheriff went to take out his notebook.

"Man, really? Sheriff, I am so sorry. You see, I just got out on leave and I ain't seen my girl in nearly six months." His face reddened. "I was gon' propose to her this afternoon. I guess I just got a little too excited. But fair's fair, I did the wrong thing and I'm truly sorry, sir." The young soldier's eyes fell to his lap in shame.

Sheriff Everett paused and put his notebook back away. "Well, I guess no harm's been done here. But you just mind yourself, boy. I don't wanna have to have your body towed out of that ravine further up there, then have to tell your sweetheart the bad news."

The soldier looked up at the sheriff, his face beaming with relief. "You mean it? I can go?"

"Yeah, go on now, get."

"Thank you so much, sir. I won't forget this." The soldier saluted the sheriff.

"Just you be safe out there, you hear? And good luck with that," Everett replied, nodding over to the ring box he'd just noticed. The soldier blushed, then started up his engine. Everett banged his palm on the roof of the Buick as the soldier pulled away slowly.

Chapter 8

"So then one faggot says to the other, 'well, ain't that just a pain in the ass' and the first one says, 'you'd be used to that by now, won't ya'."

Deputy Lawrence's guttural laugh reverberated around the police station as he told his tired, worn out joke for the millionth time to the younger officers congregating around the coffee pot stand. Sheriff Everett walked back into the station just in time to hear the punchline.

"Lawrence. How many more times have I got to tell you about that kinda language? My office. Now."

Lawrence smirked at the other guys around him as soon as Everett's back was turned. Pretending to ham it up like a scolded toddler, he ran his hand through his thinning blond hair and followed his boss into his office, the door slamming behind him.

"What the hell was all that about out there? I've told you before about speaking your views on the homosexual community out loud. What they do in private is none of our business, y'hear?"

"But sir, what they do is illegal. Not to mention immoral. That not matter to you?" Lawrence hung his hands on his hips.

"If it's done in public then yes, that's our duty as officers of the law to keep these streets safe. But I am not about to waste my valuable time policing what they do behind closed doors. Do you understand me, boy?" Everett's pale blue eyes were sharp.

"Sorry, sir, won't happen again," Lawrence replied, a hint of sarcasm in his thin, reedy voice.

"Look, son, when you first came here I promised your mother I'd train you up to be a good, honest lawman. Hell, you're almost thirty years old, Jake. You're not a teenage boy, so quit making stupid jokes which are only gonna get people's backs up around here. And while I'm on the subject of your conduct, can you tell me why I'm getting reports lately of you being a son of a bitch to people around town, huh?"

Lawrence didn't answer.

"You work for these people, not to make their lives more difficult than some of them already have it," Everett continued. "You wear that badge to protect and serve, not to strike fear into them, and you would do well to remember that. This is your last warning, Jake. I want you to quit it, OK? No more throwing your weight around this town. Do I make myself clear?" Everett's voice was calm and measured, but the annoyance at having to repeat his stance on these matters yet again to Lawrence was tangible.

"Crystal, sir. May I go now?" Lawrence replied, his previous swagger diminished slightly at the mention of his mother.

Everett answered with a simple cock of his head towards the door.

Shona had been in the small tool shed just behind the beach house for well over two hours when Chloe, curiosity getting the better of her finally, decided to take her an ice cold tea and to

37

see what she was up to. As she reached the door she paused, listening in to hear the hammering of nails into what sounded like heavy boards of wood.

"What are you making?" Chloe asked, sneaking up behind Shona who almost squashed her thumb with the hammer as it slipped away from a nail.

"Where did you come from? You gave me a fright," Shona scolded, her hand pressed against her chest.

"I heard you making a racket out here so I came to see…" she paused and bit the corner of her lip when she saw Shona raise an eyebrow. "OK, you got me. I missed you, is all. That so bad?" She handed Shona the glass of tea.

"No, course not. Come see what I made for the garage. I had this idea, y'see. I thought it might be a nice gesture, what do you think?" Shona clasped hold of Chloe's hand and pulled her into her.

Looking down at the sign Shona had made, Chloe read the words she'd painted on it and smiled. "It's perfect. What a lovely thought, honey. It might even make the townsfolk a little bit more forgiving when they find out it was me who got the auction called off."

"Yeah, if there are any two people who understand how small towns can hold a grudge it's us. We got a new start here, Chloe. We should do everything we can to make it as friendly a home as we can. Keep our heads down. It's important to me to get it right this time, you know?"

"I know. How about we go over there tomorrow, face the music? We could put the sign up and start to get ready for our grand opening," Chloe said, clasping her hands together with excitement.

"Sure, the paint will be dry by then. You know what?"

"What?"

Shona stood staring at Chloe, her hands on her hips as she gazed at her, her eyes glowing. "I just cannot believe I have my own business to run, just how I wanna run it. And this place. This beautiful beach house." Shona stopped to wipe a tear from her eye with the back of a paint-smeared hand. "And you. The girl of my dreams, standing right there in front of me. I got everything I ever wanted. I don't want anything ever to change how I feel right here, right now. This is perfect."

"I know," Chloe said. "But after all we've been through, I think we deserve a little happiness." She laughed, then added, "and a little smooth sailing would be nice too. A quiet life for once, huh?"

Chapter 9

Chloe pulled the blue pickup into the garage parking lot, then, after getting out, she and Shona began discussing which task to tackle first.

"I think I'll hammer in my sign out front over there, try and get the locals on my side from the start, huh?" Shona said.

"Good idea." Chloe pulled out the keys to the garage from her purse. "But first, don't you wanna take a look inside?" She dangled the keys out to Shona.

Shona stopped and reached out to take the keys. Holding them for a minute, she fought back tears once again. She pulled Chloe into an impromptu embrace, holding her close for just that little bit too long before realizing. "Come on then, what are we waiting for?"

Shona almost dragged Chloe by the hand over to the huge garage doors and slipped the key into the padlock, then lifted the heavy chain through the handles. Pulling open the solid wooden door, she gasped as she took her first look inside.

"Looks great," Chloe commented. "Listen, I'll let you look around. Will you be OK here for a little while? I just gotta pop back over to the doctor's office. They said they'd have my results back by now."

"Oh yeah, OK. Hope they don't find nothing. But you seemed better this last week or so. Maybe it wasn't that flu after all," Shona replied.

"Yeah, better safe than sorry though. I'll pick up some dinner on the way back if you like?"

"Sounds good. I think I'll go over to the next town to get some parts to get that contraption working again." Shona cocked her head back to the car lift inside the garage which looked as if it was missing a few vital chains and rubber grips.

"OK, well don't be late, I'm in the mood for celebrating tonight," Chloe replied with a wink.

Shona's face reddened. "Shhh...folks might hear you," she said, looking around her. "Are you sure you don't want me to come with you?"

"No, it's alright. I'll walk back, don't worry. You go run your errands and get home to me as quick as you can," Chloe said, then turned on her heel to head through the green space at the center of the town square. As Chloe disappeared out of Shona's sight, an old man wearing beige slacks and a green shirt shuffled up behind and tapped Shona on the shoulder.

"G'mornin' sir, how can I help you?" Shona asked looking down at him.

The white-haired old man squinted up at her. "Am I readin' your sign right there, young lady? The new owner o' this place offerin' to fix war veterans' and police cars for free?" His face was open and friendly, his inquisitive gray eyes sharp.

"Yes sir, that's right. All services and repairs done at no cost for all military and lawmen," Shona replied.

"Oh, well, you be sure to tell the owner that that's one of the kindest gestures ever made in this town. The last guy never did nothin' for free. The new guy's most definitely welcome around here. What's his name, miss?"

"Shona Clark, proprietor of Clark's Autos at your service,

sir," Shona replied, holding out her hand for the old man to shake.

"You're the new owner?" The old man looked taken aback with surprise as Shona nodded, but his wrinkly eyes still twinkled. "It's a pleasure to meet ya, young lady. I hope you have a lotta success with this place." He shook Shona's hand, his grip as tight as he could manage, then shuffled away after tipping his cap to her.

"One down, just the rest of the town to go," Shona muttered to herself.

"Well, hello there, Mrs. Clark, and how are you today?" Doctor Thomas greeted, holding out his broad, tanned hand for Chloe to shake.

"Good morning, Doctor. I was just wondering if you had my blood test results back." Chloe asked, seating herself opposite the doctor, who in turn sat at his desk.

"We do, yes." He took out a brown file from his desk drawer, laid it down in front of him, then placed his elbows on the desk.

After a lengthy pause, Chloe's brow began to prickle with sweat. She wiped it away. "Well, come on now, don't leave a girl in suspense." She laughed nervously, then waited a few seconds more for the doctor to open his file. He did so, watching her.

"Well, when we took the sample we weren't looking for anything in particular, just a routine check for new patients, that sort of thing." He paused.

"And?" Chloe's tone this time was a little more pinched. "Did you...?"

"Yes, Mrs. Clark, we did. We found something."

When Shona returned home that evening, the sun was almost setting. The sky was all different shades of pinks and purples and, as she exited the truck, she picked the bunch of red roses off the back seat and stared into the horizon for a moment. The view from the beach house was truly one of the finest she had ever seen. Even the one in Gulfport back on her vacation with Dorothy hadn't had the same effect on her. Everything was perfect, Shona thought, slamming the truck door behind her and hopping up the steps to her front door.

Inside, the lights were off. Strange, Shona thought. The room wasn't in total darkness just yet but it was surprising to see not even a desk lamp on. Heading off in the direction of the bedroom, she placed a rose stem between her teeth. As she reached the bedroom door on the left of her, a flicker of movement up ahead at the end of the hallway caught her eye. Leaving the bedroom door unopened, Shona carried on walking into the living room. Chloe was seated in the corner on the window seat staring out onto the ocean.

"Hey," Shona whispered, after taking the rose stem out of her teeth and placing the bunch of flowers on the coffee table. Chloe remained silent. "You alright?" Shona walked over to the window and kneeled down in front of Chloe. Chloe turned to look at Shona, her face streaked with drying tears. Apart from her smudged makeup, her expression was blank. "OK, you're scaring me now. What did the doctor say?"

Chloe wiped her nose with the back of her hand and looked away again. "The blood tests came back. They found something..." she began, her voice cracking as she forced out each word.

"What? Baby, are you sick?" Shona asked.

Chloe took in a huge breath then looked deep into Shona's questioning eyes.

"I'm pregnant."

～

"Does Bertie know yet?" Lula asked, as she leaned forward in the booth opposite Dee and Edie.

"Yeah. She was watching out the window this morning as that blonde girl was hammering in signs and setting up business. How in the hell did those two even have the dough to buy that place, let alone convince ol' man Perkins to call off the auction?" Edie replied, shaking her head. "They must have a rich uncle who's croaked it, maybe? Or they robbed a bank and they're on the run," she chuckled, her eyes wide with mischief. "Poor Bert, though, she had her heart set on that place. I wouldn't wanna be blondie when she catches up with her."

"Did you see who the blonde girl was with?" Dee asked. "The dolly with the brown hair and figure to die for? I wonder if she's single?"

"You just keep your peepers off the blonde one, she's mine. I reckon from the looks of her, I got a chance with her," Lula grinned. "Where is Bert tonight anyway?"

"Over at Sheriff Everett's place asking about legalities over the auction being cancelled. She ain't happy," said Edie.

"Neither is Nurse Marion. She had big plans for that old garage too. Hope blondie knows what trouble's coming her way," Dee warned.

～

"Pregnant?"

Chloe leaned back against the window frame. "Doctor Thomas reckons about six weeks gone," she replied, chewing on a fingernail.

Shona stood up straight and took a step back. "Six weeks?" she repeated, her head spinning, the bottom falling out of her newly pieced together world. "Kyle. That night."

Chloe pressed her eyes together, squeezing a tear out of each one. They rolled down her trembling cheeks as she nodded.

Backing away from Chloe until she felt the living room doorframe press into her back, Shona turned and slowly, almost ghost-like, disappeared from Chloe's sight.

"Shona, please. Don't go out. Stay. We need to talk about this. Shona?" But Chloe's pleas went unheeded. All she heard next was the click of the door as it closed behind Shona, then the rumble of the truck's engine as it pulled away.

∽

"Janice, get me another beer, will ya? This one is as flat as a pancake," Lula shouted across the bar. Behind her the door swung open and there stood the young blonde girl she'd been talking about only half an hour earlier.

"Well, hello there. It's Shona, isn't it? You're new in town, ain't ya?" Lula's eyes glowed.

Shona walked straight past her and to the other end of the bar. "Whiskey. Neat," she barked. Receiving her shot, she downed it in one, then demanded another.

Lula sauntered over and slouched on a bar stool next to her. "We've been wonderin' when you and your," she paused and looked over to the booth where Edie and Dee were staring over open-mouthed, "*friend*...er...sister were gonna come in here and introduce yourselves. I'm Lula, that over there in the stripy cardigan is Edie and that black girl in the white shirt next to her is called Dee."

Shona stared down at her shot, then drank it.

"We see you've bought the garage. I'll be honest, that's ruffled a few feathers around here. Not least the owner of this bar so I'd keep an eye on that door if I were you. She's wantin'

45

to have a little chat with you about it." Lula chuckled at her mock threat.

Shona looked up and gave Lula a look that could have killed her on the spot. "I don't want any trouble. I don't want no chat. I'm just here for the whiskey."

"Hey, cool it. I dig you," Lula replied. "Next one's on me, OK?"

"No thanks." Shona slammed her glass down.

Lula nodded and went back over to the booth, slumping down into her seat. Dee put her arm around her. "Shame. That's the first time I've seen you smile in weeks, Lula."

"Yeah, well, I shouldn't have bothered. That girl's got issues. And attitude."

"Two peas in a pod there then, ain't ya?" Dee joked, squeezing Lula in close to her to which Lula couldn't help but smile.

"Very funny." Lula slapped Dee on her arm, then looked back over to Shona who seemed to be lost completely in her thoughts. "Damn, though, that new girl is fine."

Edie laughed. "Yeah, you got that right." She pulled her glasses to the end of her nose and peeked over the frames. "She's cute, but she's got some kinda story to her. She must, to wanna get loaded like that." Edie nodded over to the bar where Janice was serving Shona yet another shot.

"I'd like to know more about her story," Lula said, winking.

"Well, I tell you one thing, girls. I hope our new piece o' fresh meat ain't still here when Bertie gets back or you're gonna see a whole different kinda attitude around this place," Edie warned.

"Dorothy, it's me. Shona."

Shona, standing outside Bertie's bar, held the payphone

receiver away from her ear as Dorothy let out her familiar shriek of pleasure at hearing her voice. But after a few minutes of stunted silences and one-word replies to her questions, Dorothy finally asked Shona what was wrong.

"Oh Dorothy, I don't know what to do. We were just getting settled here." She took a huge breath and leaned one hand on the cubicle wall in front of her. "Chloe's having a baby." The line went quiet. "Dorothy please. Tell me what I should do. I feel so bad. I just walked out when she told me. I just left her on her own."

"You listen to me, Shona. Sober up and go home. She's gon' need you now more than ever."

Chloe was fast asleep on the couch by the time Shona had walked the half a mile back to the beach house, thinking better of driving with half a bottle of whiskey in her system. Her head felt a little clearer after her conversation with Dorothy. Shona leaned down and lifted Chloe's head up so she could sit down and lay it in her lap. Chloe stirred as Shona started to stroke her hair. "I'm here, baby. I'll always be here, no matter what. We'll get through this. Together." She pulled a blanket from the back of the couch over to both of them and watched Chloe sleep.

Chloe stirred and opened her eyes. Looking up, she saw Shona's sleeping face and smiled. "You came home to me," she whispered, relieved more than anything. Sitting up, she replaced the blanket over Shona's body and headed into the kitchen to switch on the coffee pot.

"I didn't mean to run out on you last night," Shona's voice

piped up from the kitchen doorway, startling Chloe into almost dropping the pot.

"I know. It was a shock to me too, when I found out about..." She placed her free hand over her stomach. "I can't even imagine what you must be thinking. Especially given who the father is."

Shona felt her guts twist.

"But that's in the past now. We got to look forward," Chloe said.

"I know. It's just..." Shona stared down at her boots. For a moment she looked lost. "I was worried you wouldn't want me anymore. That you'd think I'd be no good at raising a kid. That I wasn't enough."

Chloe put the pot down on the counter and rushed over to Shona, wrapping her arms around her. "Don't you say dumb things like that, y'hear?" she said, her grip tight around Shona's back. "I need you more now than ever. I don't wanna run away from this and I don't want you thinking you gotta run either. We are done running." She peeled Shona's body away from her and held her face in her hands. "I want us to be a family. All three of us. I wanna be with you always, Shona. You're my heart, you understand? I love you."

"I love you too." Shona placed her hand on Chloe's stomach and looked down at it, as if she were trying to picture what was going on inside. Her face was one of puzzled amazement.

Chapter 10

"Morning, Blanche," Doctor Thomas said with a smile as his receptionist handed him the files for his first three patients of the day. "Thank you."

"No problem, Doctor Thomas, I'll send your nine o'clock in just as soon as she's here," Blanche gushed. She was in her mid-fifties, widowed, with blue rinsed hair and a plump body, but she still thought the young, dashing doctor would look twice at her. Even though she was married, Nurse Marion also thought the same.

"Good morning, Doctor Thomas. How are you today?" Marion asked, leaning over the edge of Blanche's desk.

Appearing not to hear her, Doctor Thomas continued to read through the patient files. Marion grunted, then leaned into Blanche. "As I was saying, I definitely think there's something going on with that Clark girl. Didn't you notice how she left here the other day? Like she'd seen a ghost, she was that pale."

"For God's sake, Marion, please. Just do your job and get ready for my nine o'clock," Doctor Thomas said. He left the two women behind him gobsmacked at his outburst and closed his office door.

"Well…" Marion spluttered, her hands on her hips, her mouth hanging open like a guppy fish.

"Touched a nerve, I think there, talking about Mrs. Clark." Blanche noticed. "I think the good doctor might have a bit of a crush. Let's find out what her story is, shall we? I'll pull her file," she added with a wink.

Shona pulled up to the garage, feeling a mixture of emotions. She'd spent the weekend talking over their plans for the coming months and how they were going to cope with the changes to their lives. Shona also, from the second she stepped out into the parking lot, felt the eyes of the town on her once again. Taking a deep breath, she clicked open the padlock and opened up the garage for its first morning of business. Across the street, the blinds to the doctor's office twitched.

"Doctor Thomas, can I have a word with you? It's just I noticed something in Mrs. Clark's notes and…well, she's with child and I ain't seen no sign of a husband in the last few weeks she's been in town." Nurse Marion ran a short red fingernail over the edge of Chloe's file.

"Marion, please don't concern yourself with my patient's confidential information. Our only job is to care that mother and baby are healthy and free from harm. That's it. And you'd do well to remember my stance on that," Doctor Thomas replied.

"Well, I just think it's strange is all. She comes into town with that young blonde woman who's just opened the garage, from underneath everyone's noses," she added with an air of scorn in her voice. "I mean, don't you think that's strange? That they have the money to buy that place? Without a husband in sight for either of them." Marion nodded her head and folded her arms. Doctor Thomas exhaled.

"Marion, it may have escaped your attention, with your own husband not taking the draft, but there was a war on over in Korea not too long ago. Maybe they lost their husbands in that? You consider that? As far as I see it, it's none of our business," he said, emphasizing every word. "As long as the baby comes out healthy and is well cared for, that's the end of our involvement. I don't want no sour grapes in my office just 'cos you lost that garage to a better offer. Now, I don't want to hear another word on the subject. Understand?"

"Yes sir," Marion replied, her cheeks reddening.

"Lawrence, get the hell in here now!"

Sheriff Everett bellowed out of his office into the noisy police station where Deputy Lawrence and his fellow officers were sharing yet another tale of his antics out on patrol last night. He dragged himself away and into Everett's office, sinking down in the chair opposite the desk. Everett glared at Lawrence from the other side of the desk a few seconds before letting out a long breath of frustration.

"Why is the first thing that my assistant tells me this morning a story of how you'd been drinking on watch last night? She had a call from a guy you pulled over. Said you were more loaded than he was."

"Well, that guy's tellin' lies, boss," Lawrence protested.

"Oh really? Well I got it on good authority that earlier you bought a six pack of suds from the store." Everett crossed his arms over his chest and set his lips. "You gon' deny that too?

God damn it. It's like looking after a child. Go home, Jake. You're suspended for two days, without pay." Everett walked over to his office door and opened it wide.

"Sir, you can't do that. I'm the best you got on this force. I got a feelin' trouble's stirrin' over at that dyke bar. You need me out there," Lawrence rose out of his chair and stood in front of Everett, his dark eyes blazing.

"I need officers I can trust to protect and serve, not pick fights with local business owners without evidence or just cause. You leave folks alone and be back in two days, sober and reformed like I asked. No excuses or I'll have your badge for good, y'hear?"

Lawrence slid past Everett whose muscular, six-foot frame almost filled the doorway.

"You got my beers in there, Marion?" Jake Lawrence asked his wife as she returned home carrying two brown bags of groceries.

"What are you doing home?" Marion asked, walking straight passed him and into the kitchen, setting the bags down on the counter. "Your shift finish early?"

"Somethin' like that. Where's my beer?"

Marion walked back over to him reclining on the couch watching TV and handed him an open bottle of beer. She perched on the end of the couch and stared, waiting for him to ask about her day, even though he rarely did.

"You wanna hear some gossip from town?" she began. Lawrence grunted. "Well, I was speaking to Edie at the store and apparently..." Marion stopped chirping away when she noticed the sharp look her husband was giving her.

"For God's sake, woman, shut up. I've had a hard day and the last thing I need is for you to bore me to death with some tittle-tattle you heard from someone I couldn't give a damn about. Now, shouldn't you be in there fixin' your man his dinner?" He pointed to the kitchen doorway behind her. "And quit yappin', will ya, the game's just started," he added, turning his gaze back to the TV.

Chapter 11

"Well, I just don't have a clue how to fix cars, young lady. My husband did all that, but now he's over in Bakersfield, a good half hour drive away. I gotta be there by two this afternoon. He'll be expecting me. Mr. Perkins used to help me out every now and again, but he was a little strange. Probably thought being a judge's wife I'd be looking out for ways to catch him out. D'you think you could help me out, sweetheart?"

Minnie Barker was sixty-six years old, with light brown hair tightly permed and cut short against her small head. She wore a fitted plaid beige suit and pumps. Her thin mouth was wrinkled at the corners, yet her soft brown eyes twinkled as she looked down that Tuesday morning at the edge of a set of creepers peeking out from underneath her Toyota.

"Well, Mrs. Barker, I think I know what's causing you the trouble. If you leave her with me for an hour or so, I'll get her all fixed up for you," Shona slid out and looked up at Minnie's face, which glowed.

"Oh, why thank you so much." She paused as a cloud of worry appeared to cross her face. "Do you have any idea how much it's going to cost? I don't have a lot of cash on me," she said, running the strap of her purse through her fingers.

"For you, ma'am, no charge." Shona cocked her head towards the sign she'd put up in the front yard. "Judge Barker fits into the lawmen category by my reckoning, so I'd be honored to ensure his wife is safe on my watch." She tipped her cap to Minnie who beamed a huge smile back.

"You're a gem, young Shona. I don't quite know how to thank you. And when I tell William what you've done, I'm sure he'll be grateful too. At least let me give you a tip." She began to rifle through her purse.

"No need, ma'am. It's my pleasure," Shona assured, pushing Minnie's dollar bill-laden hand gently back to her.

"Thank you. I'll be back in an hour or so."

Shona watched her totter across to the diner, then, smiling, sank back down to her set of creepers. Just as she was about to slide back underneath the Toyota, a shadow appeared over her, blocking out the light.

"Thought it was about time I came over to say hello," the figure announced. Shona looked up to see Bertie's piercing ice-blue eyes staring down at her.

"Can I help you?" Shona asked, her eyes taking in the formidable sight of Bertie who was wearing oversized turn-up jeans and a buttoned up blue and white checked shirt. On her feet were heavy black boots with the laces wrapped around the ankles and tied in two solid-looking double bows. Shona had rarely seen another woman who dressed similarly to her.

"Can you help me?" Bertie repeated. Her gaze then travelled around the garage parking lot and into the open doors of the workshop. "Must be nice to have the money just to bypass auctions." Shona stood up. "The name's Bertie. I own the bar over there. My girls told me you been there already?"

"Yeah." Shona wiped her hands on a cloth she'd taken out from the back pocket of her overalls.

"I was gonna buy this place." Bertie took a step forward towards Shona. "Had the money all ready to make an offer at the auction. But then I saw the sign had been taken down." She began to walk around the garage, picking up Shona's wrenches and inspecting them before placing them back down. Running a fat finger over the edge of one of the work benches inside, she looked down at the layer of brake dust she'd collected. "And I go make a call to ol' man Perkins." She eyeballed Shona and placed both hands on her hips. "Says a young brunette lady offered him the full asking price, and some. Just so he'd take it off the market." Bertie waited for a response from Shona. It didn't come. "The brunette your..." Bertie paused and sucked in the corners of her mouth. "Sister then?"

Shona looked down at her boots and clenched her teeth together. "Look, I'm just here, same as you, trying to run a business."

Bertie snorted and walked towards Shona. "You bought this place from under me. I had big ideas for this place, then you two swoop in." She stood toe-to-toe with Shona, then pressed her face so close their noses were almost touching. "You expect me to believe she's your sister?" She gave a menacing lopsided grin. "I came round to say hi the other day, but your doors were closed. I thought to myself, why, that's mighty strange. Losing custom like that? Especially as your truck was still parked in the lot outside." Bertie paused while Shona thought back to that day. As soon as Shona registered why, and the sinking feeling she felt flashed it across her eyes, Bertie gave a sly smile. "Yeah, so I went around the back to see if anyone was around. I looked through the window and there I see something that no two sisters should be doing. Even in private."

Shona clenched her jaw and swallowed. *That damn window*, she thought.

"Don't worry," Bertie winked, "I won't rat on you both." She moved away and surveyed the area around them. "I'm the oldest of four sisters. I'm very protective of the women around me, and my girls over there in my bar. I'm not looking for trouble either. Just wanted to meet the person who stole my new business from under my nose. Us girls gotta stick together. There's a greater enemy out there." She motioned for Shona to look over at the patrol car parked outside the bakery. "So, I tell you what, Shona. I'll cut you some slack with this place if you come by to the bar once in a while. The girls have been dying to meet the new dyke in town." Bertie leaned in to whisper into Shona's ear. "Bring that gorgeous brunette with you as well, Chloe is it?"

Bertie left Shona and headed back over to the bar.

"Here we go again," Shona whispered to herself.

"So if it hadn't have been for young Shona then I never would have got the truck going again. She's an angel, that girl."

It was half past one that same afternoon and Minnie had spent the last half an hour or so gushing over Shona, after arriving at her husband's side with time to spare.

"She sounds it," Judge Barker replied, his gratitude evident in his smiling gray eyes. "I'm glad my girl's being looked after. Puts my mind at rest, being stuck here," he continued, setting his lips as he looked around the neat garden of his retirement home. His physical health had deteriorated over the last year and, after he suffered the latest in a long line of strokes three months ago, Minnie found herself with no choice but to bring him here.

"I know you hate not being able to look after me, honey, but it's the same for me, with you in here. I couldn't manage the day to day on my own." She patted her husband on the arm. "But, I see the gardener is taking your advice on how to trim those wisteria bushes." She nodded over to the corner of the garden.

"Yeah, well, I'm not completely useless," Judge Barker said, taking a sip of his tea. His hand shook as he lifted his glass, leaving a thin trickle of tea running down his chin.

"Oh, honey, let me get that for you." Minnie clasped her handkerchief to his chin.

"Thank you, my darling."

"Hey Bert," Lula greeted as she walked into the bar and up to the counter. Receiving only a grunt back, Lula sat on a stool next to her. "Jeez, what's got your goat?"

"I went over to the garage this morning. Checked out my competition," Bertie replied.

Lula sat forward, her eyes bright at the mention of Shona. "Yeah?" She licked her lips. "What's she like?" Bertie gave her a sharp look. Lula floundered then set herself right. "Did you find out how she managed to buy that place from underneath you?"

"Apparently her *sister* bought it for her. I tell you one thing though, about that Chloe and our new blonde friend." Bertie paused to sip her drink. Lula waited for the sentence to continue, then stomped her foot.

"What?" she prompted.

"I know for a fact they ain't sisters."

Lula's face darkened. "They're together then? For sure?" Her voice was quiet.

"Oh yeah, and I'm sure they wouldn't want this town to find out what I saw Chloe doing to Shona up against that work bench," Bertie sniggered as she sipped the shot.

Chloe entered the doctor's office for her first official check-up. Nurse Marion ushered her into the treatment room.

"Well, Mrs. Clark, how are you today? Please. Sit." Marion held out a chair for her, then seated herself at her small desk.

"I'm doing OK, considering," Chloe began.

"I'm sure. So..." Marion fixed her with her laser stare. "Is there a nice strong husband at home helping you out with all the baby furniture and...everything?" Her eyes were unblinking.

Chloe fidgeted. "Well, now, I was told Doctor Thomas would be overseeing all of my check-ups. Is he available?"

Marion shifted uneasily in her seat. "Well, he is a very busy man." She cleared her throat, "I can assure you I am more than qualified. I just want to know you're receiving all the help and support you need for this very trying time." Her voice remained pleasant but had a little more bite to it now.

"I'm sure you do. However, I'd much prefer to speak to Doctor Thomas, if that would be OK with you?" Chloe added when she saw no flicker of compliance from Nurse Marion.

"As you wish, ma'am. I'll go see if he's available. Won't be a tick."

Marion rose out of her seat and left the room.

"Vegetables have gone up in price again," Chloe announced as she climbed into the truck after her doctor's appointment. Shona had just finished locking up for the evening.

"Yeah? About that. I was thinking of maybe planting a garden round the back of the house. It gets a lot of sun there. I'll have to test the soil first, but I figured I could grow some carrots, 'taters, maybe some fruit trees? Then we never have to worry about another recession happening. What do you think?" Shona smiled as she looked back over to Chloe, who seemed lost in her thoughts, gazing out of the window, her head resting on her palm as the truck rumbled along. "Honey? You alright?"

Chloe snapped back into the here and now. "What? Oh yeah, sorry. Just baby brain, I guess. What were you saying?"

Shona laughed off her concerns. "Oh, nothing. Say, I met a friendly local today."

"Who? Not Marion from the doctor's office, was it? She's sniffing round looking for gossip. Avoid that one."

"No. But that reminds me. I need to go in there sometime and sort out our health insurance. We're gonna need it in a few months." Shona nodded down to Chloe's stomach. "It was Bertie. The woman who owns the bar? Says you bought the garage from underneath her nose. She's pretty pissed," Shona added with a wry smile.

"Yeah, well, that's too bad. I bought that place fair and square, and if this Bertie don't like it then I don't give a rat's ass. She'll just have to get used to the idea."

Shona looked back over at Chloe and raised her eyebrows, smiling. "Somehow, I don't think she will. She told me she'd seen us the other day. In the garage that day I locked up early. She looked through the side window and..."

"What?" Chloe gasped, then reddened. "Will she tell anyone?"

"No, I don't think so. I think she wants to keep me in her pocket." Shona shuddered at the thought.

Chloe sighed, knowing that the damage had been done. "Well, no point worrying about that now. We just need to be more careful. And board that damn window up," she added.

"I'm sorry. I'll do it first thing tomorrow. What should I do about Bertie?" Shona turned to look at Chloe.

"You'll just have to charm her like you charmed me." Chloe paused, realizing what she'd said. "Well, not *exactly* like that, of course."

"I only got eyes for you, baby," Shona chimed in, resting her hand on Chloe's knee. "Anyway, hopefully I'll be able to make the town see I only wanna do good there. I did a few jobs for free today. I remember how it felt when I fell on hard times. Harry taught me the right way to be and I wanna honor that. I used to thank the Lord above if anyone did me a favor. Now I finally got the chance to give back."

"I know, honey. That just makes me love you even more," Chloe replied, her brown eyes shining in the late afternoon sun. "If that were even possible."

"You really think we can do this?" Shona began, her palm resting on Chloe's stomach.

"Yes. I do," Chloe replied, without even a second to think. "No matter how it came about, this is the family I've always dreamed of."

Shona swallowed the lump in her throat, thinking of the moment she'd found out about Kyle's attack on Chloe and the rage it had caused in her heart. She'd wanted to tear Kyle apart limb from limb that day, but seeing Chloe now safe with her, Shona knew that he could never ever hurt her again. Now they could be a real family.

Chapter 12

"Another letter to Elbie?" Chloe asked over the breakfast table.

Shona looked up and smiled. "No. I thought I'd write to Dorothy, let her know how things are with everything. I thought of calling, but you know how much she likes receiving my letters." She grinned at Chloe who nodded.

"Yeah, she loves you like her own. Maybe we should invite her to stay sometime? Would you like that, honey?"

"Of course, I'd love to see her again. But I doubt she'd be able to drive this far, not with her eyesight the way it's been going lately. And it's not as if we can go back there in in plain sight in a hurry, not after how I left," Shona added.

"You really think they'll still remember?"

Shona stared down at the table. "Folks always remember the bad stuff."

"Well, I think you should invite her. Maybe she'll get the bus or something?"

"Maybe," Shona said. "You know what, I keep thinking how I always seem to end up in the wrong place. I got run out of Louisiana for who I was, or who people thought I was; then I got run out of Mississippi, through no fault of my own, then I end up in Alabama, a place that damn near almost killed me. Now here, I got Bertie already sniffing around, not happy with me muscling in on her territory." She paused and let out a heavy sigh. "I don't know, maybe we shoulda gone to a bigger city? We might have blended in a bit better." Shona began to pick at the skin on her index finger.

Chloe walked around the back of Shona and wrapped her arms around her. Nuzzling her mouth into her neck, she kissed her. "We just need to try harder to get to know folks around here. That takes time. Honey, I can't imagine one decent person not liking you when they get to know the real you." She spun Shona around on her stool to face her then cupped her face in her hands. "You, Shona, are the kindest, most beautiful person I know." She stroked away the strand of blonde hair that had fallen across Shona's face, then kissed her on the nose. "And not all bad things came out of your visit to Alabama."

"You not at work today again?" Marion asked her husband who was still in his underpants eating a bowl of cereal while watching morning TV.

"Suspended for two days, remember. Let him see how the department manages without their finest deputy," Lawrence replied through a mouthful of Sugar Smacks.

"Yeah, well, at least you like your job. I hate working for somebody else," she grumbled as she tied the straps of her white nursing shoes. She stood up and began straightening the collar of her crisp white nurse's uniform in the mirror. "If I'd have got that garage I would have been working for myself and running my own business. But then those two lousy interlopers come into town flashing their dough around like it's nuggets to them, buying up whatever they feel like it. I mean, where are their husbands, huh? You can't always go around the place doing what you feel like. Women have responsibilities." She stared at the back of her husband's head, him not even bothering to turn around to listen to her ranting on. "Jake, I think something's not right over at that garage. I mean, they just came in and undercut everyone. That ain't fair now, is it? Something's going on. Can you find out? Get it closed down, unpaid taxes or something? Anything you can pin on them. Can you do that? For me, honey?" Marion waited for a response from her husband but all she received was a grunt. "I'll see you after work." She turned and left Lawrence to gaze at the TV, lumps of cereal drying on his sweat-stained undershirt.

"Well, good mornin' there. You must be the new girl around town everybody's talkin' about." The young light-brown haired girl behind the bakery counter smiled at Shona, her eyes wide.

"Yeah. I guess. Say, could I have a slice of that pie over there and a coupla bakehouse rolls, please?" Shona dug her hands in her pockets and pulled out a dollar bill.

"Oh yeah, sure thing. My name's Alice, by the way. My family run this place." She turned to the shelves behind her, picked up a small cardboard box and placed Shona's overly generous sized slice of pie inside it, then bagged up her rolls. She looked back at Shona with earnest eyes.

"Thanks. How much?" Shona asked with a hint of impatience.

Alice's eyes glazed over. "What? Oh, um...well, don't you worry about payin' today. Call it a 'new member of the Sunnybrook community' discount." She blushed and swept away a lock of hair from her cheek. "But come in again soon, OK?"

"You sure?" Shona asked. After a vigorous nod from Alice, Shona accepted the food and said her goodbyes.

"Yep, she's definitely gonna cause some waves around here,"

Alice whispered to herself, feeling the flush of red in her cheeks.

~

Shona found herself with not one but two police cars at her garage. One needed to have the brakes tightened up, and the other needed an oil change. Jobs that wouldn't take too long but she'd spent most of the time sharing a joke with one of the cops as she collected used oil in a bucket under the car.

"I can't believe your wife puts up with you doing that, Officer Gibson." Shona laughed at the joke, looking up at the rotund figure of the cop. He laughed back and removed his hat to wipe his brow with his sleeve.

"I know, but she's used to it by now," he replied, stroking his thick fingers down over his handlebar moustache. "And anyways, I have to put up with her shoe collection. I swear she spends my pay before I've even earned it." He replaced his hat and leaned down to help Shona to her feet from the creepers she'd been lying on.

"Thanks," Shona said, reaching up her hand after wiping it on her overalls. "All done. Just gotta top you up, then you're good to go."

"Gee, thank you Shona. It's awful nice of you to do all this for free for us guys. I just wanted you to know that the guys really appreciate what you're doing over here."

"No problem," Shona replied. "I know you get the big stuff done over at the fleet garage, but if I can help in any way then I will. I had a boss once who, well, he woulda done the same so..."

"You're a welcome addition to this town, young lady," Dennis replied, before tipping his hat and letting Shona finish up the job.

"I'll second that," a new voice piped up behind the two of

them. Sheriff Everett walked up to them and tipped his cap to Shona. "Ma'am."

"Good morning, sir, I don't believe we've met yet. I'm Shona Clark."

"Yeah, I heard all about you," Everett began, his blue eyes warm and smiling. "Done quite a few good turns around here for my men. I thought it was high time I come over here m'self and say thank you." He held out a strong, tanned hand to Shona who shook it firmly.

"No problem, sir," she replied. "If you'll excuse me for a moment, I just gotta finish this job off." She walked around to the front of the car and unscrewed the oil cap.

Dennis and Everett raised their eyebrows at each other and smiled. "She's a good one, that girl. So anyway, you figured out what to buy Shirley for your anniversary yet?" Dennis asked. "You can't go home tonight without anything."

"I know. Especially after last time." Everett shook his head and hung his hands on his hips. "We said we wouldn't spend too much this year, with the house renovations and everything, but I just can't seem to think of something that'll make her realize how much I love her."

"Um...pardon me for overhearing sir but, well, if you want something real personal like, then you can't go too far wrong with some hand-picked wildflowers. There's some out back, you're more than welcome to go see if you like?" Shona piped up from underneath the hood.

Everett's face softened into a relieved grin. "You know what, that's an excellent idea. She loves poppies. I'll go take a look."

"She's making quite the impression over there with our friend, the sheriff," Edie said as she prized open the blinds in the bar and stared over towards the garage.

"I know. I can't work out if that makes her a threat or an ally to us," Bertie replied from behind the bar.

"I guess only time will tell," Edie mused.

Sheriff Everett reappeared from his exploration behind the garage, his hands full of a mixture of wild poppies and clematis. "These are perfect. Thank you, Shona, Shirley'll love 'em."

"I hope so, sir," Shona replied, smiling.

Over her shoulder, Everett caught sight of something that made his brow wrinkle all of a sudden. "Say, you been over there yet?" He flicked his head towards Bertie's bar. Shona turned around to look.

"Yeah. I've met a few of the locals," she replied with a wry smile.

"What are your thoughts?" Everett asked, his eyes keen.

"Well, they ain't too happy with me having this place. Bertie said she was after buying it too. But the others seem OK, I guess."

"I've been trying to set up a meeting with the women in there. They seem to think we're always trying to catch them out or something. I mean," he leaned into Shona, "we all know what goes on inside those four walls, what kinda place that is, and the last sheriff here would have closed it down, but I don't see the need for all that." Everett watched Shona's reactions carefully. "I wanna talk to them, understand how to make everyone's life around here a little more peaceful."

Shona nodded. "Well, I think they probably feel a bit worried. Especially because of your deputy—Lawrence, is it?" Everett nodded. "Well, he's been throwing his weight about the place, rattling cages, and I guess Bertie and the others just feel a little..." she searched for the right word. "Unwanted."

"Well, that's my next aim. To sort him out, believe me,"

Everett affirmed. "But thank you Shona, I appreciate your insight on this. And your secret stash back there," he added, looking down at the flowers he was holding.

"You're welcome," Shona said, waving him off.

≈

"Yeah, she's definitely cooking something up with ol' Everett. They look mighty pally over there," Edie noticed, still with her thumb and index finger prized between the slats of the blind.

"Come away from that window. I know that girl's hot but you're turning into some kinda Peepin' Tom," Bertie chastised. "We need to go through our attack strategy. It's about time this town had itself a little rumble. Shake up the feelings a bit. We've been taking Lawrence's shit for far too long. Those cops need to know we won't be pushed around."

"Look, I told you before I don't do anything that involves tearing up the place. I read, I plan, I advise. That's it. I don't get involved in no violence," Edie said after removing her finger from the blind and pointing it at Bertie.

"Who said anything about violence? We'll only retaliate if they start anything," Bertie replied.

"Yeah, well, you'll have to go without me."

≈

"Honey, what are you doing here?" Everett asked, his hands clasping the bunch of flowers he'd hoped to surprise his wife with later.

"You forgot your lunch bag, sweetie," Shirley Everett replied, standing outside his office. She was in her late forties with dark brown wavy hair loosely tied in a gingham ribbon. Her flowing summer dress hugged her where it needed to, yet was loose enough to look casual. She walked over to him and

68

kissed him on the cheek, then passed him a small brown paper bag containing his sandwiches. "And Eric wanted to talk over a few things for his last assignment."

Everett's son flashed his father a bright white smile. He was twenty-one years old and in his senior year of college. When standing side-by-side with his father, they were near identical, both with the same athletic, six-foot physique, kind blue eyes and fine sandy colored hair, receding slightly. "Hey Pop, it's just a few questions about some legal procedures. Shouldn't take too long, if you have the time?"

"No problem, son. I got time now if you like?" Everett held out his arm to lead Eric into his office.

Spotting the flowers, Shirley broke into a beaming smile. "Well now, are those for anyone special?" She put her hands on her hips in mock interest.

"Only for the most special woman in this whole town," Everett replied. He handed his wife the flowers.

"They are beautiful. You, sir, are very thoughtful." She kissed him again and gazed deep into his eyes. At that moment Everett's assistant cleared her throat.

"Um...sir? I have someone on the line for you," she said.

"Take a message, Julie, I'm busy right now," Everett replied, then gazed back at his wife's deep brown eyes.

"It's important. I'm sorry, sir, but I'm afraid it's bad news."

Everett looked over at his assistant. Julie had been with him since he became sheriff five years ago and in all that time he'd never seen her face make the expression it was making at that moment. Following her pointed finger, he walked into his office, with Shirley and Eric closely behind, and picked up the receiver that was lying off the hook on his desk.

"Hello, this is Bill Everett," he began. Seconds later his face turned gray. Slowly lowering himself down in his seat, he thanked the person on the end of the call and replaced the receiver, his hand lingering on it for a moment.

"Honey? What is it?" Shirley asked.

"Pop?" Eric's eyes filled with concern.

"There's... There's been a car accident. Dad was driving and...they hit a tree." His voice choked, the words catching in his throat. "Mom's gone," he murmured. He placed his hand over his face and rubbed his eyes.

Shirley strode around the back of his desk and threw her arms around him.

"I gotta get back up to Portland. Dad's in a bad way. Someone's gotta take care of the business while he's..." Sheriff Everett looked lost for a moment, before Shirley looked over at Julie.

"I'll call Headquarters, get some relief down here. Sir, you go home and sort out what you need to. Don't worry about things here, we'll be OK," Julie assured.

Everett allowed himself to be shepherded out to his car by Shirley and Eric, the latter climbing into the driver's seat. In a second they were gone, just as Deputy Lawrence sauntered through the station doorway. Looking around the room, he tried to make eye contact with each cop standing in a daze around him, each man with his hat now held against his chest. Finally, Lawrence's eyes rested on Julie, who wiped away a tear.

"So, what did I miss?" he asked.

Deputy Lawrence picked his 'acting sheriff' badge up off his new desk and pinned it to his shirt pocket. Straightening his belt, he checked himself in the mirror on the back of Everett's door and smiled. "This is my town now," he whispered to himself. He took his baton from the hook by the door, then walked into the already crowded police station breakroom.

"Now y'all listen up. I know some o' you ain't exactly on cloud nine that Headquarters refused to send relief and decided to put me in charge around here instead," Lawrence began, pausing at a small pocket of mumbling and groans from the corner of the room, "but facts are facts. Bill spent the last few years trainin' me in his ways, and now he's got some stuff he needs to take care of back home. I know Headquarters has agreed to keep his job open for him, but we have to start acceptin' that he might not ever come back. So I need to know I have your loyalty and support."

Lawrence hung his hands on his hips, his watery speech less than convincing, especially to the small crowd of officers standing pouring a second cup of coffee and sniggering. He rose himself up to his full height and set his lips. "You over there. Barnes."

Officer Barnes looked up from his cup and looked from side to side. "Who, me?" he replied. The three officers next to him stifled their laughs.

"Well, you're the only one called 'Barnes' around here, ain't ya, boy?" Lawrence replied, his temper fraying.

Barnes clenched his teeth. He raked a lock of greying hair away from his temple and shot Lawrence a look of pure contempt. The giggling crowd fell silent, the air in the room thick.

"You've served here the longest, ain't ya?" Lawrence asked.

"Yeah," Barnes replied. "Not that that mattered to the chief," he added under his breath.

"Right, well, I want you to personally keep eyes on that no good bar, Bertie's. Everett was too chickenshit to investigate that place properly, even though everyone around here knows what goes on in there. We just need to prove it. Take three of these guys and go pay them a visit. You have my full permission to use any means necessary to question or even arrest anyone in there if you see anythin' improper."

Barnes smiled. "Yes sir," he replied, nodding at three of the officers standing by who followed closely behind him as he left the breakroom.

"The rest of you, I want you to come straight to me if you see anythin' out of place around this town, or anyone actin' suspiciously, especially around Bertie's bar. There's been talk of riots around here and I don't want any folk thinkin' that while the cat's away they can make trouble in my town. We gotta keep these streets clean for our families, if you get my meanin'. We don't want our kids seeing bad influences and things that will pollute their minds." Lawrence waited for the nods and grunts of understanding from the crowd. "Understood?"

"Yes boss," came the replies, more focused and forceful than five minutes earlier. Lawrence looked around the dispersing crowd of officers and grinned.

"What the hell...? You can't do this," Bertie said as the police officers barged past her and into the bar later that afternoon. Within seconds, tables had been turned over, bottles were smashed and pictures from the wall torn down. Officer Barnes walked up to her and pressed his face into hers.

"We can do whatever the fuck we like, pal," he replied, looking Bertie up and down with disdain. "What are you gonna do to stop us, huh? Who you gonna complain to?" He grinned, then walked past her and over to the bar, then ran his baton across it, sweeping away the glasses resting on it. As they smashed to the wooden floorboards one by one, he smiled.

"You should consider yourself lucky we don't torch this place. With you all still inside, you dumbass dyke bitches," he snarled, then nodded his head towards the other officers. "Let's go, boys, I think we've made Lawrence's point." The officers left, banging their batons against anything that was still unbroken.

"I'm sick of this," Lula said, as she swept up glass off the floorboards. "There's gotta be somethin' we can do. Everett wasn't perfect, but while he's out of town Lawrence and his cronies are makin' our lives a misery. It ain't legal what they just did, Bert." She wiped her brow with her checked shirt sleeve, her eyes blazing. "We're just sittin' ducks right now."

"I know," Bertie replied, her face impassive. "But I got an idea."

Chapter 13

"How's it been around town, since the sheriff got called away?" Chloe asked over breakfast.

"Bad. I heard two guys got beaten up the other night by Lawrence's guys. Just for being seen coming out of Bertie's bar. As far as I know they're only friends but..." Shona tailed off as she chewed her toast.

"Maybe we should keep our heads down for a bit. We don't want any more questions," Chloe replied.

"Agreed. I thought we'd be safe here, but I guess folks like us aren't safe anywhere." Shona swallowed her mouthful and pushed her plate away. "I'd better go."

"Please, Shona," Chloe's face was clouded with concern. "Please be careful."

"Don't worry. I done so many favors for those cops that I'm sure it'll be fine. And I ain't gonna be looking for any trouble, believe me. Had my fair share of that," she added with a rueful smile. "I'll see you later." Shona kissed Chloe on the cheek, grabbed her satchel and headed out of the door.

"I hope so," Chloe whispered to herself. She held her flattened palm to her stomach, which was now starting to show the merest hint of a bump.

"Good morning, Shona," a light voice piped up from the door of the garage.

Emerging from the underside of a Chevrolet, Shona looked up at her visitor. The woman straightened her stripy cardigan and stepped forward, her low heeled pumps clipping on the concrete.

"Have we met?" Shona asked.

"No, not yet, but I've been hearing all about you from Bertie over at the bar. I'm Edie."

Shona sat up on her creepers and nodded her hello. "You work there?"

Edie laughed. "No, but I was in there the other night when you came in. I think Lula pointed us all out to you. I work over at the grocery store." She nodded across the street.

"OK. You got a car you want me to look at?" Shona asked, glancing behind Edie.

"Oh, no. I just came over to, um...well, I guess to introduce myself properly." Edie fiddled with the cuff of her cardigan. "You looked a bit upset in the bar that night. I thought I'd come over and make friends." She stepped into the garage and smiled down to Shona who stood up and dusted herself off, then crossed over to the tool chest. "You don't like company much, do ya?" Edie observed, staring at Shona's back. "I get that. I'm not all that great around new people either." She adjusted her cat-eye glasses and smoothed down the front of her buttoned up blouse.

"Just like to keep to myself," Shona replied. She retrieved the wrench she'd been looking for and sat back down on her creepers.

"Yeah, me too. I sometimes feel like an outsider too, being clever and all. The others over there see me as a bit of a wet rag,

75

but it don't bother me." She pushed her glasses back on her pointy nose again and squinted. "I'm used to it."

Shona, softening her voice, exhaled and looked up again at Edie. "Ain't nothing wrong with being smart. Maybe the others are jealous?"

Edie grinned and twirled a lock of hair around her finger. "Really? You think so?"

"Maybe," Shona replied before sliding back underneath the Chevrolet.

"Well, now, you're the first person to ever suggest that, Shona," Edie said. "Say, why don't you come over to the bar later? You could meet everyone properly then. You could bring your girlfriend too. Chloe, is it?"

Shona dropped her wrench. It clanged on the concrete.

"Bertie told me. But don't worry, the town won't hear a peep out of me. Maybe you could both do with making a few friends around here?" Edie said, oblivious to Shona's stillness underneath the car. After a minute or so of no response, she sighed. "Well, Shona, it was good to finally make your acquaintance. I'll leave you to it." She waited a second or two before leaving.

Shona slid out. "Shit," she whispered to herself. She looked up at the now boarded up window at the side of the garage and cursed again.

Chloe lowered the newspaper she was reading and looked over to Shona who was sitting on the window seat staring out to sea.

"They got a quiz on over at Bertie's tonight. Wanna go?" Chloe asked.

Shona snapped out of her daydream at the mention of the bar's name. After a moment of contemplation, remembering what Edie had said earlier at work, she shook her head. "Nah, I don't fancy going out tonight. I'd rather stay in with you. It's the only place I feel truly safe."

Chloe got up and crouched in front of her. "Because of what Edie and Bertie know about us?" The lone tear that tracked its way down Shona's cheek was enough of a reply for Chloe. "I'm sure they won't say anything, honey. They know how it feels to be on the outside too. Would it be so bad to try and make friends with them?"

"I guess not."

"Alright then. We try to make them our friends. Maybe that'll make us all feel a little safer, now that Lawrence is in charge."

Shona remained quiet as she snuggled into Chloe's arms.

Chapter 14

"Hey, how's it going?"

"Boy, are you a sight for sore eyes," Shona whispered back to Chloe, who stood in front of her as she was locking up the garage for the weekend. Chloe was wearing the larger of her dresses, her growing bump much more visible lately. It was mid-January, but the weather was mild enough for her only to need a light cardigan covering her shoulders. Her face, more rounded now, was still stunningly beautiful to Shona, but her brown eyes lacked their usual sparkle. Shona still felt her heart skip a beat when she saw her though. "How did your appointment go with Nurse Busybody over there?"

Chloe suppressed a smile at Shona's facial gesture. "Fine. Though she won't let up about who the father is." She wiped a stray strand of hair from her brow and looked at Shona. "There's only so many times I can tell her the same story. I don't know why she keeps poking her nose in."

Shona stepped forward, aching to reach out to embrace Chloe. "Look, why don't we just say he's dead. I for one would sure love to speak those words out loud."

"We can't. You know that. We have to stick to the story that I found out I was pregnant the week after his army leave ended.

If we say he's dead, then that frees me up to remarry. We'll have guys all over this town wanting to save me from a life as a single parent." Realizing her assumption, Chloe blushed. "Oh, I didn't mean..."

Shona stifled a grin. "All over town, huh? Well ain't you got tickets on yourself."

"Don't. I feel like a whale," Chloe groaned, rubbing her swollen stomach.

"My whale," Shona whispered while grinning in Chloe's ear as she brushed past her on the way to load up her truck.

～

"Why don't I cook tonight? You look tired," Shona said, breaking the silence that had befallen them over the mile-ride home.

"I made a meatloaf earlier, but thank you, honey. Will you rub my feet for me later? They seem to be burning more and more these days." She let out a groan as she fidgeted in her seat.

"Sure. Oh, I forgot, I got those pickles you asked for. And potato chips. You sure are getting some weird hankerings lately." Shona laughed, leaving one hand on the steering wheel as she reached behind her to pull out a brown paper bag from the back seat and passed it to Chloe.

"Thank you. I know. I never used to eat junk. Now here I am inhaling anything I can find that's bad for me."

"What my baby wants, my baby gets, right?" Shona grinned.

"Now you got two of us to take care of," replied Chloe, watching Shona's reactions carefully. The smile of pride in that thought that draped itself across Shona's face as she looked out on to the road ahead allayed Chloe's momentary worry.

As they pulled up to the house, Shona's expression changed. "What the...?"

"What? What is it?" Chloe asked, but Shona had already

shot out of the truck and was standing at the steps by the veranda and staring at the porch swing. Open-mouthed, Chloe shuffled her body out of the truck and walked over to where Shona was standing. Then she saw what had made Shona bolt.

"You sure did pick a neat spot here. The view is everything I hoped it would be and more," a croaky old voice sounded.

"Just like the picture, huh?" Shona replied, her face beaming.

Chloe looked at the porch swing where a very familiar figure wearing a light green cardigan, white blouse and green full skirt was sitting. "Dorothy!" she exclaimed, her jaw hanging open. Her smile was almost as wide as Shona's was.

"So are you two gonna help me inside with my bags or just stand there catching flies?" Dorothy asked. Shona and Chloe looked at each other, unaware they had been staring open-mouthed at their guest for the last ten seconds.

"What are you doing here?" Shona asked, racing over to embrace Dorothy. Almost crushed in her arms, Dorothy let out a laugh and slapped Shona on the back.

"Well, seeing as though I ain't heard from neither one of ya for the past few months since your last letter, Shona, I thought I'd better mosey on down here to see if I could do anything to help out." Pushing Shona gently away from her, she looked closely at her. Her knowing pale-blue eyes narrowed. "You look tired." After a moment of silent communication between the two of them, Dorothy turned her attention to Chloe, who stood watching the reunion of her two favorite people in the world. "And you?" Dorothy exclaimed, heaving her aged body off the swinging porch seat and hobbling over to Chloe. "My goodness, you're the size of a house." She laid her palm on Chloe's swollen stomach.

"Why now, ever the straight-shooter," Chloe joked, embracing Dorothy as fiercely as Shona had. "How are you?"

"Oh, I'm fine, nothing worth complaining about." The old

lady looked between Shona and Chloe. "Now, I think you two better start from the beginning. And don't leave anything out, or else I'll know." She wagged her finger in Shona's face then took Chloe by the hand and led her into the house.

Shona picked up Dorothy's suitcase and followed behind. "No change there then," she muttered, then grinned.

The sun had already set by the time Shona and Chloe had filled Dorothy in completely. They'd finished dinner, chatted about how nothing had really changed in Riverside with Frank still acting "like an idiot," and were now sitting in the living room staring out onto the ocean, the moonlight glinting on the surface of it.

"I ain't gonna lie to you both, it ain't gonna be easy," Dorothy began, tapping her tea glass with her fingernail. "But if anyone can do this then you two can." She looked between them both and smiled. "You two are strong. The love you have for each other? Well, that ain't something that can be underestimated. Folks are gonna talk about where your men are, but you stay solid and there ain't nothing you can't overcome."

Shona squeezed Chloe's hand and, instinctively, Chloe knew what to ask. "Will you stay with us, Dorothy? At least until the birth?"

Dorothy looked at Shona, then nodded to Chloe. "Why, of course I will. Ain't nothing back home to keep me there. As far as I'm concerned, my family is here, in this room."

"Alright, then that's settled," Shona announced. "I'll go make up the spare room."

Chloe and Dorothy watched Shona leave, then Dorothy leaned forward in her armchair. "Do you know how happy you've made that lil' girl? Why, I ain't never seen her so full of life and hope. I've dreamed of this moment for so long. She's got a family of her very own now to take care of. Seeing her like this has kept me going. Chloe, you've given her something she thought she'd never have."

"What?" Chloe replied.

"A future. One worth living for."

Chapter 15

"Say, did you hear about the plane crash in Iowa?" Chloe announced over the breakfast table. "All four passengers, including Buddy Holly, confirmed dead." She lowered the paper. "That's so terrible. They were all so young."

"Well, that's even more reason to grab life and live it while we can," Shona chimed in, grabbing a piece of toast from the plate in the middle of the table. "I gotta go to work. Will you be OK today?"

"Yeah, me and Dorothy are gonna go down to the beach. The sea air will do her cough good. Did you hear her last night?"

"I'll go ask Doctor Thomas for some more cough drops for her," Shona replied. She leaned over to kiss Chloe's cheek. "See you later, baby." She lowered her head and kissed Chloe's large bump. "See you later, baby."

"Get outta here, silly," Chloe said, swatting her away.

As the front door closed behind Shona, Dorothy appeared and shuffled over to the breakfast table. "Did I miss Shona?" she asked, looking over to the door.

"Yeah, just this minute. But she'll get you some more cough

drops on the way home," Chloe said, pouring Dorothy a cup of coffee.

"She's such a good girl. I've loved these last two weeks being here with you both. And I'm so happy she's found someone to look after her as well as she looks after me," Dorothy replied.

"Believe me, she does more than her fair share of fussing over me too." Chloe giggled.

"I can tell that too. God, it makes me so angry thinking back to how she was treated in the past. By her father, and by that wretched Lucy girl back in Mississippi. I'll never get over the sight of Shona lying on my floor after what those thugs did to her. That Lucy led her on, making her think she liked her." Dorothy slurped her coffee as Chloe's keen eyes fixed on her.

"I remember you telling me the story, back when I visited you there," Chloe began. "It must have been terrible for you. When I saw the mess Kyle and those Bullen boys had left Shona in, it broke my heart."

"Yeah, our girl's certainly been through the mill more than once. But she's got us here now, together. Those people are ghosts now." Dorothy drained her coffee cup and smacked her lips. "Now, I want to feel the sea between my toes."

Later that evening, Chloe found Shona kneeling on their bedroom floor surrounded by strips of clean, whitewashed wood and a small bag of nails.

"What are you making there?" she asked, leaning against the door frame.

"Well, we're gonna need a place for the baby to sleep in a few months so I thought I'd put together a little crib. I found a place that cuts the best pine wood and bought some brand new nails. It'll be perfect," Shona replied, rocking back to sit on her heels. "How big would you say they are?" Shona held her palms apart as if she were gauging the length of a marrow.

"Well, I'd say about as long as that piece you got over there," Chloe replied, pointing down at the bits by Shona's feet.

"I thought I'd make a little mobile too, and a changing table that can go over in the corner there," Shona said, excitement in her voice.

Chloe couldn't help but feel overcome with emotion. The tears began to roll down her cheeks. Shona shot to her feet and rushed over.

"Honey, what's the matter? You don't like that idea?" Shona stroked her hair and held her in her arms. "It's fine, we'll go over to the store first thing and buy something brand new, already made. I'm sorry."

Chloe peeled her damp face away from Shona's denim shirt and looked up at her, the smile in her eyes incongruous with the tears that filled them. "Do you know how much I love you? I wouldn't want a crib for our baby that was made by anyone other than you," she said, sniffing.

"You sure?" Shona asked, wiping the tears away from Chloe's flushed cheeks.

"Positive. I don't know why I'm crying. My emotions are all over the place." Chloe laughed, her eyes still damp.

"Well, there's only a few weeks to go, no wonder. It's probably a mixture of nerves and stuff."

"As long as I've got you, there's nothing I can't face," Chloe said, nuzzling into Shona's neck.

"Well, that's one thing you don't have to worry about. I'm yours. Forever," Shona whispered. "Now, do I paint this thing pink or blue?" Shona grinned, tapping a piece of whitewashed wood with her boot.

Over in the center of town, two police officers stood in the alleyway adjacent to Bertie's. They were taking note of who went in and came out.

"You really think Lawrence can run this town while Everett's away?" Barnes asked Gibson, who smoothed down his moustache.

"Has to, don't he? It's been months now and there's no sign of the boss coming back. I can't lose my job. I got no choice but to follow orders. Even if those come from that snot-nosed runt."

"Me too," Barnes nodded. "Looks like we got some action."

Both officers hushed and trained their eyes over to where two casually dressed men walked towards the side door to Bertie's. The door opened and the short, stocky figure holding it open smiled and allowed the men to pass into the bar.

"You recognize those guys?"

Gibson nodded, then took out his notebook and wrote down their names.

"Another two for Lawrence's list," Barnes remarked.

Friday morning was colder than it had been in a few weeks, but still sunny and bright. Shona tapped on Dorothy's door as she did every morning to wake her for breakfast. Not receiving the usual acknowledgement, Shona opened the door a crack and peeked inside. The blankets were heaped over Dorothy's head and only her shape could be made out.

"Dorothy? You awake?" Shona whispered.

The blood in Shona's veins turned to ice. Clenching her teeth together, she took in a deep breath to settle herself, then moved quickly over to the bed. Peeling back the blanket, she saw Dorothy's pale face and, fearing the worst, began shaking her.

"Dorothy? Please no."

The old lady burst into life and began flailing her arms. "What the hell's... What's up with you, girl? I ain't dead."

Shona fell backwards and landed in a heap at the end of the bed.

"I thought..." she gasped.

"I ain't got time to be dead," Dorothy exclaimed. "Believe me, I'll know when I'm ready to go."

Within seconds of staring at each other in shock, Shona and Dorothy were laughing, with relief on Shona's part.

"Yeah, well, you just make sure it stays that way," Shona said. "Breakfast's on the table. I'll see you after work."

"If I make it to the end of the day, you mean?" Dorothy countered.

"Mostly walking in the hills up there, and just good living really," Minnie Barker replied after Shona had asked her how she kept in such good shape at sixty-six years old. "And I have a little vegetable patch I tend, which keeps the knee joints moving nicely," she added. "Here, I wanted you to have this. I know the price of vegetables has gone up these last few months and I got more than I need so here." Minnie held out a basket of carrots, potatoes and collard greens to Shona, who took it from her.

"For me?" Shona replied, stunned.

Minnie nodded. "As a thank you for all you do for me with the truck. You won't take money, so I brought you these. And I heard your sister's having a baby and you two are coping alone with her husband out of town." Minnie paused.

Shona gave her a knowing look. "Marion?"

Minnie nodded. "Oh, but don't worry. I wasn't asking questions, she just caught me in the line at the grocery store and began gossiping. I tried not to pay any attention."

"That woman should be fired," Shona said.

Minnie watched her. "You know, I'm always willing to listen, if you ever need someone to talk to. About anything." Her eyes twinkled as if she were reading Shona's thoughts.

~

"Why Shona, twice in one day?" Minnie greeted, finding Shona on her doorstep holding a cake box later that same afternoon.

"Well, I brought this over for you as a thank you for the vegetables. Thought you could share it with the judge when you see him tomorrow," Shona replied, remembering Minnie had mentioned it that morning. "It's cherry cake."

"His favorite. You remembered," Minnie said, ushering Shona inside.

They sat at the small table and chairs in Minnie's garden. It was just before four o'clock, the shadows lengthening as the late winter sun began to lower.

"How's Chloe doing? She must be fit to pop by now." Minnie chuckled as she poured them both a glass of orange juice.

"Almost. She's just over six months along. Not long to go now," Shona replied, staring down at her glass.

"You know, not everyone in this town is as indiscrete as Marion. What's troubling you, Shona?"

Shona put her glass down. "I don't know how to say it. Oh Minnie, everyone in this town wants to know the story with us. I feel eyes on me all the time. No matter how much I try and ignore it, it's always there, waiting for me to crack. I can't stand it." She looked up, tears in her eyes.

"You can confide in me, Shona. I've been married to a judge for the last forty years. There isn't a secret in this town I don't know about. What is it, sweetheart?"

Shona took a deep breath and told Minnie everything.

Chapter 16

Outside the bar, Bertie and Dee were sitting in the Monday afternoon sunshine sipping from beer bottles.

"I think you should lay offa that girl, Bert," Dee began, nodding her bottle in the direction of the garage. "If she's charmed Judge Barker's old lady then she must be doing something right. Cranky ol' goat."

Bertie grunted, then turned her attention to peeling the label off her bottle.

"I mean, we don't even know her. She may be real nice. She don't look like trouble to me," Dee continued, watching Shona go about her business.

"Yeah, she's real nice to the cops who come in here and smash up this place while the sheriff's out of town," Bertie grumbled. "Then she expects me to keep her cozy little family situation a secret. Well, that ain't really playing fair now, is it, Deirdre?" Bertie swigged her beer and smacked her lips.

"No, I guess not, *Bertha*," Dee replied, folding her arms. "Guess I'm just jealous of what Shona and that Chloe have got going on. Hell, maybe you are too, Bert?"

Bertie scoffed but didn't reply.

"Good luck to them is what I say. I miss being with somebody at night. And you can act tough all you like, Bert, but I know you do too. How long is it now since Sarah left?"

"Two years, six months and 28 days. Not that I'm counting," Bertie added with a sardonic smile.

"Well, I'm sick of just being a one-night thing to girls around here just wanting something different from their boring housewife lives. I deserve more. We all do. And we should stick together, right? You taking out your anger on that girl over there ain't gonna change what Sarah did to you. Shona can't help looking like her."

"Well, thank you for that rousing speech. Are you finished now?" Bertie drawled, rolling her eyes as she swigged her beer.

"You ever considered the possibility that maybe Shona's just trying to make friends? Ain't easy in a town like this. And helping the cops? Well, maybe she's just trying to be nice."

"Nobody's nice without an agenda," Bertie replied. "Anyway, she owes me." She sipped her beer slower this time, her piercing blue eyes fixed on Shona's back. "Maybe I will pay her a little visit again."

Shona decided that she would go for a drink after work. It had been a few months now, since her last encounter with Bertie, but she couldn't avoid her forever. It was a new start for Shona and the last thing she wanted was to feel as trapped as she had done in the past. A life without drama was one thing, but one without friends seemed too harsh.

Bertie's was a world away from Chasers back in Mississippi, in more ways than one. It seemed like the sort of place she could relax in. About ten minutes after she'd ordered a Coke at the bar, a woman approached her. Shona looked up to see she was in her mid-twenties, red haired, wearing a white tee-shirt, blue jeans and a black leather jacket.

"Say, I ain't seen you in here before," the redhead began. "You new in town?" Her inquisitive brown eyes glinted with mischief as she chewed slowly on a cocktail stick and placed a booted foot on the bottom rung of Shona's bar stool.

"Not really. Been here six months now," Shona replied, looking back down at her bottle.

"Oh, right." Several moments of silence went by before the woman cleared her throat to remind Shona she was still standing there. "Can I buy you a drink?"

"I already got one," Shona replied, then remembered the reason why she'd gone in for a drink in the first place. "But thank you for the offer. You live around here?"

The woman sat down on the stool next to Shona. "Yeah, my name's Susie. You're Shona, right?" She leaned over and took a coaster from the bar, her arm brushing against Shona's. *Be friendly,* Shona thought, but the conversation just wouldn't come. She sat next to Susie for a few more minutes of awkward silence before Susie got the hint.

"Look, don't think I was trying to hit on you, I was just trying to be friendly. We all know you're with that pregnant woman," Susie chastised. She leaned in with her parting shot, "and if we know it then you can be damn sure the cops will cotton on soon too. But maybe as you fix their cars for free they've turned a blind eye?" Whispering in Shona's ear as she left, Susie added, "Just watch yourself. Sheriff Lawrence ain't gonna leave you alone forever."

"Friendly, ain't they?" Bertie said, placing another Coke in front of Shona a few minutes after Susie had departed.

"Some are, some ain't. I get that a lot," Shona mused, staring at the bottle but leaving it untouched.

Bertie watched her. "Yeah, well I come in peace this time," she said holding her palms up. "I wanted to ask you for something."

"What?" Shona looked up to see Bertie's eyes fixed on her.

"Help."

"With what?"

"You've got influence around this town now. You've only been here a few months yet you've got those cops wrapped around your little finger already."

"It's because I pay them the respect they deserve."

"And because you don't want any trouble, right?" Bertie interjected. "You don't want them sniffing around your place." Bertie pointed at her. "Or your home."

Shona clenched her teeth. "What goes on in my house is no one's goddamn business, you hear me?"

Bertie leaned back, a sly grin creeping across her broad face. "Loud and clear. But I think the reason you come in here is to make friends. We understand your situation. I can guarantee you we will have your back." Bertie paused again. "Some people walk in and out of your life, sure. I had it all my life with my family telling me I was no good, given my...*lifestyle*. But us girls in here? We're loyal to the end."

Shona started to feel guilty. Loyalty was a rare thing for her to receive, especially given the betrayals she'd faced in the past, and there was something about the intensity of Bertie's stare that intrigued her. The last thing Shona needed was more trouble coming her way, but the fire burning inside Bertie was compelling. And her family history sounded all too familiar to Shona. Relaxing her shoulders, she smiled at Bertie.

"You say you wanted help? What help?"

"I wanna cause a little rumble in town. Nothing violent, just a protest against how the cops are treating this place. Like we're criminals or something. I need you to stand with us, show we ain't gonna accept being treated like this anymore. They seem to respect you, and they'll take us seriously if you're with us."

"Well, why don't we just go down to the police station and talk it over with them. Like you say, you ain't doing nothing criminal. Maybe the promise of a few free drinks once in a while might smooth things over?"

"Talk to them? Are you out of your mind? They won't listen to the likes of me. They're animals, the way they come in here and trash the place. Since Everett left, it's gotten so much worse." For a split second, Bertie looked vulnerable.

"Look, we can at least try? I won't get involved in any trouble, Bertie, but I will come down to the police station with you. We'll sit with Lawrence and make him see reason, how does that sound?"

"It won't work," Bertie replied, folding her arms.

"Never try, never know," Shona replied, hearing Dorothy's voice suddenly in her head.

After Shona had finished up at the garage, she and Bertie walked across to the police station. They looked at each other and took a deep breath as they pushed open the door and went inside. At the far end, Barnes was standing behind his counter listening to a young blonde woman who seemed very agitated. Her face was streaked with tears, her palms flat down in front of him.

"He can't keep coming home from the bar every night and doing that to me, can he? It ain't right. I say no, but he just drags me into the bedroom and..." The woman paused to take a handkerchief out of her purse then held it to her nose as more tears fell.

Barnes let out a long breath and leaned into her. "Look, Mrs. Simpson, Sheriff Lawrence has already explained this to you. Cliff ain't doing anything illegal. He's your husband, you're his wife. He has rights to *that*."

"But he's so rough. How can it be OK for him to do it anyway, even when I say no?"

Barnes shrugged. "Maybe you should take the advice Sheriff Lawrence gave you last week and treat your husband a bit better. Go home to your kids, Mrs. Simpson. Make Cliff a nice dinner. Then, maybe, he'll be more tender with you."

Mrs. Simpson sniffed and somehow composed herself. She picked her purse up off the counter and turned to leave, passing Shona and Bertie on the way to the exit. Shona met her red-eyed glassy stare and felt a pang in her belly.

"I'm so sorry, Jenny," Bertie whispered as Mrs. Simpson drifted past. She didn't reply, her mind seemingly elsewhere.

"Good afternoon, Shona, how can I help you today?" Barnes sighed. He spotted Bertie glaring at him.

"Hi Jerry, can we go in to see Sheriff Lawrence, please?" Shona replied.

"Yeah, sure, I'll see if he's free. Um...your friend can wait here." Barnes looked Bertie up and down, taking in her unconventional look.

Bertie looked between Shona and Barnes. "We are *literally* dressed the same way," she said, with frustrated sarcasm dripping from every elongated word she spoke.

"Yeah, I see that. But she's politer than you," Barnes countered, pointing at Shona.

"We'd *both* like to have a word with him if it's all the same to you?" Shona's deep blue eyes were convincing, melting Barnes into submission. It wasn't often that Shona used her feminine charms on men, but this was a necessity with a man like Barnes.

"Well, OK then. Come through." Barnes lifted the desk hatch and led them towards Everett's office. "Someone to see you, boss," he called out after he'd knocked on the door.

"If it's that Simpson dame again, you tell her what I told you. I got better things to do with my time than to give a shit what happens in Cliff Simpson's bedroom. He ain't breakin' no law, he can do what he wants." Lawrence's annoyed voice

94

bellowed through the closed door. Pushing it open, Barnes led Shona and Bertie into the sheriff's office. With his feet up on the table as they entered, Lawrence looked up and grinned.

"Well now, Miss Clark," Lawrence greeted, chewing on his gum slowly as he took in Shona's slim figure dressed in well-fitting jeans and a short-sleeved black shirt which revealed her neckline just enough for Lawrence's mind to wander. "To what do I owe the honor of your visit here?" He leaned back in his chair and clamped his hands together behind his head. Seeing Bertie enter after Shona, Lawrence lowered his legs and sat up straight in his wooden chair. "What's that doin' in here?" he asked, pointing. The look on his face was of pure disgust, a look which Shona recognized only too painfully. For once, though, it wasn't aimed at her.

Bertie chose not to respond, but the look on her face said it all.

"We came to talk," Shona replied. "About Bertie's bar, and if your men could cut them a little slack over there. They ain't doing no harm." Shona reached over to clamp a hand on Bertie's rounded shoulder. "And Bertie here would be honored to offer your boys the first drink on the house after their long and tiring shift. In recognition of their outstanding service to the community."

"Much as I'd love to take up your offer, Shona, I cannot guarantee my boys won't take it upon themselves to instinctively carry out their sworn duty." He leaned forward and gave Bertie a nasty smile. "We all know what your bar is, we just can't prove it. Yet. I don't want that filth goin' on in my town, so we will do what we can to find the evidence to revoke your license." Bertie's face creased with compressed anger, the corner of her eye twitching. "Now, get this trash the fuck out of my office," Lawrence snarled, looking at Shona but pointing at Bertie.

"Well, that was a total waste of time," Bertie said as they reached the sidewalk outside.

"Just don't give them a reason to think anything illegal is going on in there. Maybe invite more families in for a two-for-one on burgers or something?" Shona looked at Bertie.

Bertie's shoulders sagged in her oversized shirt. "Is it so bad that I just wanted to run a bar people like me could go without being stared at?" she murmured.

"I know. But they're staring now, Bertie. You gotta be smarter about it. You can't beat cops with force, only compromise. To survive in this world when you're like us is to fit in, not stand out." Shona's words came straight from the heart.

For a second Bertie seemed to ponder that thought until behind her appeared Dee, Lula and Edie.

"Hey girl," Lula said, draping a lazy arm around Bertie's shoulders. "You been over to stick it to that Lawrence? I just seen Jenny Simpson cryin' her goddamn eyes out again. We need to stand up to this asshole."

Bertie locked her now-fierce eyes with Shona, whose heart sank, knowing what was coming. Turning around to her friends, Bertie nodded. "It's time, ladies."

Shona returned home exhausted. After a full day of work, she'd then spent a wasted hour in the police station, then a further hour trying to convince Bertie and her friends why it was a bad idea to make enemies of the police. But all of her reasons fell on deaf ears and that night there was sure to be something bad happening in town. Bertie was so riled up by the time Shona had left her that she thought it best to stay home that evening.

"Hey guys, I'm home," she called out after dropping her

96

satchel by the door and walking into the living room. "Chloe? Dorothy?"

Shona walked along the hallway, finding Dorothy in her bedroom reading. Outside, she found Chloe lying on a bench fast asleep.

"Hey baby, you OK?" Shona whispered in her ear after bending down to kiss her on the cheek.

Chloe murmured and opened her eyes. Seeing Shona, she attempted to sit up, but her swollen belly made that movement less than fluid. "Oh, my, is it that time already? I meant to do the housework, honey, I'm sorry. I just felt a little funny so thought I'd get some fresh air. Must have fallen asleep." Chloe half-laughed.

"Don't worry, I'll go see to it. You stay here and rest." Shona lowered Chloe's head back to the little cushion on the bench.

"But you've been working all day," Chloe began.

"Yeah, and you've been growing a human," Shona replied, smiling. She kissed Chloe's stomach. "Relax, OK?"

Chloe closed her eyes and within seconds she was fast asleep again.

"She alright?" Dorothy appeared by Shona's side.

"Yeah. I guess it's just a little hard to adjust to how things are now," Shona added, her gaze lifting to the messy yard, then out on to the peaceful looking ocean. "It's like everything we wanted, we got, but then this happens." She motioned her eyes down to Chloe's bump. "Oh, don't get me wrong, it's just amazing the chance we got now. For a family, you know? I never in all my dreams thought I'd have a kid. I thought…"

Dorothy reached out to hold Shona's hand as she paused. "You thought it'd just be you two. Being young and carefree," she concluded.

"I love Chloe more than I ever thought it was possible to love anyone. I'd crawl to the moon for her. I just wanna make everything alright. She's been through so much."

Shona choked back the tears and felt the old lady squeeze her hand.

"It'll be OK, you know? It'll be hard and I don't pretend to know anything about having children, not having any of my own, but you will both find your way. And whatever those folks think about it in town, well..." Dorothy nodded her head, "we've faced worse, haven't we?"

Shona lifted her eyes to the sky and breathed out a long sigh. "Oh yes," she agreed, smiling.

"That's the spirit. Now, you tidy up in there and I'll start dinner. Like the old days, huh?" Dorothy tapped Shona on the cheeks with both hands and grinned. She shuffled back into the house, leaving Shona to follow seconds later after pulling a blanket over Chloe to keep out the evening chill.

Chapter 17

The drive to work that morning was one of trepidation for Shona. The cool breeze was calming, but her waters were stormy. As she drove, she replayed in her head the heated conversation she'd had the day before with Bertie and feared the worst.

She passed the garage, which at first glance looked intact, then carried on her circuit around the town square. As she reached the first row of stores, she let out a groan, her suspicions confirmed. Windows had been smashed in, with the most badly damaged ones being boarded up temporarily by the owners until the repairs could be carried out properly. Further up the road, she saw the planters at the edge of the doctor's office being put the correct way up by Blanche and Marion, who were both visibly upset. The police station windows were also broken, in more places than any other building, unsurprisingly. In the green space at the center of the town square, there were flowerbeds ripped out and litter from the garbage pails strewn carelessly around. The place was a mess.

When Shona finally pulled up at the garage, she saw one word was painted on the heavy green doors:

Half an hour of wire brushing the door down and three coats of paint later, the word was finally erased from the doors. Shona was kneeling down cleaning the paint off her hands when Bertie's shadow loomed over her.

"Was this you?" Shona asked, looking up, her face stony.

"Not personally, no. But while you were at home playing happy families, we were all out here making history. Staking our claim to a future where you *can* have a family like yours, you know what I mean?" Bertie raised an eyebrow, encouraging Shona to get her hint. "You know, Shona, you need to think carefully about which side you're on. Us girls are tired of being pushed around by Neanderthal men. I can't promise your place here won't get caught up in the crossfire next time."

"Is that a threat, Bertie?" Shona stood up and glared at her.

"Just a friendly warning. Choose wisely, girl."

Chloe and Dorothy noticed that Shona had been quiet all through dinner and now, as they all sat on the couch together, Dorothy took the opportunity to ask what was wrong.

"Why can't people just all get along together?" Dorothy asked after Shona had filled her in on the events of last night.

"People just always wanna fight about something," Chloe added, shifting in her seat, then fanning herself.

"I suppose they were just trying to speak up for themselves and get the cops to leave them alone. But they ain't gonna leave them alone now. They'll be all over that bar now looking for reasons to close it down. Even though most of the damage last night was actually done by the cops, so I heard. Oh, they tried to make it look convincing to the townsfolk caught up in it. Lawrence told them that Bertie's gang struck first, but Alice was telling me that the cops were instructed to get anyone who goes to the bar fired. That's why the bakery and the grocery store seemed to get the brunt of it all. Alice and Edie managed to keep their jobs though after agreeing to help pay for the damage, but I bet they'll all be a lot quieter now over at the bar. Lawrence is picking them off one by one, turning the town against Bertie and her girls. I'll be surprised if she's still in business by the end of the month if she doesn't pipe down."

"Then you need to stay away from those girls. They sound like trouble. The cops might hit the garage next and we all don't need any more attention brought to us and our setup," Chloe huffed.

"You're right. We got our dream home and I got my whole world in this room right now. I don't want nothing to ruin that."

Chapter 18

As the warmth of April 1959 grew day by day, so did Chloe's baby bump. Shona, her stomach churning with nerves, was never more than ten feet away from the telephone on the garage wall.

Then it rang.

Three minutes later, after apologizing to the customer that had just pulled up for his oil change, Shona was wrapping the chain around the garage door handles. Bounding over to her truck, she jumped inside and sped off, nerves and excitement fizzing through her veins as she fought to control the grin that had spread broadly across her face. "This is it," she said for the hundredth time as she raced home. Minutes later she skidded into the driveway, sand and dirt billowing up from her tires.

"Dorothy, I'm home. What's happening?" she yelled as she burst through the door.

"In here," Dorothy called back.

Shona found her and Chloe in the kitchen, Chloe leaning over the kitchen counters with Dorothy rubbing her back. A tray of tea glasses lay smashed on the floor next to the sink.

"Baby, are you alright?" Shona asked, running up behind her.

"Watch that glass," Chloe's ragged voice rang out between heavy breaths.

"We need to get her to the hospital, Shona," Dorothy said. "There's a bag already packed in the bedroom next to the dresser. Go get it."

Shona sprinted into the bedroom and found the bag, and then ran back to the kitchen and took Chloe's free arm, her other one tightly held by the old lady who was walking Chloe to the front door.

"You got the keys?"

"Yeah," Shona replied.

"Good, then let's go," Dorothy said.

"Are you sure this is it?" Shona asked. Chloe groaned as another contraction shuddered through her body.

"Did you see the puddle on the kitchen floor?" Dorothy snapped. Shona nodded. "Then I'm sure. Now come on."

Between them, they managed to get Chloe down the couple of steps from the porch and into the truck. Shona ran around to the driver's seat and hit the gas.

"It's OK, baby, I'll be with you every step of the way," Shona said to Chloe, holding her hand.

"You'd better be. I can't do this without you. And promise me you won't let them give me any of that twilight sleep crap. I read about it in *Woman's Day*. I think it's bad stuff."

"OK, baby, I'll tell the doctor." Shona tried to comfort her along the way to the hospital, but Chloe's eyes were filling with terror by the second at what was happening to her. Shona hadn't realized fully until this moment just what a massive thing Chloe was about to do. Shona looked past Chloe to Dorothy who was sitting by her side still rubbing Chloe's back.

It'll all be OK, the old lady's eyes silently communicated back.

The next four hours that passed were the longest of Shona's entire life. Sitting in the less-than-private hospital waiting area next to the delivery room that Chloe's gurney had been wheeled into, she paced the floor, her nails bitten down to their beds, as Dorothy sat staring at the posters on the wall opposite.

"Eight hours," the old lady said all of a sudden.

Shona stopped pacing and stared at her, her own face blank. "What?"

"Eight hours. That's the average for the first one. I read it in that magazine you brought home last week."

We're only halfway? Shona thought. Down the corridor, a painful groan echoed out, causing Shona's own heart to twist when she heard it.

"Why won't they let me in there?" Shona yelled, pointing in the direction of the delivery room. "She needs me. I promised I wouldn't leave her."

"Look, calm down. Even fathers of babies don't go in there. They ain't gonna understand who you are, now, are they?" Dorothy replied. "She's in good hands. The doctors know what they're doing. You told them about the twilight sleep, so you've done all you can."

Another hour passed before finally a nurse came into the waiting area to give them both an update.

"Are you Mrs. Clark's family?" the young nurse asked, looking between the expectant faces of Dorothy and Shona.

"Yeah. What's happening? How's Chloe?" Dorothy asked. Shona remained silent, the questions catching in her throat as she prayed it wasn't bad news.

"She's doin' OK. There have been some complications, with her refusin' pain relief, but the doctors are doin' all they can."

The nurse's words were like bee stings to Shona. "Please, I need to be in there," she begged. "I promised I wouldn't leave her."

"I'm sorry, I can't let anyone in there. I'll come back out in a little while when I have more news."

The nurse walked away and back into the delivery room, closing the door firmly behind her.

"I can't stand this," Shona blurted out, kicking the garbage pail by the door.

By the ninth hour of Chloe's labor, the atmosphere in the waiting area seemed to grow heavier by the minute. Lots of nurses were coming and going, their faces graver each time the delivery room door opened. Dorothy had fallen asleep in her high-backed chair but Shona was standing watching the door, her hands rooted in her pockets. The loud groans from the delivery room had quietened down, but rather than being replaced by a baby cry, all that filled the air was an ominous silence.

The delivery room door opened and the nurse from before appeared. Her concerned eyes looked over at Shona, her hands clasped. Shona looked down at the nurse's apron. It was mottled with dark red blood.

"We're havin' a little bit of trouble gettin' baby out. Mrs. Clark is getting tired and not pushin' hard enough," she said, a worried look in her large brown eyes.

"Get out of my way. I need to be in there." Shona barged her way past her into the delivery room.

"Ma'am, you can't be in here," another nurse said, taken aback by the commotion by the door.

"I need to know what's happening," Shona replied, looking around the semi-dark room. There were three nurses bustling around, removing heavily blood-stained towels from Chloe's bedside. There was a doctor leaning over her, checking her pulse with one hand and staring at his watch. He looked up when he heard Shona's voice.

"Are you related to Mrs. Clark?" he asked. Shona nodded. "Then I'm going to need your help." He beckoned Shona to the opposite side of Chloe's bed, over to which Shona bounded.

Chloe, white as the sheet she was lying on, looked

exhausted. Her hair was matted to her forehead with sweat, her eyes closed, her breathing ragged.

"I need you to calm her down," the doctor said softly. "Her heartbeat is racing. It's putting the baby under a lot of stress. Can you do that for me?" His chocolate brown eyes eased Shona into action.

Shona picked up Chloe's free hand and began to stroke it. "Hey," she began, catching herself before she whispered a word she shouldn't in public. "Chloe, it's me. I'm here."

The doctor monitored Chloe's vital signs as Shona's soft voice poured into Chloe's ear.

"It's working. Keep talking to her," the doctor said, smiling. Seconds later Chloe's head lifted, her eyes opening a crack.

"Hey," Shona murmured. She shrank down to her knees, her head level with Chloe's. Taking her opportunity while the doctor's head was turned, she stroked her hair and put her mouth close to Chloe's ear. "Come on, baby, you can do this."

Chloe turned her head to face Shona. "Promise me you won't leave?" she said, her voice cracking.

"I promise. Now with the next contraction you need to push, and push hard. Our baby wants to come out, but it needs a little help," she whispered.

Chloe nodded. There was a moment of silence before her face screwed up in pain.

"Push. Now," Shona ordered. Chloe lifted her head off the bed and let out an almighty groan, her teeth gritted, eyes clamped shut.

"Here we go," the doctor confirmed, resuming his position between Chloe's parted legs. "That's the head fully out," he announced seconds later.

"That's it, that's it, keep going. You're doing great!" Shona yelled, squeezing Chloe's hand. "Almost there, just one more push. You can do it, come on."

After one final massive push, Chloe fell back to the bed,

her chest heaving up and down, her body completely spent. Shona looked on in bewilderment as the doctor lifted the motionless baby up, inspected it, then passed it over to the nurse standing over him. Their faces were unreadable as the baby disappeared out of sight over to the table in the far end of the room. Shona looked down at Chloe who was in a state of complete exhaustion, then back over to where the baby was.

Nothing. No sound at all.

∾

Outside the delivery room, Dorothy paced the floor waiting. Over half an hour had passed since Shona had gone in there and she had begun to fear the worst. She sat down in her chair and leaned her head back against the cool tiles, her eyes closed.

Please. Please, God, let them have this one, she prayed.

Moments later, a smile crept across her face as a baby's first cry filled the silence.

∾

Shona looked down at the baby sleeping peacefully in Chloe's arms. The feeling inside her was indescribable, her mind completely blank.

"What do you think?" Chloe said, looking up at Shona.

"He's perfect. Just perfect," Shona murmured. "I'm so proud of you."

"Now, you'll have to stay with us for the night so we can keep an eye on you both," the doctor said, appearing beside the bed. "But you can go home tomorrow. You did very well, Mrs. Clark, and your sister here was a godsend."

Shona looked at Chloe, both of them suppressing their knowing smiles.

"Oh, and that little tyke's gonna need a name. We need it for the register," he added before nodding and leaving them alone.

"What are we calling you then, little one?" Chloe gushed, gazing down at her son.

"How about David?"

Chloe's eyes widened. "David? But that's..."

"Your brother's name. I remember."

Chloe, tears now streaming from her face, nodded. "Perfect."

Dorothy was waiting on the veranda for Shona and Chloe to come home with David for the first time. Her hands were clasped to her chest in anticipation and excitement. She had seen David briefly the previous night and couldn't wait to hold him again.

"Here he is," she called out as Shona helped Chloe out of the truck. Shona then reached over the seat to pick up the Moses basket.

"Hi Dorothy. Gosh, what's that I can smell? Is that chicken pie?" Chloe asked.

"Sure is. Come in and get settled, then I'll serve you some," Dorothy replied, taking the basket from Shona to allow her to help Chloe into the house. As soon as David was settled into his crib, Chloe and Shona met Dorothy in the kitchen and sat down to tuck into Dorothy's delicious looking pie.

"How are you feeling, sweetheart?" Dorothy said as the three of them sat back in their chairs with full stomachs.

"I'm fine now. Just exhausted. And a little sore," Chloe replied, wincing.

"Not surprising. Well, don't you worry. We'll take turns looking after that little guy in there."

Shona looked between Dorothy and Chloe, the words not able to form in her head for her to express her feelings.

"I think I'm gonna go lie down for a while," Chloe said, getting up from the table.

"OK, baby. I'll keep watch."

They both watched as Chloe disappeared into the bedroom.

"I'm so proud of you both. You know that," Dorothy gushed. "I made something today. I'll go and get it." She rose and went into the living room, then reappeared holding a little brown knitted bear. "For David." She handed it to Shona. "Walt and I, as you know, were never blessed with a child of our own. I've always wanted an occasion to make one of these."

Shona took the bear from her wrinkled hand and gazed lovingly at it. "Dorothy, it's perfect. Thank you so much. But, well, Chloe and I were talking before and we were wondering if..." Shona paused. "Well, we know it can't be official like, but would you like to be David's grandma?"

A look of pure joy crossed Dorothy's aged face. "Shona, that would truly be the greatest honor of my life. I accept."

Shona grinned and sat back in her chair. "I am the luckiest person on this earth right now. What more could I ask for?"

"Another slice of pie?" Dorothy ventured, to which Shona laughed, nodded and held out her plate.

Chapter 19

C hloe was in the bedroom going through her wardrobe. She pulled out top after top, skirt after skirt and sighed as she held each up against her much more rounded body. She picked up her favorite red skirt and red and white polka dot blouse. It had always been Shona's favorite outfit of hers too, accentuating her perfect curves. Curves that had turned to lumps though, even three weeks after having the baby.

"Goddamn it," she grimaced as she pulled the two sides of the blouse together. Her chest was far too swollen for the buttons to meet the holes. Giving up, Chloe then swept it off in a huff.

"Probably no damn point trying you on either," she scolded the skirt before throwing on a loose undershirt and elasticated shorts. She stood in front of the mirror and closely inspected her face. She was still undeniably beautiful, but her eyes had dark circles beneath them, her hair lank and outgrown. Her skin looked paler, even though the Californian sun was getting hotter with every day that passed closer to summer.

"No wonder Shona doesn't want to come near me lately," she whispered to the mirror.

"You OK in there?" Dorothy's voice sounded from outside the bedroom.

"Yeah, just doing a little bit of spring cleaning of my closet," Chloe replied.

Dorothy pushed the door open and saw Chloe standing in front of the mirror, lost in her thoughts. She looked over to the bed and saw a huge pile of clothes, some of Chloe's best ones. "They might not fit now, honey, but it won't be long before the baby weight drops off. You'll see," the old lady said, still standing in the doorway.

"I know. I just never thought I'd change so much. Physically. I doubt Shona will ever come near me again, judging by the whale looking back at me in that mirror." She sat back on the bed and placed her face in her hands.

A loud bark of laughter rang out from Dorothy, making Chloe jump a little.

"Are you serious? Shona is more in love with you now than she ever was. And as for whether she still finds you attractive? Well, you could be dressed in a sack cloth and she'd still be making eyes at you. Anyone can see that." The old lady shuffled over to the bed and sat down next to Chloe.

"Then, why haven't we?" She paused. "You know..." Chloe's face reddened.

"Listen, honey, that baby in there is younger than some of the food we got in that pantry. You are both so exhausted, and Shona working long hours at the garage is just what has to happen right now." Dorothy clasped her wrinkly hand over Chloe's. "You both need to forget *that* happening in here for a little while yet." She chuckled. "No, the only thing you two should be doing in here is getting some shut-eye."

"Yeah, I know. I'm just a mess of emotions right now. One minute I feel on top of the world, the next I feel like jumping off it. I don't know whether I'm coming or going, Dorothy," Chloe said, rubbing her palm over her face.

"I tell you what, why don't you put David's crib in my room for a bit? I sleep like the dead anyway, so I'm sure he won't be any trouble. It'll give you and Shona some space to reacquaint." Dorothy flashed a little smile.

"Really? You wouldn't mind?"

"Of course not. Now, you go take Junior out for a bit of fresh air. Do you both the world of good. We'll sort everything out later when Shona gets home."

Chloe looked at Dorothy and smiled. "You know what, I might just do that." She leaned over to kiss Dorothy on the cheek, then rose up off the bed.

Chloe wheeled David's buggy along the sidewalk, stopping for a moment at the news stand. She picked up a copy of *Vogue* and began flicking through, frowning when she saw models in their elegant poses wearing the latest Dior fashions and Chanel suits. Pastel pink high waisted dresses reminded her of the old days working at her father's factory, but even though she'd hated being ogled by the less-than-polite workers there, she still couldn't help but think of how good she'd looked back then. After putting the magazine back down, now feeling a little downcast, Chloe carried on walking. Up ahead of her was a store that sold the sort of clothes she was much more used to wearing these days—patterned summer dresses, halter neck tops, white shorts with an elasticated waistband and pleated floaty skirts. They were comfortable, but no matter what color combination she tried on, they just weren't flattering. Sighing, Chloe took to the counter two tops that looked exactly like the two she'd bought the previous week. Afterwards, she headed over to the grocery store with a list Dorothy had handed to her just as she was leaving. There wasn't much to get, but it would save Shona doing yet another chore on her way home. Inside the store, Edie sat behind her register talking to Nurse Marion. They hushed their conversation at Chloe's entrance.

"Why, Mrs. Clark, how are you and baby doing?" Marion began, rushing over as Chloe struggled through the doorway with the stroller.

"I'm fine, thank you for asking. We're both doing well." Chloe nodded her thanks, then set about browsing the aisles. Cocking an eyebrow, Marion returned to the register to resume her conversation with Edie. About five minutes later, Chloe appeared at the register with a small basket hooked over one arm, her other hand pushing the stroller.

"How're you getting on with motherhood, Chloe?" Edie broached, her keen eyes watching Chloe's reactions.

"Fine, but thank you for asking," Chloe replied, feeling as if she were beginning to sound like a broken record.

"Well, if you ask me, a woman like you shouldn't be doing this on her own. When's your husband home?" Marion chipped in. "You got your folks close by?"

"My father is away on long-term business and my mother is at home in Alabama. I live with my sister and a family friend now. How much, Edie?"

Edie flashed a sympathetic smile. "That'll be three dollars forty-five," she replied holding her hand out for the bills Chloe was offering her.

"Thank you. Have a nice day," Chloe said after taking her change.

"Look at them," Lula said, nodding her head in the direction of Shona and Chloe, the former picking David out of his stroller and cradling him. "The way Shona looks at that Chloe. Makes you jealous, don't it?" She clenched her teeth together in frustration, after finally having seen her competition.

"You're just gonna have to try a little harder then, ain't you. Because after that Chloe's lost her baby weight she's gonna be the town's Hot Mama. And you won't have a cat in hell's chance of prizing them two apart," Dee teased.

"Well, we'll just see about that," Lula replied.

~

"How's my little monster been today?" Shona asked as she lifted David up in the air, then held him close to her. David gurgled and grabbed her blonde locks in his pudgy fists as he wriggled in her grasp.

"He's been fine, slept most of the day. I got your lunch here," Chloe replied, handing her a small brown paper bag containing a bologna sandwich and an apple.

"Thank you," Shona replied, taking the bag from her. Unable to resist, Chloe left her fingers on the bag a second longer than she'd intended to, feeling her heart flutter as they came into contact with Shona's. "Baby, no, we gotta be careful. People might see that," Shona warned, but her own heart raced too. "Why don't we have an early night tonight, huh?"

"Yeah, OK. I hate it that we can't just be open about how much we love each other. I mean, with all the hate and the killing that's gone on in the world these last few decades, would it really be so bad for folks to see two people madly in love, just holding each other's hand?"

"Maybe one day it'll be OK? But for now, we just gotta deal with it. I hate it as much as you do. God, I just wanna throw my arms around you both and shout it from the rooftops, 'I'm in love with the most beautiful girl on the planet, and have the most perfect life with her and our boy,' but I know I can't. The worst thing is there are people in this town in normal relationships that aren't happy. Some of the things I hear the guys saying about their wives? I could never think that about you." Shona's words were loaded with emotion.

"I know. It's just not fair. Listen, I gotta go. But come home soon, yeah? I'm holding you to that early night idea." She bit on her bottom lip, feeling butterflies in her stomach.

"As soon as I get this truck fixed, I'm coming home. You can bet your bottom dollar on that," Shona replied, aching to kiss Chloe right there and then.

Chloe pushed the stroller away, looking back over her shoulder to Shona, who grinned and skipped back over to the truck.

∾

Marion had stopped at the corner of the garage, just out of sight, seconds after Chloe had arrived. Four minutes later, she was striding away in the other direction after hearing every word of her conversation with Shona.

"Sisters, my ass," she muttered to herself. "That poor baby." Her face like stone, she headed straight over to the police station.

∾

Shona had fixed the truck in record time and in less than twenty minutes she had cleared her tools away, locked up for the night and was skidding into the driveway and jumping out of the truck.

"I'm home. Chloe?" she called out after slamming the front door shut. Within seconds a screeching cry rang out from the bedroom. Chloe appeared and was standing in the hallway in front of Shona holding David. He'd been sick on her shoulder and was red-faced and screaming through the second wave of vomit.

"Shhh...it's OK, sweetie," Chloe soothed, rocking David from side to side. "I can't seem to settle him. I fed him earlier but he seems a little grouchy tonight."

"Here, let me try," she whispered, reaching out to take the baby from an exhausted looking Chloe. Gently, she began singing in David's tiny ear. "I need you so, that I could die, I love you so, and that is why, whenever I want you all I have to do is dream."

Within seconds, David was settling, gazing up at Shona with his large eyes, which slowly began to close. After cleaning his face with a towel Chloe handed her, Shona looked lovingly down at him as he snuffled softly and thrust a fist into his wet mouth. Several gurgles and sneezes later, David was lying contented in Shona's arms.

"Oh my, how d'you do that?"

"Not sure. I guess he's just worn himself out. I used to listen to that song all the time when I first fell in love with you." Shona blushed, as did Chloe. "You look beautiful, by the way."

"Liar," Chloe joked, but smiled back. "I smell. I haven't showered or changed yet. I'm such a letdown. I wanted tonight to be special for us."

Shona leaned into Chloe, David nestled between them. "I don't care, you're still the most beautiful girl I ever saw." Wrinkling her nose, she added, "But maybe a quick shower wouldn't hurt."

Chloe reached out to swat Shona but she deftly swerved away and reminded Chloe with her eyes that she was holding their most precious possession.

"OK, I'll go clean up. I felt Marion's prying eyes on me again today. Anyone'd think she was writing a book on us," Chloe said. "You OK to keep watch?"

But Chloe didn't need to bother asking. Shona, completely in her own world, gazed down in awe at the miracle lying peacefully in her arms.

~

"Shona'll have a heart attack when she sees you," Dorothy said, appearing at the bedroom doorway the following morning. "You look a peach, kid."

"Oh Dorothy, you really think?" Chloe replied, smoothing down the six-inch border hem of her new skirt.

Dorothy gave a knowing smile. "David's all ready in his stroller. I just need you to pick up a few things while you're out if that's OK?"

Chloe took the small note off the old lady and waved goodbye.

An hour later, after running all of her errands, Chloe pushed the stroller into the park in the town square. Seating herself on a bench, she fanned herself, eyes closed. The heat of June was increasing as the days went by.

"Excuse me, ma'am, do you mind if I sit here?"

Opening her eyes, Chloe looked up to see a man, around thirty years old, wearing a smart gray flannel suit and fedora hat, motioning his hand towards the empty far end of the bench.

"Of course," Chloe replied, shielding the morning sun out of her eyes with her hand as she looked up at his handsome face.

The man sat down and took out the newspaper he was holding underneath his arm. He grunted as he read over the front page headlines. "I still can't believe that," the man muttered, shaking his head.

Curious, Chloe looked over. "What?"

The man smiled. "Oh, just Patterson getting himself knocked out in three. Lost the title. There'll be a rematch, though, no doubt." He caught Chloe's glazed look and laughed. "Not a boxing fan, huh?" he said, half-embarrassed that she'd heard his mutterings. "I'm Robert, by the way." He held his hand out for Chloe to shake, which she did, accidentally knocking the stroller with her arm. David woke and began to cry.

"Oh, my. I'm sorry about this." Chloe reached into the stroller and picked David up, bobbing him up and down to quiet him. Her haste to do so only made David's cries worse.

Robert watched, not sure whether to help or to leave Chloe to it. After a few minutes he reached out his hands. "Here, may I try? I got a little trick I saw once."

Chloe held him out to Robert, who stood up next to her. Holding David close to his smart pressed button-down white shirt, he swayed from side to side, all while rubbing David's back gently. As if by magic, David's cries turned to snuffles, then soft breathing.

Chloe stared up at Robert open-mouthed. "How on Earth did you do that?"

Robert smiled. "I've had a lot of practice," he said, laying David back down in his stroller.

"How many do you have?"

Robert looked at Chloe and blushed. "Oh, no. I'm not married. I meant I got a lot of nieces and nephews. I've acquired quite the knack." He sat back down on the bench looking nervous all of a sudden. "I hope you don't mind me asking but, um...would you care to have coffee with me? I mean, if you're not busy?"

It was Chloe's turn to blush. "Oh, I'm sorry. I *am* married and, well, my husband's away on business at the moment." The lies came a little too easily for her. So much so that she gave a completely different line to the one she and Shona usually used.

Robert's face flushed. "Gee, it's me who should be sorry. I just assumed that... Well, you don't have a ring on there." He nodded down at her left hand. "So I just assumed... Damn, I'm such a heel." He rose to his feet. "It sure was nice meeting you, ma'am. I hope I didn't cause too much offence?"

Chloe shook her head. He tipped his hat in farewell and strode off, kicking out at a piece of grit on the sidewalk as he passed it.

Before Chloe had chance to process what had just happened, an old couple shuffled up to her. The lady, after looking down at David sleeping in his stroller, looked at Chloe and smiled. "I hope you don't mind us saying, dear, but you and your gentleman make such a lovely couple."

It was past midnight when Chloe woke and squinted at the bedside clock. Unable to get back to sleep, she quietly rose, so as not to disturb Shona who'd flopped into bed hours before, exhausted after her long day at work. Padding barefoot onto the veranda, she stared out to the ocean which was just about visible under the milky-white moonlight glow. *"You make such a wonderful couple."* The old lady's words pounded her brain, repeating over and over again and no matter how much she loved Shona, no matter how good she was with David, Chloe knew that they could never be open to the town, to any town, about who they were to each other. Never be a "wonderful couple'" in the eyes of society.

But it was the dream Chloe had had before she'd woken that stirred her the most. One of an alternative, normal life. With Robert.

PART 2: APRIL 1960

Chapter 20

They had decided to celebrate David's first birthday with a picnic on the beach. Cooper, their new golden retriever puppy Shona had bought for David as his present, was splashing about on the shoreline with David scrabbling in the sand. Chloe looked on with a huge grin on her face, Dorothy shaking her head and laughing at the scene in front of her as she sipped at her tea glass.

"Sorry I'm late. I had to pick up those parts from out of town," Shona greeted, sitting cross-legged on the sand next to Chloe's deck chair.

"I didn't hear you leave this morning. Or come to bed last night. Everything OK?" Chloe asked, not looking at her.

"Yeah, I stopped off at Bertie's for a few drinks, and to catch up with everyone. I didn't wanna disturb you so I slept on the couch." Shona paused. "That OK?"

Chloe remained silent and stony-faced. Dorothy looked between them and rolled her eyes. "You two stop whatever it is that's going on here. Today's about that little ankle biter over there." She nodded her head towards David who was trying, unsuccessfully, to ride Cooper like a horse.

Chloe and Shona looked at each other, an apologetic smile on both their faces. Chloe looked over to David and Cooper fooling around. "I don't know which one is more a bad influence on the other," she said, watching Cooper dig a huge hole in the sand. She covered her face with her palms as David started to mirror him, getting sand all over his head and face. "I think they both take after you, Shona," Dorothy replied with a smile.

"Yeah, they sure do. I taught 'em well. I guess some part of me has definitely rubbed off on Davey, even if he ain't my biological kid." Shona dug into the sand with a small piece of driftwood she'd found.

"Does that bother you?" Chloe asked.

Shona didn't answer. Seconds later she stood up and dusted the sand off her denim work pants. "I gotta go. I promised I'd drop those parts off before lunch."

"Go? But we're about to blow the candles out," Dorothy replied, looking up at her.

"I won't be long, promise." Shona bounded off, leaving Dorothy to fire a questioning look to Chloe, who seemed to be off in her own world entirely. David trotted up to Dorothy with a shell he'd found, Cooper bounding up a few steps behind him.

"Shell," David babbled in his newly acquired voice. He held his chubby hand out to Dorothy. Inside she saw a pretty pink clam shell.

"For me? Why, thank you, kind sir," Dorothy said. She plucked David up from the sand and sat him on her knee.

"Gam-ma," David replied.

His response startled Chloe out of her daydream. "What did he say?"

"He called me Grandma," Dorothy replied, equally stunned. Feeling the tears prick her eyes, she nuzzled her face into the back of David's hair.

"Oh, my," Chloe gushed, her own eyes moist. "He's only ever said 'mama' before now."

"I'm truly honored," Dorothy replied. "I only wish Shona had been here to hear him say it." She looked over to the beach house where Shona was leaning against her truck. "Something ain't right with that girl at the moment."

"I've noticed," Chloe agreed.

They all sat out on the veranda, with Dorothy and Chloe on the porch swing and Shona in a deck chair sipping from a bottle of Coke.

"I heard a story today that more and more white schools are starting to desegregate. Finally got tired of all the black sit-ins, I guess. God, Cuban would have loved that." Shona paused to reflect on her fond memories of Cuban. It was two years now since his death but it still felt raw, especially given the manner of his death.

"He'd love it even more if that new guy gets elected as president. Kennedy seems like a nice guy," Chloe added, smiling. "You still miss Cuban, don't you?"

Shona wiped her palm across her eyes. "Yeah. When I hear about change happening, the tide shifting, I think, why couldn't he have just made it? Just a bit longer. Goddamn that Kyle Chambers. He's got a lot to pay for," Shona added, scrunching her hands into fists.

"Well, Cuban'll be up there somewhere watching down over all of us," Chloe said, looking over to the sunset.

"Yeah, I know. I think of him when we're sitting on the beach around the fire. We'd be jamming together, him playing his guitar, me tapping out a beat. It'd be swell."

Dorothy's ears pricked up. "I'll be back in a minute," she said, lifting her aged body off the porch swing and setting off into the house. Minutes later, she returned with David in her arms. "I heard a cry," she said, sitting back down with him wrapped in his blanket and snuggled in her arms.

"Gram-ma," David murmured.

Shona sat bolt upright in her chair. "What did he say?"

"Grandma," Dorothy repeated. "He's said it before but never like that. Who's a clever boy?" she whispered down to the now-sleeping face of David.

"Said it before? When?"

"A few weeks ago. On his birthday. You left early, remember?" Chloe said. "I would have told you but you didn't get back until late. It must have slipped my mind by the morning when I found you on the couch. Again," she added.

Shona sat in stunned silence. After a few moments, the look in her eyes suddenly changed. Without a word, she rose out of her deck chair and headed down onto the beach towards the water's edge. Dorothy passed David to Chloe and set off after Shona.

"Are you going to tell me what's going on in that head o' yours?" the old lady scolded after reaching Shona's side. Shona's stare into the distance didn't break. "Hey, I asked you a question." Dorothy swatted Shona's arm, stunning her to attention.

"What? What do you expect me to think, huh?"

Dorothy looked at Shona and saw the tears in her eyes were one blink away from falling.

"Think about what? Shona, talk to me."

"Chloe got 'mama'. You got 'gram-ma'." Shona paused, but Dorothy knew now exactly why she was so upset. "What do I get, huh?" The tears were now rolling freely down her hot cheeks. "Who the fuck am I, Dorothy?"

"Now you just listen to me. I don't pretend to know what official title to put on it, maybe one day in the future they'll think of something, but you are just as much that baby's momma as Chloe is. You've been with him from day one. And I know for damn sure Chloe feels the same way too." Dorothy paused. "If you two would just talk to each other about this, instead of you being out at all hours avoiding the issue, then we'd all be a lot happier around here."

Shona stopped kicking out at the ocean. "I just don't know what to do. When he was a baby it was different. I had a way with him, you know? I felt needed. But before long he'll be going to school and more people will be asking more questions about that bastard of a father of his." Shona slung her hands on her hips. "I just don't know if I'm cut out for all this. Maybe Chloe's better off finding a husband instead. Someone she doesn't have to explain away every goddamn time somebody pokes their nose in."

"Do you love her?"

"Of course."

"Then talk to her about this. That's your family over there. Some of us don't get that chance in life to be a parent." Dorothy's voice quivered. "So when it comes along, you put your own fears on the back burner and face up to the hand God dealt you. Because it's a good hand, Shona. The best you could ever wish for."

Shona sniffed and wiped her face, and then wrapped Dorothy up in a tight embrace. "Promise me one thing," she whispered into the old lady's ear.

"What?"

"Please never leave us. I can't do any of this without you."

"I ain't planning on going anywhere just yet, Shona," Dorothy chuckled, slapping Shona on the back.

Chapter 21

David was growing fast, and so was Cooper. They both lolloped into the kitchen that Sunday morning in August, nearly knocking Chloe off her feet as she served up the breakfast. She and Shona had made a pact to try harder on their relationship and, over the last few months, they had never been happier. With all four of them sitting around the breakfast table, Cooper in his basket by the back door, the conversations flowed and the house was once again full of laughter.

"Why don't we all go down to the beach this afternoon?" Dorothy said.

"That's a great idea. Shona?"

Shona nodded back at Chloe. "I'll get the football out of the shed. We can have a game."

"Me too?" David piped up from his high chair.

"You too, sweetie," Chloe said, ruffling his fluffy black hair.

Dorothy smiled and leaned back in her chair, taking in the harmony around her in that moment. It was the most perfect scene, her family full of joy once again.

Shona was at the water's edge pitching a football over to Chloe, who caught it, albeit clumsily. Cooper was barking and trying to pick up the football but his jaws couldn't quite fit around its girth. He then nudged it with his nose until David picked it up and mis-kicked it back to Shona who ran after him, grabbing him up underneath his armpits and whirling him around. Chloe waded through the ankle-deep water to join them and was greeted by a tender kiss from Shona. The three of them twirled and danced in the water as if there was no one else in the world in that moment. They were broken out of their solace by a soaking wet Cooper who bounded up to them and jumped up on his back legs to join the embrace.

Sitting in a deck chair watching from the beach, Dorothy took in the scene, completely content.

"My beautiful family," she whispered to herself.

Then, with typical simplicity, she closed her eyes for the last time.

Chapter 22

"Are you ready?" Chloe asked Shona who was standing on the veranda staring out to the ocean. She walked over and laid a hand on Shona's shoulder.

"Yeah, just give me a few minutes, OK? I just need to get this right." Shona wiped her eyes with her palm, her heart broken at the loss of Dorothy.

Chloe looked down to the crumpled piece of paper that Shona was clutching. "You've been working on it for days, honey. I heard you recite it last night. It sounded perfect. Don't worry, baby. You'll do Dorothy proud, I know it."

"I just wanna say it right." Shona let out a strangled cry and bowed her head. "I don't know if I can do this, Chloe. Dorothy was...was..."

"She was our family. The glue that held us together. I know. But I promise you, you can do this. You trust me?"

"Yes," Shona whispered back.

"Then go out there and just speak from that enormous heart of yours." Chloe took Shona's face in her hands and kissed her on the forehead. Leaving her to compose herself, Chloe went back around the house to the garden where Dorothy's simple wicker coffin was waiting to be laid to rest, beside the rose bushes and flower beds she so lovingly tended during her all too short stay with them.

"I remember the first day I laid eyes on Dorothy Clark," Shona began to the row of people sitting in front of her.

In the center was Chloe, with David on her left and Minnie on her right. A few other grey haired ladies sat on either side of them. Dorothy's coffin lay on two long pieces of wood, the rope to lower her threaded underneath. Two officials from the local church stood by ready to perform the ceremony.

"She was standing at the cash register of a grocery store chewing the ears off the owner about her broken gutters. I'd been travelling around for a long time and wasn't doing so good. I think she only turned around and noticed me 'cos I smelled so bad." Shona paused as a little ripple of laughter worked its way across the row. Chloe's encouraging eyes prompted Shona to continue. She cleared her throat.

"But I left in such a hurry that I dropped the few bits of food I could afford. Next, she's standing there with my stuff all bagged up, saying she wasn't 'running no delivery service.' Yet there she was. She could tell I was in trouble, she knew I needed help but I was too dumb to ask for it at the time. Stubborn, that's me. But so was Dorothy. She wouldn't take no for an answer and took me back to her little cottage, gave me a place to stay and helped me find a job. She gave me a purpose, somewhere safe to finally settle down. Until..." She stopped and looked over at Chloe who looked down at her feet for a second.

"Until I had to leave her. But as soon as I was safe...I mean, settled again, I wrote her to invite her to come stay. Do you remember, Chloe? When she was sitting on the porch swing up there? It was one of the happiest days of my life, seeing her again. And now, here we are, on one of the saddest." Shona's voice quivered but she cleared her throat again and licked her dry lips, determined to finish her speech without taking the folded up paper out of her top pocket.

"My momma died when I was real young so I didn't really have anyone to help me to be who I wanted to be. Until I met Dorothy. She never had no family either, just her husband Walt. They're together now, for always. And I know we'll all meet again one day." She swallowed hard to try and steady herself as she concluded her speech. "Dorothy was the mother I needed in my life when my own passed, and the grandma David was blessed with having, even if it wasn't for very long. Not long enough. She gave me so much more than I could ever thank her for. She gave me her kindness, her wisdom, her patience and her heart. And you know what?" Shona pointed at Chloe and David, her hand trembling. "We gave her the one thing she always wanted. A family she could call her own. The family she deserved. I love you, Dorothy. I'll always love you. And I will never, ever forget you. Thank you for being my best friend."

Chapter 23

Shona returned from work and trudged up the porch steps as if her boots were made of lead.

"Hi, baby, work OK?" Chloe's soothing voice was accompanied by a gentle rub of Shona's shoulders as she embraced her.

"Same as always."

"Oh, OK. Well, I've made your favorite dinner. And I've got a bowl of warm water ready with some salts in it to soak your feet." Chloe took Shona by the hand. "Come, sit."

"No, it's fine. I'm not really that hungry. I think I just wanna get washed up and go to bed."

Chloe nodded, feeling completely helpless as to how to mend Shona's shattered heart.

The sound of soft weeping was the first thing Chloe heard when she came into the bedroom later that evening after bathing David and reading him his story.

"Oh, honey, come here," she said rushing over to the bed to gather Shona up in her arms.

"I just can't believe she's gone. She promised she'd always be here. She said she'd always look after us." Shona heaved between sobs.

"She was an old lady, Shona. She couldn't have lived forever.

She just knew it was her time. And that day she passed, she couldn't have been happier, watching us all together. That was the last thing she saw. She'll always be with us. Always telling us off for something," Chloe added, her voice cracking as she reminisced. "We just have to honor her memory by being the best we can be. Be a family. That's what she always wanted for us. She loved you more than anything, you know that."

For the rest of the long night, Chloe held Shona as her sobs ebbed and flowed until, exhausted, they both fell fast asleep.

Shona had spent most of the following afternoon banging drawers and slamming tools back into the chest. She'd trapped her finger in one of the hinges of the tool chest more than once that day and this time kicked it over in sheer frustration. Finally, the last customer of the day decided to find out what was going on with her.

"Shona?" Minnie Barker's soft voice sounded. "Are you OK, dear?" She walked over to Shona, who was now sitting on an upturned bucket nursing her bloody finger.

"I cut my finger. That's all," Shona replied. She rose up off the bucket and leaned against the garage wall.

Minnie looked down at her hand and saw an oily rag acting as a makeshift bandage. "Here, let me see that." She inspected the wound, then looked around the garage for a first aid box. Locating it, she took out a Band-Aid and patched Shona up. As she did so, Shona caught a whiff of Minnie's scent, rosewater. It was unmistakable, the smell so familiar to her these last few weeks after holding Dorothy's favorite cardigan to her nose night after night.

"How's things at home?" Minnie asked.

"I don't know what to do, Minnie. I know Chloe's feeling Dorothy's death too, but I kinda feel like I should be feeling it worse, you know? Like it should be mine. She didn't know her as long as I did. Does that sound strange that I should feel that way?"

"No one really gets the monopoly on grief, Shona. It affects different people in different ways. Chloe cared a lot for Dorothy, but in a different way to you, that's all. Dorothy was like a mother to you. It should hurt you more, but it doesn't always work like that." She clasped Shona's face in her wrinkly hands. She was so like Dorothy it made Shona's heart ache. "You all need to remember the good times and work together to grieve. Ain't nothing so lonely as a time like this when you're doing it in different rooms. Close up for a few days. Be with your family."

Minnie stroked Shona's cheek, then nodded her farewell. Thinking over what she'd said, Shona sat back on the upturned bucket, her thoughts a swirling mess in her head.

Chloe looked up at the little Mickey Mouse clock on David's bedroom wall. It was past seven and she had just finished reading him his bedtime story, all the time wondering what time Shona would eventually find her way home. For the last few weeks now, it had been the same routine and Chloe couldn't help but feel the pang of loneliness in her heart, especially since Dorothy had passed. Switching off the bedroom light, she looked down at David's angelic sleeping face. It broke her heart to see how like Kyle he was. Same black hair, same dark eyes, but his personality was completely different to his father's. David was much more like Shona. He was kind, playful, cheeky but with such a spirit inside of him that he could have easily come from her as much as he'd come from Chloe. But lately, the one thing Chloe was missing the most was Shona being present in their lives like before. For the fourth time that evening, she broke down in pitiful sobs and buried her head in a couch cushion.

"I need you, Shona. I'm breaking apart," she wailed over and over again, the cushion muffling her enough so as not to wake her son.

~

Shona had been lying back on the roof of the truck staring at the setting sun for over an hour. No matter how much she knew she loved Chloe and David, she couldn't shake the feeling of being trapped in the same routine. Minnie's words had struck a chord with her, but going home just seemed like an argument over something trivial would always be waiting for her. She understood that Chloe was feeling trapped herself, but Shona had to work. They'd discussed the way things were going to be before Chloe had given birth but now it felt like the rot was setting in. Knowing she needed to talk things over with Chloe, Shona climbed down and set off for home.

When she got there, she took a few moments to settle herself, then jumped out of the truck and hopped up the porch steps.

"I'm home. Sorry I'm late, I had a few drop-offs to make," Shona shouted down the hallway into the empty atmosphere. "Chloe?"

Shona popped her head around the doorway into the living room but there was no sign of Chloe. What she did see was a complete mess. There were cushions out of place and a dirty dinner plate, complete with congealed gravy stains, left on the coffee table. Lots of David's toys hadn't been put away and a huge pile of creased clothes sat in a heap on one armchair next to three days' worth of newspapers littered up the sideboard.

"What the hell?" she whispered to herself, bemused at the state of the room. On closer inspection, the hallway was in an

135

equally messy state as she turned into the kitchen. There she found the sink filled with unwashed dishes and the floor sticky with whatever David had splashed out of his dinner bowl.

"Chloe?" Shona repeated, louder this time.

Chloe came whizzing into the kitchen, her face like thunder. "Quit your yelling. I just got David off to sleep."

Shona looked at Chloe and for the very first time ever she was surprised, almost repulsed. Her hair was matted with grease. She had a huge gravy stain down the front of her grubby white short-sleeved blouse and her face was completely devoid of make-up. Her eyes looked hollow, with dark circles hovering underneath them.

"I'm sorry for shouting. Are you OK?" Her own gaze travelled around the messy kitchen. "Can I help?"

"Maybe if you weren't out until late every night, I might be able to manage to get everything done around here. I need help every day, Shona, not just when the mess gets too much for you to stand." Chloe's face was bright red from the exertion of trying to keep her voice low so as not to wake David. "Where you been anyway? In that bar again?"

Shona put her hands on her hips and clenched her mouth. "No, actually," she replied. She strode out of the kitchen and into the living room and began sorting through the pile of clothes on the armchair. "I was just thinking about stuff and pulled over for a bit, you know." She found the pair of jeans and blue denim work shirt she'd been looking for, then frowned. "Honey, I don't mind the pants being creased, but I really ought to be wearing an ironed shirt for work." She held out the creased shirt. "Doesn't give off a good impression to customers now."

Chloe, her face quivering like a rumbling volcano, took the shirt off Shona, looked down at it, then moments later threw it back at her in rage. "Are you serious? I tell you I need help and all you can come back with is that?"

Shona peeled the shirt away from her face and held her hands up in defense. "Hey, settle down, it's fine. Don't worry about it. I can do it myself if it's that big a deal."

They stood glaring at each other. Shona relented, throwing the shirt back onto the clothing pile. "Look, why don't I run you a bath, huh? I'll keep watch on the boy."

"I look like shit," Chloe huffed as she looked down over herself.

"Give me five minutes," Shona replied in a quiet voice, then padded into the bathroom.

~

Chloe came out of the bathroom wearing a pair of yellow cotton shorts and a crisp white undershirt, looking and smelling completely brand new. She wandered into the living room in search of Shona, a dreamy relaxed smile draped across her face. Shona was busying herself plumping up cushions, the pile of creased clothing now ironed and folded, all the dirty dishes now gone.

"Wow, you have been a busy little bee," Chloe marveled, letting her eyes drift around the neat and tidy room.

"I just wanted it to be all nice for you when you came out. You enjoy your bath?"

"It was perfect. I feel much better now. I'm sorry I snapped at you. I just miss you sometimes when you're out all day. Is that so bad?"

Shona sashayed over to her. "Well, I'm here now. How about we reacquaint ourselves." She wrapped her arms around Chloe. "Gosh, you smell so good, I could just eat you all up."

Chloe squirmed a little in Shona's grasp, pulling away. "Baby, I'm not in the mood. How 'bout we watch a little TV, snuggle up?" Her face looked weary, and normally Shona would want nothing more than to do that, but she felt her own frustration bubble over this time.

"We ain't *been* together for months now," she fumed. "Is this how it's gonna be forever now we got a kid?" As soon as she'd let those pent-up words leave her lips, Shona immediately regretted it.

"A 'kid'? His name is David," Chloe shot back. "You don't have the first clue how tiring it is bringing up a 'kid', as you call him? Or what I'm going through right now?" She drummed her finger against her temple, her eyes shooting wildfire at Shona who looked on bemused as Chloe began pacing the floor. "I'm dealing with a lot of crap in here at the moment. I'm stuck in these four walls every goddamn minute of the day thinking about what happened to me back in Alabama. Every time I look at David, it's a reminder of what Kyle did." Chloe stopped, her body swaying before she regained her focus. "I'm so lonely, Shona. I'm not coping. My head. It hurts."

"I didn't mean to say any of that..." Shona began, her feet frozen to the spot.

"Yes, you did. The truth comes out when you don't get what you want, doesn't it? Yes, this *is* how it's gonna be now we got someone in the house who's old enough to walk in on us doing stuff he might not understand. And after what I've just told you about how I feel? How can you be so selfish?"

"Selfish?" Shona yelled back. "You make it sound dirty what we do in the bedroom. We might not be conventional like other couples, but what we are ain't wrong." Shona paused, remembering their first night together at the Fortua. "You taught me that."

"Yeah, well, I'm just getting sick of your bellyaching about not getting your own way."

"It's not my fault you had a kid!" Shona retorted.

The air in the room seemed to completely evaporate.

Chloe stared open-mouthed at Shona, stunned into silence. "It wasn't my fault either. Shame on you, Shona."

She turned and disappeared into the bedroom.

Shona sat in the bar draining her fourth beer. She'd walked around town for an hour or so after storming out of the beach house, devastated at the cruel thing she'd said to Chloe about that fateful night with Kyle. It was the last thing she'd ever wanted to say, especially after she'd seen the state Chloe had gotten herself in, yet the strain on both of them at the moment was becoming too much to bear.

"Beer, not Coke? Rough night?" Lula asked after sidling up next to her.

"You could say that," Shona replied without turning to look at her.

"Next one's on me."

Shona lowered her eyes to her almost-empty bottle and nodded her thanks, unaware that Lula was moving her arm closer and closer to Shona's, inches from touching her hand.

After settling him back off to sleep, Chloe had come out of David's bedroom, half an hour after her argument with Shona, to find the living room now empty. She looked through the drapes to see the truck still in the driveway. Without thinking, she picked up the keys from the table by the door, slipped on her shoes and jumped into the truck.

Sitting on a bench not too far from Bertie's bar, Alan Walker sat watching the front door carefully. The conversation he'd had with Sheriff Lawrence a few days earlier still resonated loudly in his memory.

"So I want you to keep eyes on that place. I wanna know everyone who goes in, how long they're there for, everything," Lawrence had said to him before his smile turned nasty. "You know what's at stake, Walker. I could have your little diner closed in a heartbeat. Terrible rat infestation down that alleyway next to your place, ain't there? Or how about an inconveniently timed outbreak of food poisoning?"

Walker shuddered as he remembered the cold sweat trickling down his back as Lawrence had threatened his livelihood. Now, as he sat watching the door to Bertie's bar, and the alleyway to the side, he knew he had to come up with a list of names for Lawrence to interrogate. Walker had heard the rumors about the clientele there, but it still didn't give him any pleasure when he wrote the seventh name down on his notepad.

The next hour or so dragged on. It was almost nine o'clock at night when a pale blue truck roared down the street and parked underneath a light. He saw a brown-haired young woman leap out of the truck and stride up to the large window on the front side of the bar. The young woman pressed her face to the glass and stared in, recoiling in what looked like anger, then walking over to the entrance. As she disappeared into the bar, Walker licked the nib of his pencil and pressed it to his notepad.

"So then she went straight in there, didn't come out for a while so she must have been meeting someone. Chloe Clark, that's right. I guess what Marion told you about her and that broad from the garage has been right all along. Yeah, of course I wrote her name down too. Don't worry, I'll stay here until closing."

Walker replaced the receiver and stepped out of the telephone booth at the corner of the street, his eyes still fixed on the front door of Bertie's as he lit up another cigarette.

∾

Chloe exited the bar five minutes after entering. She'd stood just inside the entrance looking over to Shona, who was sitting at the bar talking to a black-haired girl wearing a trilby hat and leather jacket who seemed to be laughing at everything Shona said, but before she had plucked up the courage to go over to her, her anger had turned to confusion and hurt. *One time I didn't want it? Is that all it takes for you to go elsewhere?* Dazed by that crushing thought, Chloe had turned back around and left.

∾

It was almost two a.m. by the time Shona returned home. Mindful not to turn on the light and wake the house, she held her palm against the wall to trace her way into the living room but as she did so the moonlight shining through the window caught the outline of a strange shape on the floor parallel to the couch.

"Chloe," she exclaimed, racing over to her.

Opening her heavy eyelids, Chloe started to come round. "What? Oh, I fell asleep on the couch waiting for you. Must have rolled off," she slurred, still waking from her deep sleep.

"Shit, I thought..." Shona began, lifting Chloe up and laying her down on the couch. "I'll go check on David. You just rest, OK?"

Peeking around David's door, Shona could see he was fast asleep. She came back into the living room to find Chloe crying. Sighing, Shona walked over, sat next to her and slung an arm around her quivering shoulders.

"Don't cry. I shouldn't have said what I said earlier. It was unforgivable. I'm sorry."

"I saw you," Chloe said.

Shona looked surprised. "What?"

"At that stupid bar. That girl in the hat drooling all over you. I know I don't look like when you first met me but I never thought you'd lose interest so fast." Chloe's words came thick and fast before Shona could process what she was saying. After several seconds of her rant, Chloe coughed and spluttered.

"You came over to the bar?"

"I had no choice." Chloe stood up and paced the floor. "I needed to know why you go there all the time and now I do. Look at you now, you're drunk."

"And you're suspicious."

"I got good reason to be, ain't I?"

Shona paused. "Wait a minute. Did you leave David here all on his own? Chloe?"

"Don't. Please, Shona." Chloe buried her blotchy face in her hands. "You couldn't make me feel any more like a failure right now if you tried."

"Stop it, both of you," a tiny voice squeaked from the doorway. Shona and Chloe turned to see David standing there in his pajamas rubbing the sleep from his eyes. His little hand clutched at his teddy bear's brown paws.

Chloe ran over to him and scooped him up. "Don't worry, sweetie, we were just playing a game. Let's get you back to bed." When she returned, she stood three feet away from Shona, eyes fixed on her. "We need to talk this through. We can't let that happen again."

All Shona had to reply with was a weak nod.

Chapter 24

"Well, good morning, Shona. How are things?"

Shona looked up from her sandwich to see Eric Everett standing in front of her. He was the image of his father —same handsome face, muscular build and fine sandy hair. It had been cut shorter since the last time Shona had seen him.

"Hi Eric. How's your father doing?"

"Oh, he's still caught up with settling Grandpa's business affairs. He still can't walk or talk after the accident, so Mom and Pop wanna be close, in case he..." He paused and smoothed down the front of his brand new, perfectly pressed police uniform. "I said I'd stick around here until they get back, hold the fort, you know? And what better job for an Everett to get, huh?"

"The town will be glad to have you, Eric. You want me to look at the car?" Shona nodded behind him.

"Yeah, if that's OK? It's making a clunking noise."

"No problem. Hey, when you speak to your pop next, say hi for me."

"Will do, Shona. I'll see you in an hour," Eric grinned and tossed his keys to her.

As she was closing up the garage for the night, Shona saw Bertie approaching, her expression grim.

"Hey. What's eating you?" Shona asked as she looped the chain around the garage door handles.

"Didn't you hear? We were raided last night. That goddamn Lawrence has started throwing his weight around again. Since that riot down at Cooper's Donuts last year he'd been ordered to stop his men from hassling us too obviously. But it's starting to creep in again. His men arrested two guys recently on the sidewalk for doing nothing more than being seen coming out of the bar. Said it was for being drunk and disorderly, but I know that's bullshit. I should know, I was the one serving them." Bertie looked caught between upset and livid.

"Sorry to hear that," Shona replied.

"Yeah, so, Dee and Lula are over at the bar now and Edie will sneak over here when she finishes her shift at the store. I came to ask for your help." She walked up to Shona, looked around them both, then leaned in close. "This situation is getting way out of control now. I've tried to play nice and keep things low key, as I was advised to, otherwise I'd go out of business," Bertie rolled her eyes, "but they hang around most nights and arrest my drinkers on their way home for no good reason at all. Last night, it was my best friend. All he was doing was having a beer after work with his friend. That's it. I've just been over to the cop shop now to ask Lawrence to let those guys go. He's had them overnight already. What more does he want? He's got nothing concrete to charge them with and he knows it. But he's just being a punk ass. Said they were 'disturbing the peace.' How, I'd like to know. By putting a tune on the jukebox he didn't like? No, Lawrence needs to be reminded that he's only keeping that office chair warm until Everett decides to come back. He wasn't perfect but at least he kept things civil between us."

"What do you want from me, Bertie? I got no influence here," Shona protested, her hands on her hips.

"I need you to join with us. We need to rise up against those bastard cops who think they can push us around. It worked at Cooper's, didn't it? People started to listen. We need to show them that we're people too. Hell, we might even one day get some laws changed. At least get the ones we do have now stuck to. No matter what you seem to think, you are popular with the folks in this town for all you do for them here."

Shona shook her head. "I don't want to get involved, Bertie. We already had this conversation. Anyway, I ain't got no influence around here. Not really. Yeah, I do the cops a favor with their cars, but Lawrence would shut me down in a heartbeat if I start causing him trouble."

"I seen that Minnie Barker come in here all the time, bringing you coffee and stuff," Bertie replied, leaning against the wall and picking at her fingernail. "You know who her husband is, right? He may be retired now, and a few marbles short of a set, but he's still got a lot of friends in high places in this town. And there are quite a few who owe him a favor or two."

"I ain't using nobody. Minnie's a friend of mine. I won't ruin that."

"Look, I'll level with you, Shona. I'm gonna organize something a little stronger than the last piss-poor skirmish we had. I got some contacts of my own, up in San Francisco. The Daughters of Bilitis, they're called. Some group made up of women like us. They said they'd get the bus in, as many women as we need, to show these cops they can't keep pushing us around. We'll be throwing a damn sight more back at them than donuts and paper plates, I can promise you that. Now, I need to know if you want a part of this or not." Bertie's eyes fixed on Shona, waiting for her reaction.

"No, Bertie. I don't wanna fight nobody. I don't want no part in violence. I've seen enough of that in my life already. The way I figure it, we should all try and get along in peace. Or at least try to stay out of each other's way."

Bertie looked furious but remained calm. "I knew it. You're the type who wants everyone to fight so that you can reap the rewards when times change and your life gets that little bit easier because of someone else's sacrifice. You're the type to do nothing." She shook her head with contempt. "You got it all sorted out now, haven't you? Gorgeous girl at home. Rich too," Bertie added with a wink, then her head inclined as she thought of another angle. "Say, maybe Chloe could help too. Money always talks."

"No, I don't want Chloe involved in anything. She needs calm, rest. We both do. You don't have the slightest clue what we've suffered these last few years. We've had our fair share of heartache, Bertie," Shona replied. "You have no idea what we've been through to get to this point." She slammed her fist into the garage doors, causing Bertie to flinch. "I just wanna keep my head down. For the kid's sake, you know?"

"I'm sure you do, Shona. But consider this, if we ever do get the laws around here changed then you won't have to live in secret anymore."

"And if I don't help you? Shona asked, folding her arms.

Bertie's expression hardened. "Well, loose lips sink ships, as they say."

Bertie left Shona to ponder that thought.

It was almost a week before Shona next went over to the bar, deciding to let a few days pass for Bertie to calm down, but, after the stifling heat of that day, the thought of an ice cold Coke was too much for Shona to resist.

"Bertie won't be happy to see you in here," Lula said, uncapping a bottle and placing it in front of Shona.

"She around?" Shona asked, taking a swig.

"Nope."

Shona scanned the near-empty saloon area, nodding to Dee who was writing furiously in a notebook in one corner booth.

"She's writin' a letter to the Chief of Police," Lula said. "Tryin' to get Everett back as soon as possible. Oh, there's talk he's comin' back, but no date set yet. Lawrence is out of hand. We need to do somethin'."

"What about you, Lula? Are you up for a fight alongside Bertie, or up for a discussion alongside Dee?"

"I could ask the same of you, Shona," Lula replied. She put down her copy of *The Ladder* and leaned her elbows on the bar, her face inches from Shona's.

"You don't make change by fighting," Shona replied in a low voice. "You make it by changing one heart, and one mind at a time. Through educating people that we're no different than they are. We just love in a different way, no worse, no better. That's how you get peace." She paused to swig from her bottle as Lula leaned back from her and smiled.

"I'll be honest, I'm tired of fighting," Dee announced as she approached the bar and sat next to Shona. "My family have been through enough already, being black. We have to live on the other side of town, so we stay out of the firing line. But me being the way I am as well as black, well, that's just way too much for folks around here to comprehend. I agree, Shona. Words will change the world, not violence. I ain't doing no bad shit. I'll hold a sign, protest or whatever, like they're doing down in the South, but no violence. Not from me."

"Amen to that," Shona said, clinking her bottle with Dee's glass.

Lula rolled her eyes. "Well, I've had enough of this shit too, you know. I wanna fight, even if you two don't. We should let the bastards know who they're dealin' with, arrestin' our friends like that. They hate the way I dress, the way I look. Just because all their wives and daughters can't help but stare at me," she added with a glint in her eye. "No, Bertie can count me in for a fight, no question." The buckles on the wrist of her leather jacket clanged on the bar top as she banged her fist down on it.

"Well, good for you, Lula, but not everyone in this town wants a riot," Dee replied, then turned to Shona. "Say, can I read you my letter, see if it sounds OK?"

"Sure," Shona smiled, glad that there was at least one person in town who thought like her.

Shona returned home that evening with Lula's words still ringing in her ears.

"I don't care what they say to you, what they threaten you with, I don't want you joining this riot," Chloe said after Shona had filled her in over dinner on her conversation with Lula, and the threat she'd received from Bertie last week. "There's too much to lose and nothing to gain. We came here in peace, not for more fighting, remember?"

"Of course I remember," Shona replied, reaching for her hand across the kitchen table.

"Good, because I'll be honest with you, Shona, I just don't think I can take any more. You know how much I'm struggling. I need you more than ever, Shona. We both do." Chloe's face was pale, the dark circles still prominent underneath her dull eyes.

"I ain't got any intention of doing anything to ruin what we got here. We've been through enough. I was thinking, maybe we could speak to Doctor Thomas. See if he can prescribe you something to help with when you're feeling down? Or maybe just be someone you can go talk to?"

"I think that would help me. I'm due to see him again soon. I'll ask."

～

Bertie sat forward in her booth as Dee and Lula filled her in on their conversation with Shona, each giving different opinions on Shona's stance on the matter.

"Well, the way I see it she's an important ally to us. She could make the difference. I need to make a few calls, I think."

Lula noticed Bertie's furtive grin. "What are you cookin' up?"

"If she won't come willingly, maybe she needs a reason to hate Lawrence more than the rest of us put together," Bertie replied, rising out of her seat.

Chapter 25

With the weather so blissful that Friday afternoon, Shona and Chloe had taken a picnic down to the beach. They lay there on a towel looking on as David and Cooper splashed about on the shoreline.

"This is exactly what I needed," Chloe gushed as she breathed in the salty sea air.

"I know. I never want anything to change ever again," Shona replied, stroking Chloe's hair. "I don't know if I could take it."

"I went to see Doctor Thomas this morning. He said I can go and see him any time I'm feeling a little overwhelmed by my emotions. He seemed to actually understand." There was a light in Chloe's eyes as she spoke, like a weight was starting to lift from her shoulders.

"That's really good, honey. I'm glad." Shona wrapped her up in an embrace and kissed her forehead.

As the afternoon turned to evening, they began packing up the hamper and set off back up the boardwalk to the beach house.

"I'll get started on dinner. Can you put David in the tub for me?" Chloe called out as she put the sandy beach towels in the laundry hamper, then headed into the kitchen. She looked out of the window that faced out on to the driveway and froze. Sheriff Lawrence was getting out of his car with Barnes. Out of the second car stepped two other women, one dressed in a formal looking two-piece navy blue suit. The second woman was Marion, wearing her crisp white nurse's uniform.

"Shona!" Chloe yelled, then went to the front door, ripping it open before the sheriff could knock.

"Good afternoon, Mrs. Clark. I don't believe we've been formally introduced. I'm Sheriff Lawrence. That there's my deputy, Barnes, and of course you know Marion over there." He motioned his hand towards his wife who stood looking stony-faced by the car she'd arrived in. The suited woman faced Chloe, her arms folded.

"I know who you are, *acting* Sheriff Lawrence. Shona, can you come out here, please," she yelled again as calmly as she could muster.

"What is it?" Shona replied, flustered. In her arms she held David, who was still dressed in his bathing suit and tee shirt, his toes sandy. "What the hell's going on?" Shona gripped onto David tighter as she glared at Lawrence.

"We got a call down at the station 'bout an hour ago confirmin' suspicions we've had for a while about you two and the boy there," Lawrence began, looking up at Chloe and Shona from his position at the foot of the porch steps. The woman in the suit strode over to him. "This is Barbara Haskins. From the Children's Bureau."

"Children's Bureau?" Chloe gasped, then looked in horror at Shona who remained outwardly cool.

"What suspicions?" Shona asked through tight lips.

Lawrence smirked and looked back at his wife who nodded. "Well, Marion here heard you two talkin' a while back, outside your garage. She's concerned for the boy's safety. Reckons there's somethin'," he paused, as if searching for the right word, "improper goin' on here."

"Well, she heard wrong, didn't she? We were talking about a couple of friends of ours, that's all," Chloe said, sticking her chin out.

"You ain't got no right coming here, Lawrence. You know it. We ain't done nothing wrong," Shona spat back.

"You've been seen on numerous occasions goin' into that queer bar in town. Don't try to deny it now."

"By who? Anyway, there's no law against going to a bar."

"Barnes, hand me that there notepad from Walker."

"Here you go, boss," Barnes piped up, passing the notepad to his boss.

Lawrence opened it up, his evil stare not lifting from Shona. "Jerry Stone, Dee Francis, Edie Foster, Lula Bell, Jimmy Anderson, Ronnie Becker, Shona from the garage..." He grinned as he read the last name. "Chloe Clark."

Shona and Chloe stared at each other. "That night I freaked out and came to find you," Chloe whispered as a sinking feeling churned in the pit of her stomach.

"So what?" Shona said. "Lots of people go in there for a drink after work."

Lawrence smirked. "Come on now, miss. We all ain't stupid around here. You can try and talk your way out of all evidence we're buildin' on you two, but there's one thing you haven't thought of." He flicked his head towards the beach house. "The whole town knows beach houses like this only have *two* bedrooms. So...if the kid has one room, then where do you two sleep? And...where did she leave the kid that night at the bar?" Lawrence added before flicking his hand to his deputy who stomped up the porch steps with intent. The suited woman followed him, as did Marion.

"What are you going to do?" Chloe exclaimed, blocking the entrance to the house with her body and shielding Shona and David.

"I'm sorry, ma'am," the suited woman said, not sounding in

the least bit sorry. "But in the interests of the child, and his safety, we have to take him into the care of the state until we can determine the facts of the case. We cannot have him exposed to dangers of this type of lifestyle." She held Chloe back, while Marion barged past her and reached out for David.

"Over my dead body you will," Shona raged, turning her back to Marion until she almost wrestled David out of her arms.

"No! Momma, no!" David screamed, tears gushing down his face. Cooper barked, gripping his jaws around the hem of Marion's tunic.

"Get that mutt off my wife or I'll have it shot," Lawrence growled. Barnes reached for his revolver.

"No, wait!" Chloe shouted, looking at Shona. She grabbed Marion's free arm. "Please, don't do this, Marion. You know I'm a good mother. You've seen how happy David is. Please, I'm begging you, please."

"It's not right for the boy, Chloe," Marion hissed back. "You can't bring up a healthy minded child in this," she paused, a look of revulsion on her tight face, "relationship." David screamed in pain from his arm being pulled. Shona let him go.

"No, Shona, don't let her take him," Chloe wailed, but Marion had already whipped David away and was halfway to her car.

"We'll be back to question you both later," the suited woman said. "For now, rest assured the boy will be well looked after."

Lawrence climbed back in his car, Barnes in the driver's seat. David sat in the back of the second car on Marion's knee, the woman in the suit driving. Both cars pulled away slowly as if elongating the torment for both Chloe and Shona who stood watching as David tapped his tiny palms on the window and screamed. Chloe sank to the ground, inconsolable. Shona, in complete shock, stood watching the cars disappear, all sounds around her muffled, her vision blurring.

"Why did you let him go?" Chloe bawled, her face red and soaked with tears.

"Because they were hurting him. I couldn't bear it," Shona replied, her voice barely audible. She reached down to pick Chloe up off the ground, placed her gently on the porch swing and kissed her forehead. "I'll be back later. I gotta go sort this out."

"No, I'll come with you," Chloe replied, wiping her face and trying unsuccessfully to compose herself, but Shona had already leaped down the steps and was in the truck roaring away.

∼

After barging past anyone who dared to step in her way, Shona kicked the door of Sheriff Lawrence's office wide open.

"What the..." Lawrence spluttered, wiping fresh coffee off his blue shirt.

"I wanna know two things, and maybe then I might let you keep your teeth, Lawrence," Shona roared, not giving a damn for the three cops who had hurried up behind her with their cuffs ready and revolvers aimed. "Who called you, and where is David?"

Lawrence stared at her for a moment then waved his men away. "Well, they are two very good questions." He sat down in his chair. "The first question I'm not at liberty to answer, and the second, well, that ain't none of your goddamn business now, is it?"

"You tell me where my boy is or I swear..." Shona ripped away the chair in front of her and slammed her palms on his desk, her face almost puce.

Lawrence leaned forward, grinning again. "He's not your

kid, though, is he?" The malice dripped from his voice. "He's not even related to you. As far as I am concerned, you have no legal say in what happens to that boy."

∾

Shona sat on a bench outside, her head spinning, her emotions raging like wildfire inside her. She knew that the second she'd laid a finger on Lawrence she would have been arrested and thrown in the cells, doing her and Chloe, and David, no good at all. A tiny part of her, however, regretted not at least getting one punch in at Lawrence, even if just to wipe the smug grin off his face. No, there was only one person she could think of that could possibly help her and Chloe now.

"Shona, it's late. Are you OK?" Minnie Barker's concerned face appeared in the crack of the open door seconds after Shona had wearily knocked on it.

"They've taken him, Minnie. They've taken David," Shona managed to squeeze out, her voice quivering.

"Oh my, you'd better come in," Minnie said, putting her arm around Shona and leading her inside.

∾

Shona sat at the bar and ordered a beer and whiskey chaser. Serving it to her, Lula smiled. "You look as if you need those." Shona ignored her and held out a dollar. "On me," Lula replied, waving away the dollar.

"Come to talk us out of it?" Bertie asked after sidling up behind Shona. Shona turned to see a determined looking Bertie, then looked over her shoulder at the group of angry women she didn't recognize as regulars, sitting in a booth. On the table in front of them was a vast array of baseball bats, hockey sticks and protest placards.

"No more violence?" Shona read. "A little ironic, don't you think?" She nodded her head towards the weapon-strewn table. "And no, I haven't come to talk you out of it." She slugged down the last of her beer, then followed it with the shot. "Someone needs to take these bastards down. I lost my kid today. I only have one request," Shona said.

"Name it."

"I won't hurt anyone. Some of the cops have done nothing wrong. But if we see Lawrence out there, he's mine."

A sly grin appeared at the corner of Bertie's thin lips. "Agreed. Welcome to the party, Shona."

Shona stood in the restroom of the bar looking down the black balaclava she'd borrowed from Bertie and began scrunching it through her tight fists. Taking in a huge deep breath, she stared at the reflection of a woman she hardly recognized. The care-free soul who'd thought her traumatic life was finally starting to change seemed to be all but gone.

"No more hiding in the shadows. No more pretending that the world will accept you without a fight. The time for action is now," she said, slipping the balaclava over her blonde hair. Pulling it down and adjusting the eye holes so she could see clearly, she took one last look at herself. "I tried to live a quiet life. But I gotta fight back now. For my family. Please forgive me, Dorothy."

"They're all out there," Edie reported, her thumb and forefinger prizing open the blinds.

"Ready?" Bertie said after turning to Shona.

"Ready," Shona replied through tight lips.

"Then what are we waitin' for? Let's go crack some skulls," Lula roared, banging her bat against the bar. The others in the bar cheered and stormed out the exit onto the sidewalk, then recoiled when they saw in the near distance the wall of police officers.

Edie shot a look towards Bertie, then at Shona, both standing front and center. "Are you sure this is a good idea, Bert? They look like they mean business."

"We need to make this look like police brutality. If that means we take a few hits ourselves, then so be it," Bertie hissed back.

Edie switched her stare to Shona who fixed her gaze on one man in particular, her lip curling at his menacing grin.

"Let's do this," Shona commanded. She walked forward, then picked up her pace until she was almost at the middle of the street. Bertie gave the rallying cry and the rest of the group ran after her.

"C'mon, boys, let's put these bitches down," Lawrence roared. He reached into his pocket and pulled out a grenade.

Shona's blood turned to ice. "Get down!" she yelled behind her, watching in horror as the grenade whistled over her head and into the crowd of women behind her. Every heart was in every mouth as the grenade hit the concrete, bounced once, then twice before exploding into a huge cloud of smoke. Relieved it was not real, Shona turned back to the approaching men and let out a murderous battle cry. In less than thirty seconds, the rest of the women had caught up with Shona and were now fighting hard with the police officers. Wood clanged against metal shields, bats and batons crashing together, the crunching sound of them hitting arms and legs filling the air.

"Bertie, I'm hit," cried Lula, her nose a bleeding mess.

"Come on, Lula, fight," Bertie replied, trying to fend off two young officers who had rounded on her. Within seconds she too had been battered to the ground.

The gravel was swathed with pools of blood and vomit from those hit so hard in the stomach that they writhed on the floor in agony. Lula looked down at the young police officer she'd hit hard enough for blood to now pour down his forehead. She spat on the ground next to him then, whooping like a wild animal, brandished her bat in the air and ran off to strike down her next victim.

With Lawrence in her sight seemingly distracted by his men dropping like felled trees around him, Shona clenched her teeth and began to pace forward, as if oblivious to the melee around her. Lawrence was the only one in her crosshairs at that moment and every ounce of anger and hurt at what he'd done to her family was fizzing through her veins. Bending down halfway towards him, she picked up a baseball bat that someone had dropped in the chaos and swung it.

"Batter up," she growled into the cacophony.

All around her, as she stalked closer to Lawrence, women were running around in the white smoke from several more grenades that had been flung at them. Lula had joined a small group of women who were wearing masks and clattering into police officers who battered them to the ground as if they were bowling pins. At the far corner of the street a police car had been set on fire, one Shona had fixed earlier that week. White smoke was replaced by black, as thick acrid fumes began to suck the oxygen out of the air, each sweat-soaked face Shona passed becoming grubbier by the minute.

Seconds later, as if a light had been switched on in her head, Shona stopped walking and dropped her bat. About three feet away from her, lying prone on the ground, was a face she recognized. It was Eric Everett, his brand new police uniform thick with the dirt and grime he'd picked up after trying in vain to fight off his attackers. A nasty head wound poured with dark red blood. His body was motionless and about to be set upon once again by a mob of stick-wielding rioters.

"No, leave him! Stop!" Shona yelled, ripping off her balaclava, then crouching down to shield the body.

"What's your problem? He's the enemy," one of the rioters, a young woman wearing a yellow bloodstained tee-shirt and dirty white shorts, sneered back. In one hand she held a plank of wood with three hideous looking nails sticking out of it.

Shona looked up and flashed a murderous looking grin. "Back off, he's mine."

"No problem," the woman set off about her next conquest.

Eric moaned and tried to lift his head. A few feet away from him was another cop coughing spurts of blood.

"It's Shona. Stay still, I'll be back in a minute," Shona whispered into Eric's ear. He must have understood because he hadn't moved a muscle by the time Shona pulled up at the side of the road in her truck. Spotting Dee looking completely bewildered with what was going on around her, Shona called her over.

"What are you doing?" Dee asked, running over to find Shona trying to heave Eric up.

"He's hurt. Bad. Now, help me. I gotta get him to the hospital."

"If Bertie sees this, she'll go crazy," Dee said, shaking her head as she lifted Everett's son's legs over the tailgate, laying his body with a thud onto the back of Shona's truck.

"We came out here to get their attention, to try and make a difference. Not to kill anyone."

Chapter 26

The sun had barcly risen when an exhausted Shona pulled up outside the garage. She stepped out of the truck, letting out a low whistle as her red-rimmed eyes took in the destruction all around her. Windows had been smashed to smithereens, the street littered with splintered wood and broken bottles. The car that had been set on fire was now cold but had left an ugly black stain on the bright grey road. Shona had returned home briefly from the hospital to explain to Chloe what had happened in town but had altered the story slightly, not wanting to worry her even more, knowing that Chloe was teetering on the edge of the abyss at the moment. Losing David had caused her enough heartache already without her facing the prospect of losing Shona too.

Eric Everett had needed seventeen stitches in his head wound and had a concussion but was otherwise going to be OK. Over the three hours she'd been in the emergency room, Shona had seen several injured cops brought in, but before the police force from the neighboring town could be deployed, Lawrence had fired several gunshots in the air to call off the rioters.

Shona, in the cold light of day, felt disgusted with herself for getting involved. As she'd driven down the highway to the hospital, all she could hear in her head was Dorothy's croaky voice: "This isn't you, Shona."

A few hours later, after sweeping up the shards of glass strewn around the parking lot, a familiar voice piped up behind her. Turning around, Shona saw Minnie standing there holding a basket covered with a red and white checked dish towel.

"A bit of a skirmish in town last night, then," Minnie said, eyeing Shona. "Edie in the store told me what had happened to the place. I was surprised she still had a job after what she told me, but she said she was wearing a balaclava so no one recognized her. Those women from San Francisco apparently did most of the damage around here. Everyone I've talked to this morning is glad to see the back of them. But why did you get involved, Shona?"

Shona looked at the ground, feeling the weight of Minnie's knowing stare. "They took my boy, Minnie. I had to do something."

Minnie's face creased. "Oh Shona, it's not like you to get involved with violence. That's not the way to change things. You know that." Her voice was soothing yet scathing at the same time. She handed over the basket and placed a hand on Shona's shoulder. "Here, it's just a few things I baked yesterday. I'm going to see William later. He still has a lot of friends in the office. Maybe he can talk to someone about all this business with David?"

"I'd appreciate that, Minnie. It can't be legal, what they're doing," Shona replied, holding the basket against her chest.

"I know. But you need to keep out of trouble, Shona." Minnie paused. "Maybe William can give Bill Everett a call, see if he's able to come back yet. I know it's been a few years, but this town needs a decent man to cut out the rot that's set in since Lawrence took over." Minnie's eyes misted over, then refocused. "Always remember what's important, Shona. Family."

Shona nodded and waved goodbye to Minnie who climbed back into her car and set off. She looked over to the bar. The front windows were all smashed, the red and white striped awnings slashed and torn down. The door was scuffed and in need of a repaint. She pulled the garage doors closed and set off across the street to the bar.

"Hey Lula, Bertie around?" She walked up to the booth nearest to the door where Lula was sitting staring at the wall.

"Where did you slope off to last night?" Lula asked, not bothering to make eye contact.

"Nowhere. Where's Bertie? I need to speak to her."

"Nowhere, my ass. You were seen, Shona. Helpin' that Everett boy into your truck. Word is he's recoverin' in hospital now. Two other police officers too, so I hear."

"It got way out of hand last night, Lula. People got hurt."

"Yeah, I know they did." Lula paused, then turned to look Shona full in the face. Shona recoiled. Lula's nose had clearly been broken. Around her left eye, she had a dark blue bruise and a three-inch cut across her eyebrow. "But I didn't notice you throwin' *me* on the back of your truck. Why should you give a shit, though, huh? Too busy playin' nice. Tell me, Shona, why did you even want a piece of this action anyway?"

Shona felt guiltier the longer she looked at Lula's injury. She'd been angry last night but she'd never wanted anyone to get seriously hurt. Apart from Lawrence. She tried again to apologize but Lula had already turned away.

"You can't blame her," Bertie said after walking up behind Shona. "We all feel a little disappointed in you, especially after all your big talk last night about helping the cause." She was also nursing her own memories of last night; her lip was cut and her left arm bandaged at the wrist.

"I'd like to help pay for the damage here," Shona said, pulling out a small wad of bills from the top pocket of her denim jacket.

"I don't want your money, Shona. I wanted your support."
Bertie's reply, like Lula's, was soaked in disappointment. It was
the first time Shona could recall seeing a vulnerable side to
Bertie, but there it was.

"Take it. Call it a donation from the community." Shona
reached over and tried to place it in the pocket of Bertie's shirt,
but Bertie stepped backwards.

"I can't take your money, Shona. I just wanted your help
and the only way to get it was to give you a reason to fight with
us. I had to make you as angry at Lawrence as we are."

Shona noticed a strange flicker in Bertie's eyes. It looked
like guilt.

"What? *You* made that call to the authorities," Shona hissed,
feeling her heart thud. "You got my kid taken away?"

"Don't you realize what's going on in this town, Shona?
Every day, people like us are being persecuted for trying to live
a normal life. I lost the love of my life because she couldn't
handle the shame of who she was. The sideways looks, the
whispers behind her back, people around here judging us.
Three years together, then one morning she's gone. Just like
that." Bertie fought to contain the emotion now flooding
through her words. "Why the hell should *you* get what we can't
have, huh?"

The room fell silent. Both women stood toe-to-toe, then
Shona pressed her face into Bertie's. "Leave me and my family
the fuck alone, you piece of shit!"

Incapable of holding in her rage any longer, Shona tore the
backyard of her garage apart seconds after Bertie left, her half-
hearted apology for the phone call still hanging in the air. Oil
drums, old crates and various boxes of nuts and bolts were

kicked around with Shona finally ending up in a heap on the stony ground, a sobbing mess.

"I gotta get him back. I gotta get him back," she repeated over and over again.

Almost an hour passed before Shona felt composed enough to drive home. It was still only midday, but she didn't feel in the mood to be working. She needed to be somewhere where she could think, without people around her. Solitude was sometimes the only company she wanted. About half a mile in the opposite direction to the beach house, Shona saw a car broken down at the side of the road. Next to it was a young woman who, after spotting Shona's approaching truck, began waving her arms to flag her down. Shona felt her right boot press slightly harder down on the gas pedal, but her better nature overwhelmed her desire to drive past. Sighing, she clicked on her turn signal and slowed the truck down, pulling in behind the red Pontiac.

"Having some trouble?" Shona called over as she climbed out of her truck and grabbed her tools from the back seat.

"Yeah, I heard a noise like nails being fed through a grinder, then it just cut out. You a mechanic?" the woman shouted back, wrinkling her nose in surprise. Shona was used to that comment by now. Normally she'd throw a witty comeback, but today wasn't the day for it.

"Yeah. Want me to take a look or just tow you back to town?" Shona asked as she began walking over.

"Well, if you don't mind taking a look? I'd be really grateful. I'm not having the best of days and this just topped it all off." She wiped her eyes and ran a hand through her tousled sandy blonde hair. She was around twenty years old, wearing brown slacks and a white tee-shirt. Her light brown jacket was edged around the collar and lapels with a thin line of dark brown fur. Her pretty face was stained with dry tears, her tired looking eyes heavy lidded.

"You OK?" Shona asked.

"Not really. I've only been back home from college a day, then I get a call from the hospital saying my brother's in bad shape. I've been there all night, then this damn heap of junk lets me down on the way back." The young woman kicked the tire in frustration. Shona nodded, completely able to empathize with her on that. "I'm Alison, by the way." She held her hand out to Shona who shook it.

"Shona. Now, let's have a look under the hood."

"I really appreciate this, Shona. My dad usually takes care of all this stuff but he's out of town."

Shona buried her head in the engine bay looking for the fault. Less than an hour later, the car was all fixed up and Alison was back behind the wheel. She reached into her jacket pocket and pulled out her wallet. "How much do I owe you, Shona?"

Shona shook her head. "No charge. It was just a bit of grit in the fan belt and some wires to tighten. But my garage is just in the town back there, so if you ever need anything else, you know where to find me."

"Thank you, Shona, I'll remember that," Alison replied, then set off again on her journey.

Chapter 27

"I know it don't mean anything to you, but I genuinely am sorry the way things turned out with the kid. I didn't think they'd actually take him away from you," Bertie began after strolling into the garage and leaning against the car Shona was fixing that Wednesday morning.

Shona stuck her head out from underneath the car and looked up at her in disbelief. "What the hell did you think they would do? It's all but sent Chloe over the edge again. You know no one will accept two women to bring up a kid together, like as a couple."

"I know. But that's gonna change one day, you'll see. The wheels are in motion, and that's why us standing up to the police is the right thing to do," Bertie replied.

"One day maybe, but not in our lifetime. You can protest and stomp your feet all you want, but the law is the law. They're kicking people out of the armed forces for being like us, no matter how good their service record is. They don't want queers in their society, Bertie, full stop. I can't believe you let me think that violence was the way to make them listen. All we can do is live a quiet life." Shona slid back underneath the car and clanged her wrench loudly against the bracket she was trying to loosen.

"Well, you say that. But I heard on the grapevine that because you were seen helping Everett's son and those other police guys, then we might be able to broker at least a truce for now. Give us time to plan our next skirmish without being raided every night." Bertie grinned as Shona slid out again, more forcefully this time.

"For God's sake, Bertie, you get a truce and all you wanna do is keep fighting? You and your girls not get beat up enough last time?" Shona pointed her wrench at the still healing cut on Bertie's bottom lip.

"What choice do people like us have, huh? It'll always be them winning. A truce just means they want us to keep quiet, stay obedient. Well, fuck that."

"I can't help you," Shona replied. "I won't help you. We ain't friends. Just leave me the fuck alone."

"Good morning, Shona, how have you been?"

Bill Everett was standing at the garage doors looking ten years older than the last time Shona had seen him. His sandy hair was a little thinner at the sides, the lines on his face more pronounced.

"Sheriff Everett!" Shona exclaimed, her face beaming. They had only known each other for a few weeks before his tragic family news, but they had already forged a bond, and, since Lawrence had been in charge, she'd missed Everett's strong calm leadership. "How have you been? Are you back in town now?"

"Not quite. We got the news about Eric being in the hospital, so we came straight down. I'm leaving Shirley here to look after him while I go back up to Portland. Dad's still not..." He tailed off, then smiled back at Shona. "I see your place is doing well."

"Yeah, I'm making a living," Shona replied, wiping her oily hands on a towel before offering Everett a coffee.

"No thanks, I can't be long. Shirley's just across the street picking up some groceries. I just wanted to come over here and see how you were doing. And to thank you for what you did the other day."

Shona blushed. "Oh, don't worry, it was nothing. Anyone would have done the same. Your son needed help and I..."

Everett held up his hands to protest. "No, no, I don't mean what you did for Eric. I'm truly grateful for that too but what I meant was what you did for my daughter. Alison?" Everett waited for Shona to remember. "She told me about 'a woman called Shona who saved her bacon at the side of the road' on Saturday morning. I'm truly thankful you came along. Some of those tow truck guys might have taken advantage..." He tailed off, then refocused his eyes.

"She's your daughter? I didn't know. She never gave me her last name," Shona replied. "But you're welcome."

"She said you wouldn't take any payment either?"

"No, sir."

Everett stared at Shona and smiled. "Well now, if that's the case then I'm just going to have to do something else to repay you. How about I recommend this place to all my friends and family so they can bring some more business your way. They'll pay, of course. I just want them to have the best mechanic I know on their vehicles."

Shona nodded and shook Everett's hand. "Thank you, sir, that would be swell. But I won't charge the police officers. No matter what Lawrence thinks of me, that ain't changed around here since day one."

"So be it, then. You're a one-off, Shona, a real asset to this town." He turned to walk away. When he was at the edge of the sidewalk, Shona called after him. "Yeah?"

"Come back to work soon," Shona said, her eyes imploring him.

"We'll see," he replied.

Chapter 28

For the first time in nearly a week, Chloe dared to go out in public. It had been six hellish days since David had been taken away. Six long days of desperate phone calls to every Children's Bureau officer she could get the number for, but no one would give her any more details than "your son is safe, he's being cared for." Walking the half mile into town, she'd decided that she couldn't stay cooped up indoors for much longer. The townsfolk would already be churning over the different stories they'd been told, each one putting their own opinion in for good measure no doubt. She had barely eaten or slept that week, and not felt like cooking at all even though she knew Shona needed to keep her strength up for work. With that in mind, the bakery was her first port of call.

"Good morning. I'd like one of your chicken pies, please," Chloe asked, her voice barely audible.

"Hi Chloe," Alice chirped, giving her an inquisitive look. "How's Shona today?"

"And four of those fresh baked biscuits if you please," Chloe said, ignoring Alice's question.

"Sure thing." Alice bagged up the biscuits and boxed up the

pie. She took Chloe's money, smiling as she spoke. "Shona's real nice, isn't she? Always comes in here for her afternoon snack."

Chloe didn't respond, but noticed Alice's fresh face, sparkling eyes and bright green summer dress. The ribbon in her light brown hair reminded her of how she used to look and hearing her talk about Shona sparked a pang inside of her.

After sitting in the park area in the center of town for the last half an hour thinking about what Alice had said, and the way she'd said it, Chloe stood up and headed over to the garage but as she reached the sidewalk she saw Shona in a heated exchange with two police officers, one with his handcuffs at the ready.

"Oh no, what now?" she exclaimed, then raced over, the brown bag containing her box of pie and biscuits flapping in the breeze as she ran.

"Shona, what's going on?" Chloe said.

"Nothing, it's fine. These gentlemen were just checking up on their cars, right, guys?" Shona raised her eyebrows at the police officers.

"Um... Yeah, so I want it ready by this afternoon, OK?" one officer replied. He put his handcuffs back on his belt, then smiled at Chloe as he led Shona a few feet away from her and his partner. "Shona, look, you know I hate to do this, but the boss wants me to pull you in for what happened the other night. I know you helped some of us and I appreciate that, but what do I tell Lawrence if I don't?" The young police officer took his hat off and wiped his sweaty brow.

"Just tell him you didn't see me do anything other than just stand there," Shona whispered back. "I didn't get involved, so he can't touch me for any felony. He knows that, he's just sore about it, Donny."

"OK. But I can't promise he won't send Barnes over here. He's his little pet now. Bring back Bill Everett, that's what I say."

Donny walked back over to his partner, gave him the signal to leave, then tipped his cap to both women.

"What was all that about?" Chloe asked again, her stare more pointed this time.

"Lawrence," Shona replied. "What smells so good?" She looked down at the bag Chloe was holding.

Minnie's car pulled up. She gave them both a beaming smile and almost leapt out of her seat. "Shona."

"Hi Minnie, you OK?" Shona asked as Minnie trotted up to them.

"I'm fine, dear. How are you both today?"

"We're doing good. How's William?" Shona asked.

"Oh, he's OK. One of his better days, actually. We got to chatting about the old days when he was in his prime, ruling on all the important cases here in town. Oh, the memory that man has," she paused and bit her lip, "well, when he's not confused. But anyway, we got on the subject of that nasty piece of work Lawrence and what he's done to you and your family and he was furious. Especially after everything you've done for me. Then we talked some more and, well, we might just have come up with an idea." Minnie's eyes sparkled.

Minnie had followed Shona and Chloe back to the beach house after Shona had quickly locked up the garage. Now sitting on the couch in the living room, Chloe and Shona waited for Minnie to begin speaking.

"The way William and I see it," she said, leaning forward in her armchair, "the only reason they had to take your boy away was because they assumed you two were living as a couple, right?"

Chloe and Shona looked at each other. "Well, yeah. But we

can't deny that now, can we?" Shona replied, sweeping her hand through her hair.

"But you haven't confirmed it to anyone other than me, right?" Minnie's eyes were keen.

"Only Doctor Thomas, but he's bound by oath," Chloe replied. "Shona?"

"Only the girls at the bar, but they won't say anything. Many of them are in the same boat," Shona replied. "They pride themselves on their loyalty. Well, apart from Bertie, but her call to the police was anonymous so they won't be able to chase that one up. And I made sure she knew how much damage she's done. I actually believe she's sorry for what she did," Shona added. Both their hopes grew higher as Minnie began telling them her idea.

"But that's so simple," Chloe gasped when Minnie had finished speaking. "Why didn't we think of that?"

"Doesn't matter now," Minnie replied with a sense of glee. "We'll put the plan of action in place first thing tomorrow morning."

Chloe couldn't hold back any longer. She wrapped Minnie up in a tight hug and held her while she composed herself. "I don't know how to thank you for this, I really don't."

"It's the least I can do after all the good deeds Shona's done for me these last few years. I just hope it works."

Chapter 29

Sheriff Lawrence pulled up outside the beach house still mystified by the call he'd received an hour ago from the Children's Bureau. "Meet me at the Clark residence at 3 p.m. There's been a development," the voice had said. Stepping out of his truck, he could see that she was already there.

"Well, good afternoon, Barbara. What are we doin' here?" Lawrence said as he made his way over to the suited woman from last week.

"We've had new information passed to us by a trusted source, not some random anonymous tip-off," Barbara said with disdain. "I'm here to assess the suitability of the residence where the child is to live."

"I thought we'd already decided what was in the best interests of the child."

"Sheriff, did you or anyone else who reported this case to me actually check the living arrangements in that house *before* calling me?" She gestured towards him with her clipboard.

"They're all built the same way, these beach houses." His confident grin turned to a snarl.

The front door opened and Chloe appeared, Shona standing behind her.

"Good morning, Mrs. Haskins. Won't you come in?" Chloe said, not bothering to acknowledge Lawrence's presence.

"Thank you, I will," Barbara replied, following Shona and Chloe into the house. Shona slammed the door as Lawrence made a move to follow. He stood outside, impatiently waiting. Not even five minutes had the chance to pass before Barbara reemerged. She stormed down the porch steps towards her car, her face red with embarrassment.

"On behalf of the Children's Bureau, ma'am, all I can do is apologize," she called back over her shoulder. As she fumbled with her car door handle, she shot a look of pure annoyance at Lawrence. "Sheriff Lawrence here gave us false information, but I really should have checked myself. I'll be in touch as soon as I get back to the office." She roared away up the driveway.

"What the... Get out of my way." Lawrence pushed past Chloe and Shona and stormed into the house. Shona grinned at Chloe.

Lawrence stalked along the hallway hunting for the master bedroom. When he found it, he swung the door wide open. The room was beautifully furnished, with crisp white linen on the bed and a blanket with little red flowers sewn on it. The drapes matched perfectly and all around were soft cushions. The handmade pine dressing table was painted white and an assortment of hairbrushes and makeup was lined up neatly. It was unmistakably a woman's bedroom and, as he walked up to the double bed, Lawrence let a sly grin drape across his face.

"Just as I thought."

"So, now you've invaded my privacy, *Acting* Sheriff Lawrence. Are you satisfied?" Chloe said, appearing behind him with her arms folded.

"Oh yeah, I'm satisfied. Satisfied that we had that kid taken away from you pair of..." He paused, looking for the most offensive word he could think of. "It's disgusting, and illegal, what you were doin' in here."

"What are you insinuating?"

"Insinuatin'?" Lawrence replied with a snort. "Look, if that's the kid's room through there," he pointed to the room directly across the hallway, "then where the hell does *she* sleep?" He jabbed a finger towards Shona.

Shona stepped forward, her face expressionless. "In there." She pointed at the much plainer-looking door about three feet further along the wall to the door to David's room.

"What?" Lawrence said, the grin melting from his face. "But that's not possible."

Shona went over to open the door. Lawrence was out of Chloe's room and into the snug single bedroom in two bounds. Sure enough, inside was a neat and tidy, perfectly laid out bedroom, complete with single bed, desk, chair and wardrobe in the corner. Muttering several curse words, Lawrence flung open the wardrobe door to see all of Shona's work shirts ironed and hanging up. Her spare pair of work boots sat nestled in the bottom. On the back of the desk chair hung her jacket and on the desk was her comb and a few coins. He turned around to see both Chloe and Shona watching him, their faces set.

"Will that be all, *Acting* Sheriff?" Chloe purred.

Lawrence, with a sharp intake of breath and without another word, stomped out of Shona's room and out of the house.

He hadn't noticed the smell of wood shavings and fresh paint.

PART 3: SEPTEMBER 1964

Chapter 30

S tuck in the same routine as before, and with David getting more boisterous by the day, Chloe had found it harder and harder to cope with the exhaustion. Her visits to Doctor Thomas were weekly now, an hour each time, where he could talk her through her raging emotions. When September came around, she was almost relieved that David was ready to start preschool. He'd turned five that April and, with his black hair and dark eyes, was looking like Kyle more and more each day, a fact that especially bothered Shona who was now spending most of her time at the garage.

"Sorry I'm late. I stopped off for a Coke at the bar," Shona said as she walked into the kitchen to find Chloe cleaning up the dishes from her and David's dinner.

"We already had dinner. I left you some on top of the stove," Chloe replied without turning around. She busied herself at the sink washing the dishes and placing them on the drainer.

"Have we got everything ready for tomorrow?" Shona asked sorting through the pile of neatly folded laundry and finding David's best pair of blue shorts and white tee-shirt.

"I've already picked out his outfit. It's hanging up in his room."

Shona looked hurt. "I thought we were going to choose what he was gonna wear on his first day together?"

"You weren't here," Chloe replied, turning to face her as she dried the bubbles from her wet hands with a dish towel.

Shona leaned against the counter. "OK. Well, I'll eat, then go read him his story."

"He's already had it. It's half past eight, Shona," Chloe shot back. The frustration in her voice was obvious. "You should be here for those things, not drinking in some bar that you said you weren't going to go to anymore. I thought you wanted to stay away from those girls?"

"They're OK. There's been no trouble these last few years since the police laid off them. Bertie has rights now since she registered with the Tavern Guild, and Lawrence knows he can't touch her now, or anyone who goes in the bar. The town's sick of his shit now anyway. They just want a quiet life. You remember when Lawrence was warned to leave me alone too, because of all that embarrassment the Children's Bureau suffered when the papers got hold of it? Well, it's been over a month since he last snarled at me in the street. I think he's mellowing." She laughed, then stopped as Chloe shot her a sharp look.

"It's not funny, Shona. If it hadn't been for Minnie and her quick thinking, we would have had the whole town chasing us out. Again."

Shona's grin melted away.

"If Judge Barker hadn't made that call to the Children's Bureau to get them to come and check the house afterwards, we might never have gotten David back. You should be glad Lawrence is staying away from us now, not gloating about it. A 'low profile' is exactly what we should be keeping. I don't need you worrying me sick all the time by drinking in that bar and getting all riled up by those table-banging radicals pushing their luck." Chloe threw her dish towel onto the drainer and left Shona to eat her dinner in the kitchen alone.

Chloe was just about to leave the spot on the end of David's bed where she'd been sitting for the last twenty minutes when he turned over and looked at her.

"Momma?"

"Go back to sleep, baby. I was just checking in on you."

"Will it be OK tomorrow?" David said, rubbing his eyes.

"Oh, of course it will be," Chloe replied, rushing up to tuck him back in. She tapped his chin and smiled. "You'll make lots of new friends and learn so much. Now close your eyes. You need a good night's sleep." She kissed him on his forehead and smoothed down his covers.

When she returned to the living room, Shona was already sitting on the couch. She smiled up to Chloe where their eyes met in a mutual apology. "He OK?"

"Yeah. I think he's a little worried." Chloe sat on the couch next to Shona, who lifted up her arm naturally for Chloe to snuggle underneath. "I think I am too."

Shona kissed Chloe on the head. "Why's that, baby?"

"Well, I heard that the principal is a bit of a force. It's not ideal, but Fairview is the only elementary school in the town. It's our only option. The other three in the book are miles away. What if the principal asks a lot of questions about us? I just want a decent education for our son. He deserves that." Chloe bit at her fingernails as she spoke.

"Just relax. We've lived in this town for over five years now. We're just as good as anyone at that school, with just as many rights now. Well, you have them as his mother," Shona added with a mirthless laugh. "Just tell her that you've heard all good things about her school and that it's our first choice. Then get the heck outta there."

"Yeah, I guess. I wish you could come too."

Shona shook her head. "No, I won't come this time. It looks better if it's just his mother with him on his first day." She paused and picked at a loose thread on the arm of the couch.

"You know you mean the world to David, don't you?" Chloe affirmed, stroking Shona's arm.

"I love him like he was my own. But there are some things you gotta do that I can't be a part of. Maybe that'll change in the future. But right now, this is the best we can hope for."

"I guess."

"Anyway, I was thinking, with David at preschool in the daytime, you'll have so much more time to take up your hobbies again. I'll go up in the attic and get your painting things down, how about that? I ain't seen you paint for ages."

Chloe's face lit up. "Oh, would you? That would be amazing. Thank you."

"Of course. I'll make you some new canvases too this weekend. I've got some wood out in the shed that will work just fine. Hell, maybe you could paint me?"

Chloe blushed, remembering the painting she'd done, purely from memory, of Shona on her horse Storm, back in Alabama when their feelings for each other were unknown. Having her sit for her in person would be exhilarating. "Thank you, Shona. That really means a lot to me. It'll be nice just to be normal again. To be me," she added, her eyes glowing in the semi-darkness of the living room.

"I've missed you," Shona said as she kissed the top of Chloe's head. "I've missed us."

Chloe nodded, then snuggled deeper in Shona's arms.

Principal Margaret Miller strode down Fairview Elementary school's main hallway, her Chanel heels clicking on the perfectly polished parquet flooring. She had just that year turned fifty and had been in charge of the school since the last principal retired ten years ago. As she approached a patch of dull wood on the ground in front of her, her face creased into a frown.

"Bennett, get over here," she barked.

Henry Bennett, the janitor, scurried over to her. He wore blue coveralls and had a wooden broom tucked underneath one skinny arm.

"Yes ma'am," he said, tipping his blue cap to her.

"When I said I wanted this floor polished to the point where I could see my face in it, I meant the entire floor. Not just the parts I can see. Look down there." She pointed to the patch just behind a coat stand that Bennett had missed.

"Right away, Mrs. Miller," Bennett replied, taking out his polishing cloth. He maneuvered himself behind the coat stand and began buffing the floor. "Oh, by the way, you have a visitor waiting in your office. Polly asked me to let you know if I saw you. It's your son, I think."

Miller looked surprised, then set off back to her office.

"Is he in there?" she asked Polly, who was sitting at her assistant's desk outside Miller's office taking a phone call.

Polly clamped her palm over the telephone receiver and nodded. "He didn't say what it was, but he looked pretty nervous."

Miller entered her office to see her tall, well built, twenty-three-year-old son standing by her window looking out onto the green space where the third-grade children were playing. He was wearing grey slacks and a smart blue shirt. "Hello, Jonathan, to what do I owe this pleasure?" She kissed him on the cheek, then sat at her desk.

"Hi Mom, I was just passing by and I..."

"Get to the point, son. I'm a busy woman."

Jonathan ran a hand through his dark brown hair. "Well, I know we've had this conversation before but..."

Miller's heart sank. She knew what he was going to say. It had been the same conversation they'd had for the last year, and no matter how much she'd wanted the idea to go away, the subject kept coming up.

"I've made some more inquiries and the draft office said I can join this month." He watched his mother's reaction, then his eyes hardened. "You're not going to talk me out of it this time, Mother. It's what I want to do. I can't wait tables all my life —I need to be doing something that matters. It won't be long until they make us enlist anyway. I want to go over there on my terms."

Miller pursed her shiny red lips and smoothed the back of her short brown hair. "Are you finished?"

Jonathan straightened his back. "Yes."

"Good. You're not going. I forbid it."

Jonathan scowled and thrust his hands in the air. "I'm twenty-three years old, damn it. I don't need your permission."

Miller tapped a maroon fingernail on the mahogany wood. "Why? Why do you want to put yourself in danger? Wasn't losing your father in France enough for you? Growing up all these years without him with nothing to remember him by other than some old photographs? You were only three years old when he died on that beach," she paused, her eyes moistening, "and now you want to put me through all that again?"

Jonathan fell silent.

"It's a war that can't be won. That's what all the newspapers are saying. We've tried to bring order to Vietnam, but we're meddling in another country's regime. What are you going to be fighting for? Do you even know?"

"It's what I want, Mother," Jonathan replied. He walked

towards her, leaned down and kissed her on the cheek. "I'll write as soon as I get there."

After he left, Miller stormed up to the door and slammed it. Leaning against it, she felt her whole body tremble. After a minute or two, she composed herself, smoothed down the front of her peach Chanel suit and checked her hair in the small mirror by the door. As she did so, there was a knock and Polly's long face peeked through the crack as she pushed the door open.

"Sorry to bother you, Mrs. Miller, but your nine o'clock is here."

Miller walked back to her brown leather office chair and seated herself back down, straightening her name plate on the desktop.

"You can go right in," Polly said as she opened the office door. Chloe nodded her thanks and smiled at Principal Miller.

"Hello, I'm Chloe Clark, my son David is starting preschool today and I was told you wanted to see me?"

"Yes, of course, Mrs. Clark," Miller began, pausing when she saw Chloe redden slightly. "It is *Mrs.* Clark, right?"

"Yes, but my husband isn't with us. He's away," Chloe replied.

"Away where?" Miller pressed, noting the lack of a wedding ring on Chloe's finger.

"He's in the military. *Was* in the military. He died. He was in the army." Chloe smiled but could feel a bead of sweat drip between her shoulder blades.

Miller's face twitched. "Seems like a common desire around here today, the army," she muttered back.

"Pardon me?"

"Oh, nothing. I'm sorry to hear about your husband. So, Mrs. Clark, that's not a local accent you got there. Where are you from originally?" Miller smiled and leaned back in her chair.

"Alabama. But we moved here to get a fresh start and..." Chloe stopped, noticing a flicker in Miller's eyes.

"We?"

"Me and my sister. She's been staying with me since David's father died." Chloe shifted uncomfortably in her seat and wiped her brow.

"Oh, I see. You mentioned a fresh start?" Miller's inquisitive blue eyes were penetrating. "From what?"

Chloe licked her lips. "Nothing really. Just wanted to get away from the painful memories, plus we just wanted to live by the sea, you know? Sea air, good for you, isn't it?"

"Well, I can't argue with that. Lived here all my life. OK, Mrs. Clark, well, thank you for coming in today. I'm sure our school will offer the best possible education for your son. Polly will go through all the forms with you." Miller stood up and showed her out to Polly who was waiting with a clipboard.

"Thank you, Principal Miller. I'm sure it will," Chloe said, her face flushed.

∾

Shona came out of David's bedroom later that evening wearing a beaming smile.

"He had a great first day, couldn't stop going on about it." She sat down next to Chloe on the couch. "You OK, honey? You've been quiet all night."

Chloe lifted her head off her hand and sat up straight. "Yeah, it was just this morning when I met the principal. She's a bit of a dragon."

"Really? In what way?"

"Just the questions she was asking and the look on her face when I answered. I felt like a criminal."

Shona laughed. "I ain't never met a woman you can't give as

good as you get back to." She laid her head back and closed her eyes.

"Yeah, I know. But it was just the way she looked at me when I told her David's father was dead. It just came out. She acted like I wouldn't be able to cope without a man around, like David is suffering or something. Bet she has her man around doing everything for her." She turned to face Shona. "We've done OK so far with David, haven't we? He's a good boy and he's happy, don't you think? Shona?"

Shona was fast asleep, snoring softly. Sighing, Chloe sat back in her seat and stared at the TV.

~

"So, you liking preschool, baby?" Chloe asked as she combed his hair after breakfast.

"Yeah. I get to play with the red wagon today," David replied.

"That's good. You like red. How's your teacher, you like her?"

"She's funny and kind. She has brown hair like you, Mommy."

"Really? Well, that's good." She paused and pushed David out to arm's length to admire him. "Now, aren't you such a handsome little boy. Go get your shoes."

David stayed still and looked at Chloe with his dark brown eyes. "Mommy?"

"Yes, baby?"

"Why don't I have a daddy?" Chloe's heart froze. It was the question that she'd dreaded. "I see other kids with their daddies. Bobby Kelly in my class says his daddy picks him up at home time. Bobby said everyone gets a daddy when they're born. Where's mine?"

Chloe bent down to stroke her son's face. "Um... Well, you

got me and you got Shona to look after you. You love Shona, right?"

"Yeah."

"Then don't you go worrying about what Bobby Kelly said, OK?"

"OK, Momma. Can I have macaroni and cheese for dinner?"

Chloe laughed. "Of course you can. Now scoot. Go find those shoes."

Chapter 31

Shona burst in to find Chloe in the kitchen after retrieving a letter from the mailbox outside.

"It's from Elbie!" Shona yelled. "I recognize the postmark. And that spidery handwriting," she added, laughing.

"Well, go on, open it!" Chloe exclaimed as she dried her soapy hands on a dish towel.

Shona ripped open the letter and read the first few lines. "He's all good, his daughter's doing well and, oh my, she's just had another baby. A boy this time. His first grandson. Oh Chloe, he'll be tickled pink about that." Shona clutched the letter, her eyes shining. "I gotta write back, tell him about David starting preschool and everything." She ran into the living room and over to the bureau. Taking out a piece of fresh white notepaper, she began composing her return letter.

"I wrote a letter to my mom yesterday, telling her the same thing. It's on the bureau with some other letters I need to send out. Could you put the one to my mom in Elbie's envelope, please, before you seal it? And ask if he still doesn't mind mailing it for me from Tennessee?"

"Uh-huh, sure," Shona replied, not looking up.

"OK, well I'd better get the little guy off to school. I'll see you after work?"

"Mmm..." Shona replied, deep in thought.

Chloe and David left Shona chewing the end of her pencil, thinking of all the stories to tell Elbie. Half an hour later, she slipped her letter in the envelope and closed it. Picking up the other mail on the bureau, she set off to the post office with a long-missed spring in her step.

Over macaroni and cheese, the family sat laughing about the day's events. Shona had closed the garage up early and was enjoying the seventh story David was telling, this one involving whose wagon was faster, his or Bobby Kelly's. Later, when he'd gone to bed, Chloe sat next to Shona who was reading the newspaper.

"It was so sad today at the school gates. David's noticing all the daddies picking up their kids. He hasn't asked again but I can see the confusion in his face. He doesn't know his daddy will be rotting in some prison cell somewhere for the rest of his life."

"That's where he belongs," Shona lay her newspaper down on her lap. "Do you miss yours?"

Taken slightly aback by the question, Chloe wrinkled her brow. "Not at all. I mean, I miss who he could have been, and who he was before I went off to college. But when I came back to Daynes and saw all those barbaric things he did, my feelings changed. I don't miss the man he is now. Not one bit."

"Then David will be fine without his father," Shona reasoned. "One day we'll tell him, but not yet. Let him think for just a little bit longer that all men are gentlemen."

Chloe nodded her agreement.

~

Early Wednesday morning, Chloe set off into town to pick up a few groceries. After her bakery run, and the usual comments from a doe-eyed Alice asking her how Shona was, she ran into Minnie who was just about to leave for her weekly visit to her husband.

"How is he doing now? Shona told me about his fall," Chloe asked.

"Oh, he's doing much better now. Damn doorstop, I tell him all the time to watch that thing when he's coming out of his room, but will he listen?" Minnie shook her head. "I think his mind is still distracted worrying about this town and the mess Lawrence has made of it these last few years. It's just not the same since Everett was in charge. God willing, one day he might agree to take his old job back. Anyway, there's me rambling away. How are you all doing? How's little David doing at preschool?"

"He's absolutely loving it. He adores his teacher," Chloe gushed.

"Yeah, I heard she's real nice. Pretty girl, 'bout the same age as you." Minnie saw a look of confusion on Chloe's face. "Oh, me and Margaret Miller go way back. She told me over our monthly game of bridge."

Chloe shuddered at the mention of the principal.

"You've obviously met her?" Minnie gave a knowing smile. "She's alright when you get to know her, just has very high standards for her school."

"I didn't know you two knew each other," Chloe replied, biting the corner of her lip as she remembered the lies she'd spun Miller about David's father.

"Don't you worry, honey. I won't say a word. I know what's at stake for you and Shona. I'd better go. William will be waiting and if this pie goes cold before I get there I'll be in big trouble."

Minnie said her goodbyes and headed back across the sidewalk to her parked car.

Heading back into the town square, Chloe sat on the bench and stared across to the garage where she saw Shona in mid-flow, talking to Eric Everett and laughing at something he'd said. As she was about to set off for home, a young couple with a stroller crossed her path. She noticed the baby had carelessly dropped a pacifier on the ground and, after picking it up, Chloe set off after the couple.

"Excuse me, sir, ma'am? Your baby dropped..." She paused when the man turned around. He looked vaguely familiar and after a few seconds both of their mouths formed into a grin of recognition. "Robert? Hi. Do you remember me?" Chloe said.

"Why, of course I remember you, Mrs. Clark," he said, tipping his fedora hat. "Ain't every day I hit on a married woman. Married myself now, well, not *myself*, but...ah shucks, there's me rambling on again." Robert's cheeks reddened as he reached out to pull his wife into him. "This is Janet."

"Hi," Janet said with a flick of her gloved hand.

"And this is our daughter, Eleanor," Robert gushed. "That trick still works," he added with a wink.

"Eleanor?" Chloe replied, taken aback for a moment.

"After my mother," Janet chipped in, then gazed lovingly between Robert and their baby daughter.

"What a beautiful name," Chloe said, her voice barely audible as her thoughts drifted to her own mother.

"Yeah, well, we'd better be getting this little one back home for her feeding. It was real good to see you again, Mrs. Clark. You take care now."

"You too, Robert. And you, Janet. You make a wonderful couple," Chloe said, the last haunting sentence leaving her lips before she'd even realized it.

She watched as they walked away, Robert's arm draped around his wife's shoulders as she pushed the stroller. "Bobby

Kelly says everyone gets a daddy when they're born," she heard in her head as she walked slowly through the square. Feeling her head spin, she turned in the direction of the doctor's office, rather than heading straight home, her thoughts a jumbled mess.

～

David flew at Shona the minute she arrived home from work. She just about caught him in her arms before he knocked her over.

"Whoa there, where's the fire?" she exclaimed.

"Shona, Shona, look what I got." He held in his little hand a certificate, its edges blunted from being carried all the way home.

Shona took it from him and read it. "Most improved student. Oh, I'm so proud of you, you're so clever," she gushed, scooping him up in her arms. "Where's your momma?"

"She's in the kitchen. I made a mess again."

"Oh, well, that's OK, buddy. Clever people are always the messiest." She sank to her haunches and ruffled his black hair. Grinning, David ran off to play with Cooper in the front yard, leaving Shona to go and find Chloe.

"Hi honey." Shona walked up behind Chloe and kissed her on the cheek.

"He spilled his macaroni all down the table. He got so excited to see you coming down the driveway that he jumped up from the table and..." She opened up her arms to emphasize the accident.

"Takes after me, alright," Shona grinned, nuzzling into Chloe's neck. "You smell real good. That a new scent?"

"That's the macaroni and cheese he wiped on me as I was cleaning him up," Chloe replied. "Yours is in the oven keeping warm. I was thinking, after I've put David to bed, we could get ourselves an early night?" Chloe turned to face Shona and wrapped her arms around her neck. Seeing Shona look over her shoulder and out of the window, Chloe stopped talking. "Are you listening?"

Shona snapped back to her senses. "Oh, sorry, I was just thinking I'd go and spend some time with David out in the yard, maybe throw around that new Frisbee thing I got him?" She refocused her eyes on Chloe. "But yeah, afterwards I'd love to snuggle up with you." Leaving Chloe to finish the dishes, Shona ran out to the yard.

Chloe, watching from the kitchen sink, couldn't help but admire the closeness of Shona's relationship with him. It was all she'd ever wanted for him, to have someone to teach him stuff. "Did Shona have to be a man to do that?" she'd asked Doctor Thomas that afternoon. Deep down, Chloe knew Shona was an amazing parent, but that the intimacy she'd once felt with her had begun to wane lately. With this gnawing away at her, Chloe made her mind up that tonight she would put this right.

Chloe bathed David and read him his bedtime story in super quick time. Climbing into the shower, she began lathering her body with her most luxurious soap and washed her hair twice, not wanting the smell of dinner to linger on a single strand. She chose Shona's favorite coconut-scented conditioner, then dressed in the red chiffon nightgown she'd bought earlier that week. She blow-dried her hair carefully, running a soft brush through it to accentuate the natural waves in her light brown hair, and applied just the merest hint of red lipstick. Looking in the full-length mirror, she saw her old self staring back, her face and body more mature though now, with more natural lines and curves. Long gone were the days when she would cake on her makeup and squeeze into tight dresses and restrictive pencil skirts when she worked for her father. Taking in a deep breath, she checked herself one more time and walked back into the living room.

Shona had taken off her denim shirt, pants and boots and was lying full length on the couch fast asleep.

Chloe sashayed over to Shona and lay down next to her, lifting up her arm to snuggle underneath. Lifting her lips to Shona's forehead, Chloe planted a soft kiss there, then another one on her temple, finally coming to rest on her lips.

"Hey baby, you smell amazing," Shona mumbled, her eyes still closed.

"I just wanted to be close to you tonight. We don't have to go any further if you're too tired." Chloe stroked her fingers across Shona's forehead, sweeping away a few loose strands of baby soft blonde hair. Her hand then drifted over Shona's arms, lifting her undershirt over her head. Running her palm over Shona's warm, smooth skin, Chloe felt the first ripples of arousal flutter through her as she slipped Shona's white shorts down over her knees and dropped them to the floor with the undershirt.

"Mmm..." Shona murmured as she sleepily lifted up Chloe's nightgown, and it joined the undershirt and shorts on the carpet. Both now naked, they lay together, skin on skin, feeling their bodies tremble in the cool evening air. Placing Shona's head on her chest, Chloe held her tightly, her breathing matching the rhythm of Chloe's own. Shivering, she reached up to the back of the couch and pulled a blanket over them both.

"I love you so much, Shona. I'm so messed up in the head at the moment, about a lot of things. But everything seems to go quiet when I'm lying here with you."

"I'll keep you safe, baby, always. Ain't nothing and no one gonna break us. I love you too," Shona replied, looking up at her. For a few seconds they gazed at each other, connecting on the deepest of levels once again. Shona, unable to keep her eyes open a second longer, lay her head back down on Chloe's chest, the perfect comfort of Chloe's heartbeat thudding against her chest sending her almost immediately into a deep sleep.

They lay there together for the rest of the night, their breathing and heartbeats completely in sync, their bodies melted together as if as one.

Chapter 32

After finishing all of her morning chores, Chloe lay on the couch for ten minutes to rest. Waking with a jump *five* hours later, she looked up at the clock.

"Oh my gosh!" she exclaimed, seeing that it was well after four. Running over to the telephone in the hall, she dialed Shona's number at the garage.

Seconds after hanging up the phone on Chloe, Shona locked the garage doors and sped off in the direction of Fairview Elementary where David had been waiting for over an hour to be picked up.

Skidding to a halt just inside the school gates, Shona jumped out of the truck and ran over to the reception where she leaned over the desk, breathless. "I'm here to pick up David Clark?" she squeezed out between gasps.

The receptionist looked up from her Rolodex and pinched the corner of her cat-eye glasses, pulling forward. "Name?"

"Clark. David."

The receptionist rolled her eyes and straightened her beehive. "No," she replied, "*your* name."

"Shona Clark."

"Relation?"

"Aunt," Shona said.

There was a long pause while the receptionist got to her feet and walked over to the filing cabinet behind her, her kitten heels clicking on the wooden floor. A few moments later, she walked back and met Shona's expectant stare with a hard one of her own. "You're not down as a nominated adult, so I can't let you take him. Is your sister at home for me to call?"

"Yeah, she's the one who sent me." Shona's patience was wearing thin.

"Hold on." The receptionist dialed their home number and in a few moments was pointing the way to David's classroom. Reluctantly thanking her, Shona headed off in search of David. She finally located Room 19 and knocked on the door.

"Come in," called a light feminine voice from inside.

Shona pushed open the door and looked around the room for David, who was playing with a red wagon on the carpet in the corner. Shona grinned and rushed over, scooping him up in her arms.

"David, I'm so sorry you had to wait, but I'm here now."

David wrapped his little arms around Shona's neck and nuzzled into her. "It's OK, I got to play with the red wagon *and* the blue wagon. Miss said I could because I'd been a good boy today."

"Is that a fact?" Shona replied, turning around to face the front of the classroom. She saw David's teacher sitting facing her, a look of complete disbelief on her face. She stood up, a hand up to her mouth and in total shock. It was a look matched instantly by Shona.

"Shona, this is Miss Adamson. She's my teacher," David said as he rolled a wagon innocently up and down Shona's arm.

"It can't be. Lucy?" Shona gasped, her eyes like saucers.

"Did you call home?" Principal Miller asked, her hands on her hips as she bore down on her seated receptionist.

"Of course I did, Mrs. Miller. But Mrs. Clark said it was fine for her sister to pick the child up as she wasn't feeling too well today."

Miller took her glasses off and chewed on the end of one earpiece. "Where is this Shona now?"

"Gone down to Lucy's classroom to pick up the boy."

"Hmm... OK, leave it with me." Miller set off back down the hallway. When she reached her office, she closed the door, sat down at her desk and picked up the telephone.

"Hello, is that Mrs. Clark? This is Principal Miller at Fairview Elementary. My receptionist has informed me that you're not feeling too good today and have therefore sent an advocate to pick up your son?" She paused. "Oh, I see, that *is* correct. Well, now may I suggest that, going forward, we make a record of your sister's contact details so we can update our records." She waited. "Oh, nothing much, just her full name, address, that sort of thing." Miller paused as Chloe replied. "So her address is the same as yours? Right. Pardon me for sounding surprised, but you didn't put it on the forms when you enrolled David. No, no, it's fine. Alright, well, thank you, Mrs. Clark, for clearing that matter up. Good day."

Miller hung up the telephone and sat back in her chair, her hands clasped together, fingers steepled and pressed against her chin.

"What are you doing here?" Shona squeezed out after what felt like an age staring in shock at the ghost from her past.

"I could ask the same about you," Lucy replied, equally bemused.

"I'm here to pick up my s..." Shona stopped herself before saying the word. "Nephew."

"Your name isn't on the list. I checked all the next of kin when I filled in my planner at the start of semester. I would have noticed your name." Lucy's cheeks were flushed, the look in her eyes alternating between shock and amazement. Finally, she couldn't suppress her smile any longer. "You look good. How long's it been now?"

"Eight years," Shona replied, her whole body ice cold.

"Eight years? Wow." Lucy shook her head and bit the corner of her lip, hardly able to believe she was standing in front of her so many years after what had happened in Mississippi.

Shona snapped out of her shock. "I have to go." She held on to David, who was still sitting snugly against her hip, his arms wrapped around Shona's neck.

"Wait!" Lucy exclaimed. "Um... I need to clear it with Principal Miller. If you're not on the list then..."

"The receptionist called home. It's fine." Shona stormed towards the classroom door, ripping it open with her free hand, David wriggling in the crook of her other arm.

"Shona... Shona, stop! Please," Lucy called after her.

Principal Miller came out of her office, appearing large in the corridor in front of Shona who almost, in her haste to escape, barged her over. "What on earth is going on here? Lucy?" Miller looked over Shona's shoulder at a red-faced Lucy.

"I just needed to check that it's OK for Miss Jac..."

"Clark," Shona interjected with an urgency that startled Lucy.

"Miss Clark, would you mind if I took David for a moment?" Miller reached to take David from Shona and beckoned Lucy into her office. "I won't be a moment. We just need to check one or two things."

The door closed. Shona watched through the window as Lucy opened her arms out wide as if to say she didn't know something. Miller let out a long breath and nodded, her hands firmly clamped on her hips. Finally, the office door opened and David appeared, still clutching his red wagon.

"Send your sister our best wishes for a speedy recovery, Miss Clark," Miller said, a forced smile plastered on her perfectly made-up face.

Shona nodded, picked up David and strode away, casting the quickest of glances back to Lucy.

"This can't be real," Shona muttered to herself. "Why? Why here? Why now?"

"I think Miss Adamson looks like Mommy. They have the same hair," David said as he rolled the red wagon he'd taken from his classroom up the back of Shona's seat.

"She's nothing like your momma," Shona snapped back. She wiped her brow and chewed on the end of her fingers as she drove, her eyes fixed on the horizon. So many thoughts were whizzing through her mind. Eight years had passed since that fateful night at Dorothy's house. Shona rubbed the side of her ribs where the first blow had landed, the memory of it flooding back. Her thoughts drifted to Chloe. How on earth was she going to tell her that her son's teacher was the same person who nearly got the love of her life killed? Would they really have to now up and leave town—again? All because of the past? It was all such a mess. But Chloe had to be told. There was no way Shona could keep this a secret.

Minutes later, they arrived home and Chloe rushed out of the house to greet them.

"Oh baby, I'm so sorry. Momma fell asleep and lost track of time." She scooped David up in her arms and smoothed his hair down. "Are you OK?"

"Yeah. Shona came and got me. She met my teacher," David said, rolling his wagon up Chloe's sleeveless arm.

"Well, I'm due to meet her next Tuesday night at parents' evening and I can't wait," Chloe replied, smiling. A flicker of dread crossed Shona's eyes. "Why don't you come with me, Shona, now you've introduced yourself to the school? I'm sure Miss Adamson won't mind," Chloe asked.

"No," Shona said, then strode straight past Chloe and David down the boardwalk to the beach. In a second or two she was out of sight, leaving Chloe open-mouthed at her reaction.

"So, are you gonna tell me what's eating you?" Chloe asked, looking down at Shona, who was sitting cross-legged on the white sand.

Shona looked up and squinted into the lowering sun. "Nothing. Just had some heat from that principal, that's all." She looked back out to the water. Somehow the words hadn't quite fallen into place in her head yet to explain how she felt about seeing Lucy again. Anger had emulsified itself with hurt, a hurt tinged with regret that their friendship had ended the way it had. All of these feelings were wrapped up in a tangible web of frustration that, because of Lucy, she'd had to leave Mississippi and a job she adored, not to mention having to leave Dorothy on her own. But what was conflicting her more was the thought that if all that hadn't happened then she wouldn't have ended up in Alabama and met Chloe.

Shona blinked hard, hoping her shattered mind would clear.

Chloe sat on the sand next to her and leaned against her

arm. "She can be a dragon. She called me while you were there. I think she bought the idea that we were sisters, so if you want to, I think you should come to parents' evening." Chloe reached out to stroke Shona's face. "I'd really like you to come with me. He's your son too. At least in my eyes, if not in the eyes of the law."

Shona blinked back the tears. "I can't. I'm sorry," she replied, then got to her feet. "I gotta go out for a bit." She walked away, leaving a confused Chloe sitting alone on the sand.

"Why Shona, this is a nice surprise. Come in," Minnie gushed after opening the door.

"I'm sorry to bother you, Minnie, but I need someone to talk to. I really don't know what to do. Something's happened and…" Shona's voice was breaking as she spoke.

Minnie wrapped an arm around her shoulder and walked Shona into her opulent living room, sitting her down on a cream-colored wingback chair. "Now you just take a minute to settle yourself. I'll go get us some tea and you can tell me all about it."

Minnie disappeared into the kitchen, leaving Shona to attempt to piece together her jumbled thoughts. Five minutes later, she returned holding a tray with two tea glasses sitting on it and a plate of ginger cookies. After placing the tray on the coffee table, she sat on the chair opposite Shona and leaned forward, her wrinkly hands clasped.

"Now, tell me what's troubling you, dear."

"I don't know where to start." After a few more minutes of coaxing from Minnie, Shona finally began to find her words. "I met David's teacher today. She's a girl I knew when I lived in Mississippi eight years ago. It was before I met Chloe and, oh

Minnie, I never in my wildest dreams thought I'd ever see her again after what happened."

"Is she a girl you knew well?" Minnie said, an eyebrow raised.

"I thought I did. But not like that, Minnie. We were never… Oh, it's all such a mess, Minnie. My head is spinning."

"Here, take a sip." Minnie handed Shona her glass of tea and waited while she took a huge gulp. "Better?"

"Yeah. Thank you."

"So, this girl was a friend of yours? Back in Mississippi," Minnie asked.

"I was working in this garage called Wreckers and Lucy would come over every day to see me. She had this boyfriend, Frank, who was treating her real bad, so I thought she just wanted a friend to talk to. And we got real tight for a while, but then Frank started to get her to dance in the bar he owned. Then he made her do more."

"More?" Minnie asked, sipping her drink.

"Yeah. With some guys who'd pay him for her company."

"I see. And how did that make you feel, Shona?"

"I didn't care at first, but one night I saw her with some guy. They were in bed and he was doing things to her that made my stomach turn. It made me sick. I couldn't control it. Back then, I hadn't dealt with the shame of who I was. That I liked girls." She lowered her eyes. "Back in Louisiana, my father and this doctor friend of his tried to cure me by making me sick when I saw pictures of women. When I saw Lucy that night with that guy, she looked so similar to a picture in a magazine the doctor made me look at while they put an electric shock through me and…" Shona shuddered, the shame of her treatment flooding back through her. "Anyway, afterwards Lucy tried to explain that she wasn't going to do it anymore. She'd spoken to Frank and told him she was gonna take college more seriously and that was that. We started to get close again, and the sight of her in that bedroom started to fade. She became Lucy again, a girl I'd grown to really like. I couldn't show it, though, in case I ruined our friendship. When I was growing up back in Louisiana, I fell in love with a girl when I was a kid and when she found out how I felt, our friendship was ruined and I had to run away. I didn't want that happening again with Lucy. And I was happy in Mississippi living with Dorothy and working at Wreckers. But then I started to get the feeling Lucy was after more from our friendship so..."

Minnie waited while Shona took another deep breath.

"One night she came round to my house. I was real nervous because I was starting to have feelings for her too. But I still wasn't sure. Until she leaned in to kiss me."

Far from looking shocked, Minnie leaned closer to Shona. "And? What happened, Shona?"

Shona buried her face in her hands for a moment, then looked back at Minnie. "She'd tricked me. She called me a 'screw-up,' then I was grabbed by this guy called Chuck. It was all a set up, you see? Lucy just wanted me to show my true colors. She must have arranged for Chuck and his friends to follow us home, then creep in and catch us in the act. The way Lucy jumped up made Chuck think that I was doing something bad to her."

"What did he do to you, Shona?"

Shona swallowed hard and blinked away the tears. "He hit me so hard I felt something in my chest crack. I couldn't breathe. Then the other guys jumped in and that's all I can really remember, other than Dorothy being by my side in the hospital."

"Oh, sweetheart," Minnie said clasping her hand over Shona's. "That's why you left Mississippi?"

"Yes. I had no choice. The rumors were already going around about what I was. They were calling me a 'monster' and a 'deviant.' Dorothy told me that Lucy had left town not long after, so the truth never got told. But it wasn't my fault, Minnie. I never did nothing wrong." Shona began sobbing.

"No, you didn't, honey. You did nothing wrong. It's Lucy who should be ashamed of herself. She befriended you, then betrayed your trust, all for some sick little game to catch you out."

"And now she's here. Living in the same town as me again. What do I do now, Minnie?" Shona asked, her red-rimmed eyes wide. "Dorothy told Chloe about Lucy years ago when Chloe visited her, but how do I tell Chloe that Lucy's here? Not only that, but is our son's teacher as well?" She tailed off and sank her face into her hands again. "Urgh, it's all such a mess. I feel so much rage for Lucy, yet I gotta play nice for the sake of the boy. We can't move again, not now. We finally got the law off our back, we got a beautiful home, Dorothy's buried here." She paused, a lump catching in her throat.

Minnie clasped her hand on Shona's knee. "Tell Chloe. Tell her everything. You have no feelings for Lucy, right?"

Shona didn't answer, but Minnie continued anyway.

"You can't pretend this isn't happening. Chloe knows about Lucy. The only surprise for her will be that Lucy's here and you should both deal with that together, as one." Minnie paused, her gaze travelling up to a framed photograph of her and her husband on the marble stone mantelpiece. "When you love each other, you share your troubles. You shouldn't deal with them yourself. Go home and tell Chloe everything. She'll only find out later, then it might be worse."

Shona knew Minnie was right. She took in a huge breath. "I can't believe this is happening again, Minnie. Will my past ever stop haunting me?"

∼

Shona walked into the hallway and turned left to go into the kitchen, but a voice from the living room opposite halted her.

"What are you not telling me?" Chloe whispered. The thread from the armrest she'd been pulling at came loose. "I always know when there's something bothering you."

Shona perched on the end of the chair nearest the living room doorway. "Today. At the school. When I met David's teacher. It was Lucy." Her words were stilted, like tiny rumbles of thunder from an oncoming storm. She waited for a glimmer of recognition from Chloe, but it didn't come. Shona took a deep breath and repeated "*The* Lucy. From Mississippi. She's here."

Chloe's open face became frozen in disbelief. "What?" she breathed. "I don't understand. Why is she here?"

"I don't know. I knew her family lived in California somewhere, so I guess it makes sense." Shona's voice caught in her throat. She swallowed, then looked at Chloe through glassy eyes. "I didn't know how to tell you. I swear I didn't know she was from this town. I never would have brought us here if I'd known that. I hate her. I was almost killed because of her lies." Her words were falling out of her with abandon now. Chloe, realizing Shona's body was slipping from the arm of the chair, rushed over to grab her.

"It's OK. Baby, I know you would never have done that. I know. We'll be fine. We don't have to see her. David won't be in her class forever. Please, Shona, calm down."

Shona's whole body was shaking.

Chapter 33

Lucy had spent the weekend in a similar state of shock. She sat in deep thought at her desk in her classroom the following Monday morning trying to make sense of it all. *How could Shona be here?* Of all the places she could have gone to after she left Mississippi, she had ended up in Sunnybrook, only ten miles from Monterey, where Lucy had moved back after that terrible night at Dorothy's house.

Lucy had always wanted to teach, but when she'd enrolled in college back in Mississippi eight years ago it just didn't feel like the right time. On her arrival back in Monterey, she'd been escorted down to the local college by her mother and enrolled at the next intake. Now that she was doing the job, she'd realized it was all she'd ever wanted in her life.

"Excuse me, ma'am, do you mind if I finish cleaning in here?" Bennett said after popping his head around the door.

Lucy snapped out of her thoughts. "Um... Yeah, of course, Henry. Go right ahead."

Bennett swept his brush across the wooden floor, then ran his polishing cloth over all the tiny chairs. He poked the edge of his cloth into the corners of each window after wiping them until they sparkled.

"All done, Miss Adamson. Sorry again to disturb you," Bennett announced, tipping his cap.

"Well now, Henry, what a brilliant job you've done there. Those windows are shining like a new penny. Thank you so much," Lucy replied, a genuine smile on her tired face.

"You're welcome. You have a great day now." Bennett collected his things, then closed the door again behind him. Seconds later, another knock came at the door and in stepped Principal Miller, a pensive look on her face.

"Good morning, Margaret. How was your weekend?" Lucy asked. Her smile eased off when she saw Miller's hard stare.

"Fine. How's that boy David getting on? Is he causing you any trouble?" Miller walked over to Lucy's desk.

Lucy's skin prickled. "He's doing great. Really great, actually. Why do you ask?" Her eyes focused on Miller a little too keenly, causing Miller to raise an eyebrow.

"Just the way that Shona woman was eyeballing you like she hated you. Almost as if she knew you or something, but they've just moved here from Alabama, haven't they?"

Lucy felt the corners of her mouth twitch. "I don't know... Don't worry, Margaret. I'll be sure to let you know if I get any trouble."

"See that you do. This is a respectable school. I don't want any fuss, OK?"

"David, can you come over here a second?" Lucy called out as her class was running off to morning break. Holding the paw of a brown bear he'd found in the homeroom box, he trotted over to her desk and stood wide-eyed, looking up at her. She pressed her hands together and placed her fingertips on her lips. "How's things at home now? I heard your momma was sick."

"It's OK. Mommy gets tired a lot, but Shona plays with me

when she's sleeping," David replied, wiping his nose with his free hand.

"Shona's your aunt, right?" Lucy probed.

"Um... I just call her Shona. That's what Momma said to do." He cuddled the bear into his chest. "Can I go now, miss? I gotta get my cookie."

Lucy smiled and nodded. Five minutes later, after snapping out of her racing thoughts, she looked up at the clock on the wall. "Shit." She jumped up out of her chair and set off down the corridor and into the yard just in time to catch the last five minutes of her break duty and a stinging look from Principal Miller who'd been covering her absence.

"You're late, Lucy."

"I'm sorry, Margaret. It won't happen again."

"See that it doesn't. You seem to be distracted today."

Lucy felt her cheeks redden.

"Anything I need to know about?" Miller stepped closer to her.

"No, nothing new to report," Lucy said.

"Well, OK then. Your annual review is coming soon. Just to remind you," Margaret said pointedly before walking off.

"Are you coming later, Shona?" David asked, in between shoveling spoonfuls of cereal into his mouth.

"What's that, bubba?" Shona replied as she tied up her bootstraps.

"There's a thing on at school. Momma said I get ice cream afterwards if Miss Adamson says I done good."

Chloe bustled into the kitchen holding a hamper and began sorting out the whites from the colors. "I didn't think you'd want to go, not with..." she paused as Shona ran a hand through her hair and picked up her satchel. "I'd love you to come, but I understand why if you don't."

"I don't want to cause a scene. This afternoon's about David. We don't need any more attention on us. But I'll think about it. See you later." She leaned over and planted a kiss on David's head, then one on Chloe's cheek.

It was three thirty and Lucy's eyes had been fixed on the entrance of the school hall for the last half an hour. Parents had begun to file in and were shepherded over to their respective teachers' classrooms to discuss their children's progress. Her heart thudded at the prospect that at any moment, around any corner, she could bump into Shona.

As she smiled at parents and gushed over their child one by one, Lucy kept one eye on her watch. It was almost an hour into parents' night and still no sign of Shona. Then, fifteen minutes before the end of the time slots, Chloe walked into her classroom and up to her desk.

"Good evening, Mrs. Clark. How are you?" Lucy said. She held out her hand for Chloe to shake, then they both sat down. Lucy, feeling the weight of Chloe's stare upon her, began straightening the paper on the desktop and lining her pencils up. She plucked up the courage to look Chloe in the eyes. "So, David is doing really well at the moment. He's mastered his alphabet and is now writing his name in very neat handwriting. He gets along with everyone in his class and hasn't been in any trouble whatsoever since he started here." Normally by now the mothers she'd spoken to that evening would be gushing and holding their husband's hand, both proud of their parenting skills, but Chloe remained motionless, as if she hadn't heard a word Lucy had said. "This is an example of his handwriting. I asked him to write down the names of the people in his family."

Chloe looked down at the piece of paper Lucy had pushed towards her. Every name was present and correctly spelled. David had even drawn yellow hair around the 'o' on Shona's name.

After a few more stories about David's progress, Chloe picked up her handbag and stood up. "Well, thank you, Miss Adamson, for the glowing report about my son."

"You're welcome. Goodbye, Mrs. Clark." Lucy stood up and held out her hand for Chloe to shake, which she did, more firmly this time. Their eyes locked for few seconds before Chloe departed, nodding to Principal Miller as she passed by.

"Who the hell does that bitch think she is, huh?" Chloe raged as she stormed through the front door and threw her handbag onto the couch next to Shona, almost hitting her.

"What? What happened?" Shona replied, shocked at her near miss.

"All gussied up like she's going on a date with Elvis himself. The gall of that woman. She's so smug. Thinks she's the best teacher in the whole damn world. 'Oh, your son is doing so well here,' she was droning on. God, she's a piece of work." Chloe's breath finally ran out as she reached the end of her tirade. She stood in the living room, hands on hips, staring open-mouthed at Shona who jumped up and wrapped her arms around her.

"I'm so sorry, baby," Shona whispered in her ear.

"I have half a mind to tell that principal exactly what kind of a woman she has on her payroll. After everything she did to you, she deserves it."

"No, you can't do that," Shona replied. "How would that make us look, huh? Think about it. You'd be outing us to the whole town. It wouldn't take a lot of digging to uncover our secrets. That's exactly what we've been fighting against happening all these years. Since we got that room converted into two and David back, the townsfolk have left us alone to get on with our lives. If we tell them who Lucy is, then it will all come out."

"OK, but if she comes near you or does anything to hurt you again, I'll tear that bitch's hair out. You should have nothing to do with her, is that clear?"

Shona recoiled, having never seen Chloe so incensed. "I don't want her anywhere near me. You don't have to say all that."

"I know," Chloe replied, running her hand through her loose brown curls and taking her coat off. "I'm sorry, honey. She's just really got my goat tonight."

"Well, there won't be another parents' night for the rest of semester so we can stay out of her way. You should get some sleep. It's late."

Shona led Chloe's weary, spent body into the bedroom.

"Momma, can I stay behind after preschool tonight? Miss Adamson's started an art club," David asked as he pulled his sneakers on the next morning.

"Since when?" Chloe replied, then kneeled down to tie his shoes.

"She told us all yesterday to ask if we could stay until five and that she'll tell Mr. Bennett to bring all the kids home on the school bus afterwards. Bobby's going. Can I go, Momma? Please?" His pleading face was too much for Chloe to refuse.

"OK, baby, if you're sure you wanna go?" She scooped him up off the ground to his feet and smoothed his hair down. "You know your momma paints, don't you?" For a moment she became lost in the memory of the day last week when Shona had sat for her. She looked up at the stunningly detailed portrait hanging on the hallway wall, stifling a blush at what she remembered happened afterwards.

"Momma?" David repeated.

"Why, of course you can. You'll be even better than me, I bet."

David grinned and grabbed his school bag, then held his hand out for Chloe as they set off on the walk to Fairview.

Chapter 34

It was half past eleven on Wednesday morning, and Lucy sat at her desk deep in thought. The letter she'd decided to try and write to Shona was covered in scribbled out sentences as she tried to find the words to explain. She was jolted out of her daze by Principal Miller who burst through her door.

"Lucy, this is getting out of hand now. I cannot believe you've let it happen again." Miller's face was the angriest Lucy had ever seen it. Her hands were clamped on her slim hips, strands of wispy hair out of place in her haste to get to Lucy's classroom.

Lucy looked back at her, then jumped up out of her seat. "Oh, damn." Seconds later she'd almost barged past Miller and was running down the corridor towards the playground, ten minutes late for her duty twice in as many weeks. Only a few feet from reaching her post, she heard an ear-splitting scream which filled the air. She looked over to the climbing frame twenty yards away at the other end of the playground.

Running over, Lucy fought her way through the crowd of children that had assembled around a boy who'd fallen from halfway up the climbing frame, landing in a heap on the grassy bank next to it. His face was streaming with tears, both hands clutching his knee. Lucy felt faint when she saw it was David.

"Oh my, now what happened here? Are you OK, sweetie?" Lucy crouched down to roll up David's pant leg. The wound was smaller than she'd feared, only a tiny graze and, after checking the knee joint was still bending fine, Lucy lifted him up off the ground and brushed the dirt and leaves off his legs. "There, there, all better now. How about we get some ice for that knee? I think I've got some cookies left too." Lucy smiled, hoping that this would stop the tears that were still flowing down David's bright red face. At the mention of the cookie, he sniffed and wiped his nose with the back of his grassy hand.

Principal Miller, after following Lucy outside, had seen the whole thing. Her face thunderous, she cast a look of pure disappointment at Lucy as she passed her on the way to the medical room with David.

"My office, ten minutes," Miller barked.

By the time Lucy had patched up David and made her way to the principal's office, Chloe was already at the school and sitting in there with Miller seated at her desk. They both stared at Lucy as she pushed open the door. Before she could say hello, David rushed past and into his mother's arms.

Chloe caught him and sat him on her knee. Her face hardened as she looked back at Lucy. "So as I was saying, Principal Miller, I'm not at all happy my son wasn't supervised. He could have been seriously hurt."

Miller laughed nervously. "I'm sincerely sorry this happened, Mrs. Clark. You can be sure I will be treating this matter with the utmost care. Lucy, would you like to explain what happened today to Mrs. Clark?"

Lucy struggled to find her voice. Moments later, the tension between them was broken by David tugging on his mother's sleeve.

"Momma, it's OK, my leg don't hurt that much now. Miss

Adamson put something cold on it. It's all better now. And I got a cookie. Can we have macaroni and cheese tonight?"

Chloe gave a tight smile to Miller and lowered her lips to David's head, breathing in the scent from his hair. "Of course we can, baby. You sure your leg's OK?"

David nodded and jumped down. He walked over to Lucy and held his hand out to shake hers. "Thank you, Miss, for looking after me."

Lucy blushed and shook David's hand. "You're welcome."

Chloe glared back at Principal Miller. "I want something done about this." She took David's hand, almost dragging him away. The look she gave Lucy as she passed could have killed her stone dead.

"Sit down, Lucy. We need to talk," Miller instructed after Chloe had closed the door behind her.

Lillian Adamson laid a tray loaded with a coffee pot and two cups on the table between her cream leather couch and the armchair Lucy had sunk into after returning home from work.

"So, are you going to tell me what's bothering you, or do I have to keep asking?" her mother began. She poured them both a cup of strong black coffee and dropped two cubes of sugar in her own.

"Nothing's bothering me. Just tired from work, that's all," Lucy replied, stirring her coffee. She sat back in her armchair, her eyes glazed.

"Well, there's obviously something on your mind. You've had that look on your face for over a week now. Is the job not going OK?"

"It's going fine, mother. Please stop asking."

Lillian rolled her eyes, then offered Lucy a sympathetic smile. "I know what it is. You're missing Ray, aren't you?" She reached over to tap her daughter's hand. "Are you regretting splitting up with him, honey?"

Lucy shook her head. "He was a loser, mom. I'm happy to be rid of him."

"He was a lawyer, darling. He had really good prospects. Oh, I know he wasn't the most tender of men, but you can't have it all. You can't be single all your life, Lucy. You're almost thirty years old. Time you got yourself a husband." She sipped her coffee. "I got a call from Margaret Miller today."

Lucy looked up. "What? Why, what did she tell you?" The hand holding her coffee cup began to shake.

"She said you hadn't been concentrating on your job lately. She's worried about you. As am I. Margaret and I go way back, what did you expect? Are you mixed up in some kind of trouble, Lucy?"

"Mom, please. Just leave it, OK? There's nothing wrong." She let out a long, frustrated sigh. "I'm gonna go to bed, I think. My head hurts."

Lillian looked at the clock on the mantelpiece. "It's only six o'clock. I've got dinner in the oven."

"I'm not hungry," Lucy called over her shoulder as she disappeared up the stairs to her room.

Chapter 35

Shona had been twisting her wrench around a stubborn bolt for the last five minutes until it finally loosened, but in the process, she lost her grip, dropping it to the concrete.

"Damn it, that's gonna be hard to reach." She wriggled underneath the truck, reaching out to grab the fallen wrench which was now only millimeters from her grasp. "Come on, nearly..." Placing the very tips of her fingers on the leather grip she at last got a good hold on it. She was about to slide out when something in the corner of her eye made her turn her head. A pair of white pumps had appeared, just about visible between the truck's front two wheels. Face down, Shona pushed her arms against the concrete to move her body backwards and out from underneath the truck. Now sitting on her haunches, she looked up at her customer. Her expression darkened immediately.

"What the hell are you doing here?" The wrench weighed in Shona's clenched hand as she spoke.

The hard swallow in Lucy's throat was clearly visible.

"I don't want you here. Get out," Shona continued. Her face creased into the most disgusted look Lucy had ever seen. It pained her like a slice through the heart.

"I came… I came to…" Lucy stuttered, then licked her dry lips and tried again after clearing her throat a few times. "I needed to come over here. I never expected to see you again. I didn't think I'd ever get the chance to explain to you about what happened that night."

"And you won't never get too neither," Shona interjected. "Get the fuck off my property or by God I'll…" She stepped forward, her face reddening with eight years of pent-up confusion and anger.

Lucy took a step back and looked down at her white pumps. "Shona, I don't blame you for being angry with me. I would be too. But please, you gotta let me explain. Please."

Shona curled her lip and walked back to her tool chest at the far corner of the garage.

"I'm not going anywhere until you hear me out," Lucy continued, walking over.

Shona spun around to face Lucy, her eyes glassy.

"Why? Why are you here? In the one place I'm finally in. And happy. Goddamn it, I've finally got everything I could ever want after all those years of fighting, hurting, being attacked for who I was." She wiped her face with the back of her oily hand and pointed her wrench in Lucy's face. "All those months we spent together back in Mississippi, me trying to be your friend and save you from that asshole boyfriend of yours. You doing all those disgusting things for money and still, there I was, believing in you. Then, when I finally think I've made a friend, one I could trust, you think it'd be sport to lead me on, didn't you? Thought it'd be a real big tickle to try and catch me out so you could tell the rest of the town what a dirty pervert I was. Is that about right?"

"No, of course not. That's not how it was, Shona. All those months we were friends, how could you not see how I felt about you? I was falling for you." Lucy's own tears were rolling down her cheeks now, but her voice was dripping with frustration at how Shona had remembered that night.

"What? Are you crazy? You liked me? You had a boyfriend! You were a fucking prostitute, Lucy. All those men that you were with every night, and now you tell me it was *me* you were wanting? And I'm supposed to buy that crap?"

"Yes," Lucy whispered. "I came over that night to Dorothy's house to tell you how I felt about you. I hadn't told a soul I was going over there. I didn't want Frank to know, let alone anyone else. When we sat on the couch together, oh my, the feeling in my stomach, it was like I had a million fireflies in there. All I wanted to do was tell you I was in love with you, Shona." Lucy shrugged. "I'd fallen for you. And all I wanted to do in that moment was kiss you. I was praying you'd kiss me back and tell me you felt the same. Oh Shona, there were so many times we spent together when I was sure you would if I ever made the first move. So that's what I did." She walked up to Shona and grasped her wrists. "I swear on everything I hold dear, I never arranged for Chuck and his friends to be there. Chuck was a creep who followed me everywhere. I would never want you hurt, not in a million years."

Shona ripped her wrists away. "Then why did you say what you said?" Her eyes blazed raw anguish.

"What?" Lucy replied.

"You said, 'I knew you was one of those screw-ups,' when Chuck burst into the house. If you didn't set it all up, then *why* did you say that if you weren't expecting him?"

Lucy covered her mouth with both hands. "Oh my God, Shona, I saw him there and I thought he'd tell Frank and then the whole town would know if I had kissed you. I wimped out." Her eyes filled with shame. "I had to make it look like you were forcing yourself on me."

"You just left me there. They could have killed me, and you

just saved your own skin. And you say you were in love with me?"

"Shona, I'm so sorry. I was so scared. He was obsessed with me. He said so to the judge at his trial. I read it in the paper afterwards. He was so angry that I wanted you, and not him, so he took it out on you. Afterwards he never got the chance to get to me because that next morning I called home and my parents came to pick me up. That car ride back here was the longest of my life, Shona. How could I ever explain to them what had happened to me? To you? I hated myself for what I did, Shona. I still do."

"And so you should," Shona spat back. "You called me a 'screw-up.' That's the one thing I can't forget hearing. I don't remember a lot that happened, he hit me so hard, but I remember what you said so clearly." Shona paced the floor rubbing her head. "Then his friends began kicking me. Next thing I know, I'm waking up in the hospital with Dorothy telling me what she'd found when she got down the stairs." Shona paused and sat down on a stool by her workbench. "Dorothy said she saw Chuck and his friends running out of the house leaving me on the floor in a bad way. Then minutes later a doctor came round."

Lucy's face brightened. "That was *me* who told him to come over. I had to do something."

"*You* got the doctor?" Shona's face turned deathly pale.

Lucy walked back over and kneeled in front of her. Clasping her hands around her face, she wiped Shona's tears away with her thumbs. "I loved you. From the first moment I saw you," she laughed, "in a garage pretty similar to here. Heck, I even look the same now as I did that day." Lucy tugged at her lemon yellow summer dress tied at the waist by a thin white belt. "Talk about déjà vu." She wiped her cheek with the cuff of her white cotton cardigan. Shona looked down to her boots and sniffed.

Lucy lowered her hands and sat back on her heels. "I think about you often, you know."

"I think about you too," Shona replied. Lucy's eyes brightened. "Every time the cold hurts my ribs, I remember you."

Lucy fought back the tears. "I am truly sorry, Shona. I would do anything to take that night back. Well, just the way it ended, I mean."

Their eyes locked for a second before Lucy moved her face closer to Shona's. At the last second, Shona pulled away and stood up, her hands on her hips. "No. You can't just walk in here and start doing things like that, Lucy. It's not fair."

Lucy stood up. "Because you're with that Chloe now?"

"Yes. I am. You got that? I just want to live quietly with no drama. This town has finally backed off and left us alone after so many years of trying to catch us out. I don't need this in my life now, Lucy. I don't *want* this." She leaned back against the inside of the garage doors, the cool breeze from outside bristling over her hot face.

"Oh yeah?" Lucy replied, stung by the rejection. "And what do you think people in this town will say when they find out that you two *aren't* actually sisters or whatever it is you say you are? Things may have moved on since back then in Mississippi, Shona, but if there's one thing this town hates more than homosexuals, it's liars."

Shona let out a mirthless laugh. "And what do you think those same people will say when they find out you've slept with half of Mississippi? For money." She fixed Lucy with a stare as hard as the one Lucy was aiming back over to her. "What would your boss Miller think, huh? So don't talk to *me* about being judged."

Lucy stared at the ground. "I'm sorry, Shona. You're right." Looking up, she walked over to the garage doors and reached down for Shona's hand and squeezed it gently before leaving.

~

"I'm going out tonight, Mother, don't wait up," Lucy called up to the bedroom from the hallway downstairs.

"Where are you going?"

"I'm gonna try that new bar over in Sunnybrook. Bertie's, it's called."

"Bar?" Lillian Adamson's head shot around the top banister, her eyebrows arched.

"Yes, Mother. We've had this conversation, remember?"

"Yes, but why there? I've heard about that place. It attracts a certain *kind*, so I'm told."

"For God's sake, mother, there's nothing wrong with that place. It's just Marjory from the country club filling your head with rumors."

"They had a riot in that town, trashed the place. Most of the reprobates involved came from that bar. 'All those queers causing trouble for law-abiding folk,' that's what Marjory's husband said. And he should know."

"Mother, it was women from San Francisco who did most of the damage. Didn't you read it in the paper? They were celebrating. And you know what? I'm on their side. You can hardly blame people for fighting back. It's how they're treated, mother. People like Marjory and her husband are nothing but gossip mongers and bullies," Lucy replied with a tired sigh.

"They should think themselves lucky we allow them to live among us. In my day they would have been run out of town without even a right of reply. Or worse still, strung up."

Lucy looked up at her mother. "Can I go now?"

Lillian paused, then nodded her permission. "Put a cardigan on over that dress, at least. It's way too low-cut for a lady. What if someone from school sees you?"

"Mother, it's fine," Lucy replied, rolling her eyes. She smoothed down the straps on her best red and black cocktail dress but, feeling the weight of her mother's disapproving stare, took a red silk scarf from the coat stand and wrapped it around her neck. Pausing to model it to her mother, she reached down to pick up her purse and slammed the door behind her.

"What's the matter, sweetie? You've been quiet since you came home from work." Chloe put her fork down on her plate and lay a hand on Shona's dropped shoulder.

"Huh?" Shona replied, looking up from her plate. Her chin was still resting on her palm. "Oh, nothing. I just had a long day. Say, do you mind if I go out for a little bit? I just need to clear my head of a few things."

Chloe, tired from her own long day and not really wanting to spend the evening alone as well, nodded. "Sure. I know you need that sometimes."

Shona got up from her seat and kissed Chloe on the forehead. "I won't be late, I just... You know?"

"I know," Chloe whispered back as Shona headed into the bedroom to change her shirt.

A few minutes later she reappeared, hair combed and wearing a green and black checked button-down shirt and turn-up blue jeans.

"You look real nice there," Chloe said with a tinge of sadness. "I thought you were just going out for a drive or something?"

"I thought I'd go see some of the girls down at Bertie's. I ain't been for a while so..."

"Should I be worried?" Chloe replied after an awkward few seconds.

"Ain't nothing you gotta worry about. I won't be late."

"Who is that?" Dee whispered in Bertie's ear as she cast her glance across the bar to Lucy who'd been sitting in a booth in the corner for the last half an hour. "I've seen her before. She's kinda nice, don't you think?"

Bertie looked up and grunted. "Yeah, good luck with that one."

"What do you mean?"

"I get the feeling she's waiting for someone."

"Well, I'm sure my apple butter can take her mind off that," Dee winked and stole two whiskey sours from Bertie's drink order, then made her way over to Lucy. "Hi, I'm Dee. Anybody sitting here?" Dee placed the drinks down on the table and sat down.

Lucy dragged her gaze away from the entrance to the bar. "Umm...no, I guess not. You work here?"

"Sometimes. You, umm...with anyone?" Dee said, looking around.

"No, but I'm kinda wanting a little space tonight." Lucy winced as she smiled. "Sorry. Is that OK?"

Dee tried to be as nonchalant as possible as she rose to her feet. "Sure, don't sweat it, girl. Just being friendly." She took one of the drinks and sidled back over to the bar where Bertie was attempting, unsuccessfully, to stifle a grin. "Yeah, well, at least I had the balls to try, Bert."

"Plenny more fish in the sea, girl."

"Yeah, but she's a hot one alright. Clearly there's someone else on her mind, though," Dee added, noticing that every time the door opened, Lucy craned her neck to see who it was. Male or female, Lucy's hopeful expression saddened more each time.

The next person who walked in, however, caused a smile as bright as a sunrise on mountains to spread across Lucy's beautiful face. Both Dee and Bertie looked at each other and rolled their eyes in mock surprise as they followed the trail of Lucy's gaze.

"Hey girl, the usual?" Dee asked before uncapping a bottle of Coke and placing it in front of Shona after she'd nodded. "How are things?"

"Not so bad. The boy's doing good at school. Brought his report card home last week. Got his momma's brains for sure," Shona said, laughing as she took a swig.

"Say, Shona, your boy's at Fairview, ain't he? The preschool class?" Bertie hollered over from the end of the bar.

Shona swallowed her mouthful of Coke and wiped her mouth. "Yeah, why?"

Bertie grinned and nodded towards the booth in the corner. "That'll be his teacher then, won't it?"

Shona turned around to see Lucy's bright eyes staring at her. Dee and Bertie, as if they were watching a tennis match, flicked their heads between Shona and Lucy and back again, weighing each person's reactions. Shona tapped her foot on the ground, fully aware that there were now three pairs of eyes on her.

"What?" she grunted at Bertie, who held her palms up in surrender, then disappeared into the back room.

"Can I get some service down here?" a salty-voiced customer called out.

"Coming," Dee called back, then walked over to them.

Shona took another swig of her Coke trying to remain as low key as she could, but Lucy was already making her way over.

"Hi Shona. I've got a booth. You wanna come sit with me for a bit?" Painfully aware of how good Lucy looked, and smelled, Shona shook her head and returned to her drink. "It'd be nice to catch up properly. I'd like to clear the air properly if it was possible? Please?"

Shona lifted her elbows off the bar top and sauntered over to the booth. She sank down into the leather seat, bottle in hand still.

"How 'bout something stronger? Beer?" Lucy asked when Shona had drained her last drop of Coke.

"Why not? Of all days...I need it," Shona shrugged.

Within twenty minutes, and three beers downed, the mood began to lift.

"So, I got the job after my mother, bless her meddling, spoke to old sourpuss Miller and pulled a few strings. It's only my first proper job. I've been doing the odd semester here and there, but since I got home to Monterey all those years back, I've struggled to settle. Then I met this guy, but he wasn't what I wanted, you know?" Her light brown eyes locked onto Shona's half-drunk blue ones.

"So, why this school?" Shona slurred.

"Well, Sunnybrook is only a few miles away from home, so it seemed perfect. And my mom used to be the principal before Miller got the gig. It made sense. It used to be my preschool too, so I felt right at home. Your boy is beautiful."

"I know. Nothing like his no-good father," Shona added under her breath.

"What?"

"Nothing."

"Where did you go after Mississippi, Shona? I rang Dorothy every day for a month, but she wouldn't say. I just wanted to explain." Lucy placed her hand on top of Shona's, but it was shaken off.

"Alabama. I had no choice but to keep moving. I thought Chuck would come after me and finish the job." She fixed her stare on Lucy. "You're the reason I had to leave the best place I'd ever lived and the best job I've ever had. I had to leave Dorothy all on her own again, just when I was starting to build a life."

"How is Dorothy?" Lucy asked.

"She died. A few years ago now."

The air fell silent between them. Lucy wiped away a strand of hair from her cheek. "I'm sorry, Shona. I know how much you loved her. Is she still in Mississippi? Can you visit her grave?"

"She came here to live with us when David was born. She's buried here. I should never have had to leave her, Lucy. I was happy in Mississippi." Shona's eyes were damp as she finished her beer.

"What can I do to make this right, Shona? Please tell me."

"You can't change the past."

"I know." A smile began to form in the corner of Lucy's mouth. "But I can get us some bourbon chasers. Come on, for old times' sake. Have a proper drink with me?"

Within minutes Lucy was back at the table with two shot glasses and a bottle of bourbon.

"To old times," Lucy said, pouring them both a shot and laughing as they both downed it in one huge gulp.

Feeling the alcohol fizz through her body, Shona looked at Lucy properly for the first time since they'd found each other again. Her beautiful face was expertly made up, and her gorgeous red and black shimmery cocktail dress hugged every perfect curve. She had hardly aged a day, even though eight years had passed, but there was something about Lucy that intrigued Shona. Regardless of all the hate and anger she'd felt until this night, she had always wondered about Lucy. What would it have been like if they had kissed that night?

What if Chuck hadn't burst in?

Bertie had returned to the bar from the back room an hour later to see Shona and Lucy laughing and drinking shot after shot of bourbon, the bottle almost empty in front of them.

"I don't think Chloe will be too happy about Lucy bird-dogging her girlfriend, do you?" Dee said as she came up behind her.

"No, I don't think she would," Bertie replied, her eyes narrowing as she watched Lucy's hands wandering over Shona's arm, then disappearing underneath the table to rest on her knee.

Dee sucked in her cheeks. "Is that woman not content with having that Chloe in her bed? She has to bag another hottie too? Save some for the rest of us, why don't you?"

"Lucy and Chloe do look very similar, though, don't they? Shona's obviously got a type," Bertie tutted.

"Maybe you should ring Chloe? Get her down here and stop Shona making a big mistake. They got a kid, remember?"

Bertie looked at Dee and shook her head. "I'm not getting involved. If she wants to throw it all away for a one-nighter then it's up to her. I run a bar, not a counselling service."

By the time Dee and Bertie looked back over to the booth, Lucy and Shona had disappeared.

Chloe was climbing the walls with worry. It was way past midnight and Shona still wasn't home. Not wanting to leave David alone again, like last time, she picked up the telephone and called Bertie's bar.

"Yeah?" answered a sharp voice.

"Oh, hi, is Shona there?"

"Who?"

"Shona? Blonde hair, green and black checked shirt? Probably got a crowd of women around her," Chloe added.

"Oh yeah, Shona. The mechanic. She was here, but she left about an hour ago with a brown-haired woman. The teacher from Fairview. Hello? *Hello?*"

Chapter 36

Chloe woke up on the couch after barely an hour of sleep. There was still no sign of Shona. Fighting back tears, she busied herself with her normal morning routine: getting David washed, dressed and ready for preschool. Seeing no sign of Shona at the garage on her way to drop him off, her anxiety began to grow by the second. As soon as she got David outside his classroom, her emotions spilled over. Encouraging him to go catch the last five minutes of playtime out in the yard, she then strode straight up to Lucy, who was sitting at her desk preparing the morning's activities.

"Where the hell is Shona?" Chloe growled as quietly as her remaining self-control would allow.

Lucy looked up half in shock and half in surprise. "What?"

"You heard me. I called the bar. I know you spent the night with her. She never came home last night and she's not at the garage. So where is she?" Chloe slammed her palms down on Lucy's desk, causing her neatly folded paper cutouts to spread out.

"Look, Mrs. Clark, you need to calm down. The children will be in from play in a minute and I don't want them to hear you say something you'll regret."

"Ha. That's rich, you being all caring and responsible all of a sudden. Shona told me all about what you did to her back in Mississippi. She told me what you were. What you are." Chloe almost spat that last sentence out, leaving it hanging in the air like a stain. "The disgusting things you used to do for money. 'Slut,' that's what she calls you," Chloe lied, aiming low on purpose. "You're not responsible enough to look after my dog, let alone my child. I'll tell the principal everything."

"Tell her what exactly? Tell her that I'm the reason why your sister, who is actually your girlfriend, was beaten up because she's queer? How does that sound? You'd have that poor boy out there taken away from you again before you could finish your sentence."

Chloe was speechless, half with rage, the other half knowing Lucy was right.

"We both got secrets, right?" Lucy added, nodding to encourage Chloe to agree.

"I just want to know where Shona is," Chloe murmured.

"Shona came home with me last night," Lucy revealed. Chloe's eyes widened, then let out of huge wave of tears. "We got a cab home. She was drunk, and yes, I made a pass at her." Lucy heaved in a huge sigh. Chloe couldn't even breathe. "But no matter how much I tried, all she could do was ramble on about how much she loved you. She is completely devoted to you."

Chloe's eyes refocused as she tried to take in what Lucy was saying. "You didn't sleep together?"

"No. She passed out on my couch. I threw a blanket over her and by the time I came out of my bedroom this morning, she was gone." Lucy shook her head. "I screwed up all those years ago. I had my chance, so now I guess I'll always be left wondering. That's my punishment." She looked up at the clock. "I gotta bring the kids in now. Go sort things out with her, Chloe—she loves you."

Minnie had been sitting in her living room telling Shona all about her latest visit with her husband for over ten minutes before she stopped and wrinkled her brow. "What's the matter, Shona? You seem like you have the weight of the world on your shoulders since you got here."

"Hmm?" Shona replied, snatched from her daydream. "Oh, I'm real sorry, Minnie. I've just got a lot on my mind."

"You can tell me anything, you know that," Minnie said, laying a hand on her shoulder. "Did something happen last night? I mean, I'm not used to having guests knock on my door at 7 a.m."

"That's just it, though, Minnie. I can't fully remember what happened last night," Shona replied, then began filling Minnie in on her troubles with Chloe and her night with Lucy. Minnie listened quietly as Shona spoke. "And while I was asleep on her couch, I had a dream." Shona paused, her face reddening. "About what it might have been like that night, if Chuck hadn't burst in. Oh Minnie, we were so close to kissing, we might have ended up..."

Minnie tutted. "Oh, Shona, you think this old duffer has never had sex? I'm not too old to hear the words, y'know." She let a tiny smile cross her lips and encouraged Shona to go on.

"I think I told Lucy 'no' when she tried to take me to her bedroom last night, but I can't remember if she talked me round. It's all a blur. I'd had way too much to drink and I don't usually touch the hard stuff. Chloe is all I have ever wanted." Shona paused and rubbed her forehead. "But I woke up feeling like if something *hadn't* happened between me and Lucy last night then I'd have missed out. Does that make any sense? Lucy never knew I was starting to feel something for her back in Mississippi, and if she had kissed me back then I wouldn't have stopped her. I was so confused after everything that happened when I was a kid back in Louisiana that I couldn't read the signs with Lucy until that last moment. And just when I figured it out, and I had the chance to go for it, in burst that ogre Chuck. Then I met Chloe in Alabama and I fell completely in love. She loved me from the moment she saw me, and I her. We've been through so much together that I know in my heart I wanna be with her for the rest of my life, Minnie. So why do I feel like this about Lucy?"

Minnie leaned back in her chair. "And how *is* it you feel about Lucy?"

"Curious. Like there was so much more to happen with us. But now it can't. Do you understand?"

Minnie nodded. "Shona, this is the oldest problem in the book. 'What if I'd done this differently? What if that had happened instead?' You think other people don't feel like this sometimes?"

"Do they?"

"Of course they do. But let me ask you one thing."

"OK?"

Minnie took a deep breath. "Can you imagine your life without Chloe and David in it?"

Shona shook her head.

"Then there's your answer. Lucy is just the one who might have been, not the one who should be. Chloe is your future. It takes more than one temptation to break something as strong as what you two have. So talk to her. Tell her how you feel, before it's too late."

Lucy was staring into space later that afternoon as the class sat at their tables painting. When he had finished, David got up and walked over to Lucy's desk. He lay his still-wet picture down in front of her and grinned.

"I've finished, miss."

Lucy snapped back into reality and gazed down at the picture. What she saw nearly brought her to tears. There was a beautiful white house in the middle of the paper, with blue window frames and the ocean behind it. Standing in front of the house was a stick woman with brown hair wearing a red and white polka dot dress and red pumps. The second stick figure was wearing blue overalls, brown boots and had bright yellow hair. Between them stood a smaller figure dressed in exactly the same color clothes as David was wearing today. The stick boy was holding a hand of each of the two stick figures on either side of him, all three faces with wide smiles on their red painted lips. A yellow stick dog with a red collar was sitting next to the group holding a bone in his mouth. There was a bright sun shining in the blue painted sky and floating above the house was an angel, wearing a white blouse, green cardigan and pale blue full skirt. The angel was smiling and above her greying hair bun was a bright yellow halo. At the top of the paper David had written 'My Happy Place' in green paint.

"You like it?" David asked. "It's my favorite place in the whole world. There's Momma, and Shona, and Cooper, and me. Grandma Dorothy keeps an eye on me from Heaven." He stood back from the desk after pointing out all the figures.

"It's a beautiful picture, David. Your momma will love it. Go put it on the rack to dry. You can take it home later."

Every word Lucy spoke was harder to force out than the previous one, the lump in her throat almost choking her. David obeyed just as Polly came in to pass on a message. Standing up, Lucy excused herself and left the class in Polly's hands.

Lucy called Shona to ask her to pick David up that afternoon. She didn't feel right about going round to the beach house, not with Chloe there. It was hard enough to say what she had to say to Shona without seeing her rival in the beautiful home David had painted. When Shona arrived at the school gates, Lucy walked him over to her.

"Jump in the truck, kid. I won't be long. I just gotta talk to your teacher," Shona instructed, knowing that she had her own question to ask Lucy. David obeyed and sat in the passenger seat. She then walked over to Lucy who had hung back.

"Hi," Lucy said.

"Hi." Shona toed the dirt as she struggled to find the words to ask what she needed to know. "Um... Last night. Did we...?"

"What?" Lucy blushed, understanding the question. It felt like an age to Shona before Lucy answered. "No, Shona, we didn't. You couldn't stop talking about Chloe and how much she meant to you."

"I'm sorry. It wasn't fair of me to do that. I just—"

"I'm leaving, Shona," Lucy interjected, her face set. "At the end of this semester. I can't be here anymore, seeing you all the time. I can't be the reason that poor boy has his family ripped apart by me not being able to stay away from you. You and Chloe are his whole world and I can't come between that." She paused and looked Shona square in the eye. "I love you, Shona. I always have. And I always will." The words caught in her throat as she fought with all her might to stop the tears from falling. "So I need to walk away."

Lucy turned to leave until Shona called out to her. Lucy turned around waiting, hoping, that Shona would say the words she'd been aching to hear for eight long years.

"Do you ever wonder what might have been? If Chuck hadn't burst in that moment?" Shona asked, her own voice cracking.

Lucy didn't hesitate before replying, "I think about it more than you'll ever know"

"You ever wonder what that kiss would have been like?" Shona prodded

Lucy let out a sigh and cast her arms wide as she looked to the heavens. "Every day of my life since that night, even when I was with other people, but... Well, I guess we'll never know now."

Chapter 37

All the way home, Shona couldn't get what Lucy had told her out of her mind. In her heart, she knew it was for the best and now she had to make it right with Chloe. Stopping off at the little flower shop before going home, Shona picked out the biggest bunch of red roses they had.

"We're home," she called out, closing the front door behind her and David, who ran off into the yard after Cooper who'd bounded up to him.

Shona placed David's painting on the coffee table, then crept down the hallway with her bunch of flowers and over to the bedroom door. She opened it a crack and peeked inside. There, in front of the mirror, Chloe was about to try on a new red and white striped dress she'd bought that afternoon. Shona, without realizing she was doing it, simply stared at Chloe's body, naked save for her panties.

"Oh my," Shona managed to squeeze out between breaths.

Chloe span around, covering her modesty. Seeing it was Shona, she relaxed and smiled back. "I thought I'd treat myself." She looked up at the wardrobe door where the dress was hanging. "You like it?"

"I love it. But do you have to put it on right now?" Shona walked closer, the roses hidden behind her back.

Chloe heard the rustling of the pink paper they were wrapped in. "What's that behind your back?"

Shona brought out the flowers. Chloe reached forward and took the huge bunch. "For me?"

"No, for Cooper. Of course they're for you," Shona joked, then swept a strand of hair out of Chloe's bright eyes. "You like them?"

"You know I do. They're my favorite, but what's the occasion?"

"Can't I treat my gorgeous girl without there needing to be an occasion?" Shona's grin melted away to a more sober expression. "I wanted to say I was sorry. About everything that's been going on lately. With Lucy? I'm sorry I didn't come home last night, but I swear nothing happened."

"I know. She told me everything."

Shona recoiled. "She did?"

"Yes. I can't imagine how hard that must have been for her. To let you go. I couldn't do it." Chloe stroked her fingertips over the soft petals of a rose.

Placing a finger underneath Chloe's chin, Shona lifted her face to meet her own. "I could never want anyone else other than you, Chloe. You're my heart. You always will be, no matter what happens or who comes along." She wrapped Chloe's semi-naked body in her arms and kissed her. "So, about that dress? Can you try it on in a little bit?"

"David might come in," Chloe giggled as Shona edged her backwards in the direction of the bed.

"He's playing with Cooper. We'll be fine for five minutes."

"Five minutes, huh?"

"Well, maybe ten," Shona replied with a cheeky wink as she pushed Chloe down onto the bed. She lay on top of her, feeling the warmth of Chloe's skin on her fingertips. "I wanna make it right."

"I was worried when I saw Lucy." Chloe paused and fiddled with the point of Shona's shirt collar. "She's so beautiful, Shona. I was worried you'd want her now, not me. My body's changed since I had David. I'm not…"

Shona leaned back on her elbow and stroked Chloe's hair. "Your body is as perfect to me as it ever was." She let her palm slide over Chloe's naked chest and stomach, finally coming to rest on her hip. "Even more so now it's produced the second most beautiful thing I've ever had in my life. Chloe, how could I ever want any other woman? I was just so surprised to see her, and after she explained what happened, I was so confused. But not about my feelings for her. It was more I was confused by thinking one thing for so many years, then finding out it wasn't how it really happened. It threw me off, that's all. I needed to work that out in my head." She cupped Chloe's cheek in her palm. "But I could never want anyone like I want you. We're a family now and I won't ever let anything take that away."

"Nothing ever will. I promise. No one, not even ghosts from the past will ever break what we've got here, Shona, I swear to you. I love you."

"I love you too, Chloe." She lowered her lips to kiss her. "So much."

"Davey, are you sure you can carry that?" Shona said with a raised eyebrow as he heaved up a breakfast tray from the counter. As he did so, Chloe's coffee cup and toast plate slid into each other. His heart in his mouth for a second while the crockery settled on the tray, David then walked with short steps out to the back porch swing where his mother was sitting enjoying the early Saturday morning sun. From inside the kitchen Shona heard an entirely predictable crash of crockery hitting the deck. Rolling her eyes, she picked up a dish cloth and headed outside.

"Uh-oh," David said, staring down at the shattered coffee cup and plate. Chloe looked up at Shona trying to keep a straight face.

"Takes after you, that one," she said before releasing a loud burst of laughter.

"You got that right," Shona agreed, shaking her head, then bending down to pick up the broken pieces. After she had stacked them back on the tray, she grabbed David and tickled him, then wiped his hands clean of splashed up coffee and brushed him down.

Chloe watched her son and Shona cuddle together as Shona set about reassuring him they weren't mad at him. "I'm so lucky to have you both," Chloe murmured.

"What's that?" Shona said, looking up.

"Oh, nothing."

"Come on, Cooper, let's go play in the water," David called out to his dog who came bounding over. The two of them ran off down the boardwalk and across to the water.

Both Chloe and Shona watched on in admiration of their carefree playing. Then Shona's eyes darkened. "Say, did you hear that on the radio just now? They're marching again in protest over domestic violence. I don't know how a march is gonna do any good in ending it. The government need to pass a law or something making it illegal. Men. Goddamn bullies." She sucked in her cheeks. "Thinking they can go around beating up women—it's disgusting." Shona had continued with her tirade not noticing how quiet Chloe had become during it. "Baby, I'm sorry. I didn't mean to remind you..."

"It's fine, I know you didn't mean it. I hardly think about it now."

Kneeling in front of her, Shona placed her hands on Chloe's knees. "You're safe now, OK? You believe me, don't you?"

"Of course I do. So, what are we gonna do today?" Chloe replied, catching David in her arms as he ran back from the beach, Cooper closely following him, his fur soaked in ocean water. "How 'bout a picnic? We could take the boat out, maybe? Shona?"

"Yeah, sure, great idea. I'll go bring it out." Shona jumped over the rail around the veranda and landed on the sand a few feet below. As she began to walk over to the boat, they heard the doorbell ring.

"Can you get that, sweetie? I'll go prep the boat," Shona called back over her shoulder. Chloe rose off the porch swing and headed through the back door into the house. David and Cooper trailed behind her playing tug-of-war with a piece of rope.

Opening the door, Chloe froze. Her legs almost buckled underneath her.

"I believe you have something in here that belongs to me," the smart-suited man drawled, taking one more step up towards the door. He was six feet tall, with jet black hair and horribly familiar dark eyes. A sly grin was draped across his clean-shaven, handsome face.

"What the hell are you doing here, Kyle?"

Chapter 38

Shona flipped over the little fishing boat that was stored behind the shed and brushed off the loose sand that had collected around the rudder. Picking out the shells David had collected last time they'd gone out together, she grabbed hold of the two paddles and began pushing it down across the sandy path that ran the length of the house and towards the beach. Stopping for a moment, Shona looked out to the horizon and took in a huge lungful of sea air. It was as if the ocean was calling her. Its waves were the calmest she'd seen for a long time, the morning sunbeams dancing over the surface.

"Now, *this* is freedom," Shona said to herself before continuing on to the beach with the boat. Moments later, Cooper appeared in her path, jarring her out of her tranquility by barking in a way she'd never heard him bark before.

"What's the matter, boy?" Shona sank to her haunches to pat him, but he quivered and began to whine. With Cooper now pulling on the hem of her white undershirt, Shona strode up to the back door and into the house where at the end of the hallway she saw Chloe standing motionless facing the front door with David clamped behind her, wriggling. "Chloe, what's going...?" Shona's puzzled smile dropped off her face the instant she saw who their visitor was.

"Well, Shona Jackson, as I live and breathe," Kyle's smarmy voice began. "It is so good to see you looking so...healthy."

Bile began to rise in Shona's throat at the sight of the man who had caused so much pain to the people she loved and nearly killed her. "What the *fuck* are you doing here, you murdering son of a bitch?"

Kyle recoiled theatrically and tutted. "Please, Shona. Not in front of my *son*." David popped his head around the back of Chloe and locked eyes with his father.

Kyle looked down at his son and for the first time Chloe could recall, his coal-black eyes glinted with light. "Hey boy, come here. Come meet your father."

"No, David. Shona, can you take him? Please?" Seeing Shona's reluctance to leave her in Kyle's presence, Chloe continued to assert herself in front of the man who'd violated her. "I'm fine. I can do this."

"I'll be in here, OK?" She led David into his bedroom, then turned back to shoot a look of pure contempt at Kyle. "Don't you try anything or I swear I will finish you." The door remained open but Shona had disappeared from view.

"What are you doing here, Kyle?" Chloe asked turning back to face him, her heart thudding.

Kyle took out a letter from his top jacket pocket. "You sent your mother this. Oh yeah, we still keep in touch," he added after seeing Chloe's eyebrows raise.

"But how...?" Chloe stared at the letter in complete confusion.

"I can't believe someone as smart as you, Chloe, would make such a rookie error." Kyle sniggered as he stared at her, shaking his head.

"What?"

"The postmark. You posted it from here, didn't you? It

wasn't hard to track you down when it says 'Sunnybrook, California' on the envelope. And the way you talk about this beautiful beach house with its gorgeous white paint and blue window frames. Why, you make it sound almost unique, which it is. All the other houses along this street have green windows." He leaned back and spread his arms out wide. "So, it was hardly a challenge, darling. I did watch this place for a few days, just to make sure I was right, before I came to visit my son."

Chloe couldn't decide who she was madder at right that second, Kyle for being here or Shona for forgetting to put her letter to her mother in Elbie's envelope.

"I want you to go. Now," Chloe demanded.

Kyle took another step forward until he was standing toe-to-toe with Chloe, his six-foot frame towering over her. "No," He snarled, curling his lip.

She took a step back, her whole body trembling with the memory of what he'd done to her that night. "But how can they have let you out? After what you did to all those people. What you did to Cuban? What you did to Shona?"

"Oh, you were hoping I'd get the Yellow Mama, right?"

"If there was any justice in the world, you would have, but even an electric chair isn't enough for you—it's too quick," Chloe spat back.

Kyle laughed. "That was never gonna happen. They couldn't convict me for half of what they charged me with. The evidence seemed to just..." He blew in his hand and waved it away. "Those cops saw sense in the end, along with the dollar signs, when my mother came to visit me. Who says money don't talk, huh? It's amazing how me promising to be a good boy can reduce a prison sentence. Six years, that's all." His tone turned darker. "But it was long enough to cause me to miss my son growing up. You had no right to take him away, Chloe. No right at all."

Chloe erupted in quiet anger. "You wanna talk about *rights*? After what you did to me? You can't scare me anymore, Kyle. It's a new decade now. I got rights of my own." She set her lips and gripped the door, ready to slam it in his face. "If you don't get off my property, I will call the police."

"And tell them what? The husband you said was dead is now on your doorstep asking to see his son?"

Chloe's face froze.

"Oh yeah, I've been in town a few days now asking about you. Poor little Chloe, struggling to raise a child alone with only her *sister* for company. Which story was it again? I was 'away in the war' or I 'was dead'." He licked his lips as he taunted her. "Oh, I'm sure that will go down very well with the police when they find out you've been lying to everyone."

Shona burst out of David's bedroom and went to grab Kyle's suit lapels, but Chloe pulled her back just in time. "No. Shona, don't. That's exactly what he wants you to do. Kyle, get off my property now."

Seeing Cooper bare his teeth behind Shona and David's wide, confused eyes, Kyle stepped backwards down the porch steps. "I'm staying at the motel on the highway. I want to see my son. I *will* see my son," he said, pointing his finger at Chloe as he paced backwards towards his brand new shiny black Lincoln Continental.

Chloe turned to Shona, her eyes red and filled with angry tears. All Shona could do was stare back, heartbroken.

"I am so sorry, Chloe. I've fucked up."

"You promised me we would be safe here. You swore you'd keep me safe."

"I know. I know. Argh, I'm so, so sorry." Seeing Shona crumble with complete desolation over what just happened, she called David over and wrapped her arms around both of them, embracing them in an impenetrable hug.

"We'll fight this. He won't win," Chloe assured her family.

Chapter 39

"Hey sweetie, how was your weekend?" Bill Everett said to his daughter who'd just walked through the door with a strange expression on her face. "You OK?"

"Yeah. I think so. Just some guy asking me to get in his car. Real sleazeball he was."

"Description?"

"Black hair, grey suit. Good looking, but just a little creepy the way he was looking at me. I think it was a Lincoln Continental he was driving. A black one, with an Alabama license plate."

Everett smiled at her eye for detail. "You really are your daddy's daughter alright." He kissed her on the forehead and took the grocery bag from her. "I'll ask the boys down at the station to keep an eye out for a new guy sniffing around town before I go back up to Portland for the week. Don't worry, I'm sure he's just another douchebag who thinks he's good enough for my baby girl."

"Oh Dad, no man'll ever be good enough for me," she joked, walking over to hug him. "He was way too old for me anyway, at least forty." She winked at her father.

Kyle circled the Sunnybrook town square three times, eyeing up all the amenities like a tourist, before pulling into a parking spot just outside the bakery. Stepping out of his car, he breathed in a lungful of morning sea air and smiled. "I think I'm gonna like it here," he said, straightening his tie and smoothing down his expensive suit. Sniffing, he caught the scent of freshly baked pie and headed towards the bakery, where he swaggered over to Alice who was sitting behind the counter reading a newspaper.

"Anything interesting in there today?" Kyle asked, flashing his perfect white teeth.

Alice looked up, her face unmoved by Kyle's penetrating stare. "The usual," she answered abruptly.

"What's a stunner like you doing wasting away behind this counter?"

"Umm...I work here. Can I get you somethin'?"

"Hmmm, now then, what would I like?" He leaned into her and sniffed at length. "What is it, apart from you, that smells so good in here?"

"Pie. Pork with apple sauce today."

"Sounds good. I'd like one, please... And your number." He reached into his jacket pocket and pulled out a shiny gold pen. Sliding it across the counter to Alice, he let his fingers brush against hers. Immediately, she snatched her hand away.

"No thank you, sir." She reached behind her and found the coldest pie she had on the shelf. Sliding it into a brown paper bag, she pushed it across the counter to Kyle, followed by his pen. "That'll be thirty-five cents, please."

Kyle passed her a half dollar. "Keep the change, honey." As he turned to leave, he looked out of the bakery window, his interest newly piqued as a thought crossed his mind. "That garage. Out of curiosity, who owns it?"

"Oh, Clark's? That's Shona's place. Why?"

"This town has a woman running a garage?"

"Yeah, she's real good. Best mechanic this town has ever seen." Alice's cheeks flushed with color at the mention of Shona's name.

Kyle sniggered. "Really? You mean people actually trust a woman to repair their cars? It's absurd."

Alice glared at Kyle, who mock saluted her and left, eyeballing the garage as he stood on the sidewalk lighting up a cigarette.

Waiting for Shona at the garage that morning was Bill Everett.

"Hi Bill, how's things?" Shona called out as she jumped out of her truck and rushed over to shake his hand.

"It's good, Shona, thank you. I got some news. I spoke to the Chief of Police last week about maybe taking up my old post again over there." He nodded over to the police station. "He's been unhappy with the way Lawrence has messed up this town the last few years, so he almost bit my hand off when I offered to come back."

"Oh, Bill, that's the best news. We've missed you around here."

"Yeah, well, I've missed it too. Dad died last month, so there's really no point in me staying up in Portland now. His automobile business will be auctioned next week so, once that's over with, I'll be back for good doing the thing I love. I was no good at selling car parts," he added with a wry smile.

Shona beamed, wanting to hug him.

"Lawrence wasn't too happy with the decision, but he's agreed to transfer to Sacramento when I start back. Oh, they had to offer him a pay raise and the sheriff post over there, but it gets him out of this town. Now, you got any more of those wildflowers out back still?"

∽

Kyle pulled up outside an elaborate red brick building just over a mile outside Sunnybrook, annoyed that he'd had to wait until two o'clock for his appointment slot. He strode down the hallway, passing room after room and staring in the windows, finally reaching the office where his meeting was to be held.

"Can I help you, sir?" the receptionist asked, noting his smart suit and slicked back hair. Sniffing, she caught a whiff of his cologne and blushed.

"I have an appointment with Principal Miller," Kyle replied, placing his palms on the desktop in front of him.

"One moment please." The receptionist got up and knocked on Miller's door, then popped her head inside. Seconds later, she invited Kyle inside.

"Good afternoon, sir. How can I help you?" Miller looked up at Kyle but remained sitting at her desk.

"I'd like an update on my son's progress here," Kyle replied, sitting down before being invited to.

"And who is your son?" she replied, her tone clipped.

"David." Kyle paused, confusion crossing his face for a second.

"David what?"

He laughed. "Well, actually I don't know what surname his mother is using right now."

Miller sat forward in her chair and clasped her hands together on the desk.

"She left me very suddenly," Kyle continued, softening his tone. "We had some problems in our relationship and she just left one day, without even telling me she was pregnant. I've spent six years trying to find her, then one day she sends her mother a letter with her address and, being the concerned mother she is, she wrote me straight away and, for the interests of the child, said I should go to her daughter and make it all OK again between us. That's what I'm here to do, ma'am. I just want my family back together." Kyle fiddled with his cufflink all the way through his rambling speech.

"I do have a David, of the correct age you speak of. Would that be the one?"

"Yes. Yes, that's him. His mother's name is Chloe." Kyle leaned back in his chair, shaking his head as if relieved, then out of the corner of his eye watched to see if Miller was buying his act. "She's probably told you about her sister living with her?"

Miller's eyes became keen. "Yes, a woman called Shona." Again she leaned forward. "Why?"

Chapter 40

After sprinting the whole way to Fairview Elementary, Chloe almost collapsed over Polly the assistant's desk.

"That's fine, Mrs. Clark. Principal Miller is expecting you. You can go right in," Polly cut in just as Chloe tried to breathe out her words to ask.

Pushing the door open, Chloe saw Miller's stern face first, then Kyle. "What is going on here?"

"Sit down Mrs. Clark," Miller replied, then rose to pull out another chair for her.

"No, I can't have him here. He's dangerous. I don't want him here. Please." Chloe, adrenaline rippling through her body, fell forwards, leaning her hands on the back of the chair.

"Now, Chloe," Kyle began, turning to face her. "I'm sure we can sort all of this misunderstanding out together. Sit down."

Chloe glared at him with renewed anger. "Don't you ever tell me what to do, Kyle. Not ever." She turned to Miller. "Ma'am, the reason I left this man is that he...he." She paused, but she still couldn't say that word. "He's been in jail."

Miller's face hardened towards Kyle. "You didn't mention that before, Mr. Chambers." Looking back at Chloe, she waved her hand, insisting she sit down. Kyle began fiddling with his cufflink again.

"He was sent to jail for being involved in fraud, corruption, several assaults and second-degree murder. I have no idea why they've let him out or why he's here now, but he's dangerous. I don't want him anywhere near my son."

"*Our* son," Kyle cut in. "I made him too, didn't I?"

"You *really* wanna go there?" Chloe snapped back.

"And the reason you left me afterwards is because of Shona, wasn't it?"

Miller held her hands up, confused by the rapid-fire arguments. "Hang on a minute, I'm confused here." She looked at them both. "Mrs. Clark, you and this Shona have the same last name, yes?"

Chloe nodded, licking her lips.

"And that's the same last name you gave David? Clark, right?"

Kyle smirked. The penny had finally dropped for Miller.

"Yes." Chloe fiddled with the strap of her purse on her lap.

"But you said when you enrolled him that his father, your husband, was dead. So why doesn't David have his father's last name? Chambers?"

The seconds dragged by as Chloe thought fast. But there was no way out of this one. She took a huge breath and looked intently at Miller.

"Because I didn't want people to know his father was a criminal. That's why I lied. He's not really my husband. Shona and I both changed our own last names because I wanted a fresh start away from this animal. We're not really sisters either, we're..." She paused. "We're friends. We made a pact to stick together, as one of the things *he* went to jail for was hurting Shona so badly she was almost killed. So, you can understand why I didn't want him to find us." She stood up to leave, but Kyle thrust out his hand and grabbed her wrist.

"Chloe, please. I just want to see my son. I've changed." He looked at Miller. "I've served my time, ma'am. I'm no longer a danger to society. Surely if I was, they wouldn't have let me out, would they? I just want the opportunity to get to know my boy."

Miller lay her palms on the desk. "I'm sure you do, Mr. Chambers. But I need time to think this over. For now, I think it's best you both organize this between yourselves. Legally, *Miss* Clark, you and your friend are down on school records as responsible for David and I'm satisfied with that. For now," she added. "See me next week and I'll discuss it with you and Mr. Chambers further. My only concern is for the welfare of the child." All three of them stood up for Miller to show them to the door. After waiting for Kyle to step away along the corridor, Miller leaned in close, locking eyes with Chloe. "Maybe, for David's sake, Miss Clark, you should think about letting his father back in his life," she hissed. "No matter what mistakes you've made in the past, a boy should have a proper family around him. I don't want any trouble brought to my door, you hear? You wouldn't want to have to move David to a school out of town now, would you?"

Outside, Kyle struggled to keep up with Chloe, who, stunned by Miller's opinion, was now striding away down the hallway. He stretched out and pulled her arm back.

"Get your hands off me, Kyle," Chloe said, flinging his hand away from her.

"Look, if you don't want me marching back in there and telling Miller exactly what Shona is to you, then you'd better let me see my son."

"Leave us alone, Kyle. Go back to Alabama and leave us alone." She strode away as confidently as her shaking legs could manage.

It was three o'clock and Kyle had gone straight from the school to Sunnybrook's grocery store. He walked up and down the aisles, then found the perfect gift for David, a little brown bear dressed in a grey suit with a red tie, almost exactly the same as the outfit Kyle was wearing. At the register, he smiled at the Edie, but she glared back at him.

"Something I said?" he joked.

"I'm friends with Alice from the bakery," Edie replied, holding out her palm for the money. "She told me what you said about Shona."

"Well, maybe she misunderstood my sense of humor."

"No, she knew exactly what you were meaning. Shona's our friend, so you leave her alone or you'll have us to deal with, OK?" Edie, bolstered by the fact there was a counter between them, hardly flinched when Kyle took a step closer to her, his smile hardening.

"I was really hoping this could be my local store, so you can tell Shona from me, I ain't planning on going anywhere. OK?"

"Get off my property before I call the sheriff. I'm not joking, Kyle." Chloe stood behind the closed front door, having watched through the kitchen window as he drove up to the house that same afternoon.

"Look, I just wanna talk, Chloe. I'm not here to cause trouble. If I wanted to do that, I would have gone back in that office and told Miller all about you and this little love charade you got going on here. Open the door. I'm not gonna do anything."

Chloe opened the door a crack. "I don't want you here, Kyle. You don't scare me anymore," she said.

Kyle took a step back down the porch steps and held out the bear. "I just wanted to leave this for the boy. I know he ain't home from school yet, so surely that shows you that I'm not here to make trouble. I come in peace."

Cooper ran in from the garden covered in mud from the hole he'd been digging. Lolloping around the hallway, he distracted her just long enough for Kyle to creep inside the front door as Chloe was bending over to shoo Cooper away. Refusing to leave Chloe alone completely, Cooper sat at the end of the hallway watching Kyle with keen brown eyes.

"Kyle, I didn't say you could come in," Chloe gasped as she stood up and came face-to-face with him. He took a step backwards.

"Look, I just wanted to see if you were OK after what happened at the school." Kyle paused, his forehead creasing. "And I thought you should know something about Shona." He knew he'd got her attention judging by the stare she gave him and was savoring every second of it.

"Know what?"

"That girl in town. The one in the bakery? Alice, I think her name is."

"What about her?" Chloe interjected.

"Well, actually it's not just her. That girl in the grocery store too. They all seem to know Shona pretty well."

"What are you saying, Kyle?"

"Do you really know what she gets up to when she's out at work, while you're stuck here, day in, day out? Seems to me that she's got all the freedom, not you." His voice softened as he took a tiny step closer.

"I trust her," Chloe replied, folding her arms.

"You know, I remember how you used to boss us all around at Ellis and Bruce. God, that was such a turn on. And you coming in every day looking and smelling amazing. All the guys wanted you, but none more so than me, Chloe. I can't believe how stupid I've been. I've messed everything up."

His face crumbled and, to Chloe's amazement, tears began

to form in his dark black eyes. "I ruined everything that night. We could have been married by now, raising a family together. But I messed it all up because I was so in love with you. But what I did was wrong. Maybe not in the eyes of the law, but wrong all the same." He wiped his nose on his sleeve and pinched the bridge of his nose.

"Kyle, what are you saying?" Chloe whispered.

"I'm saying I wanna try again with you, Chloe. For the boy's sake. Seeing the way Shona is flaunting herself and her new confidence around town has really woken me up to the way you're being treated. It's not right. I said to myself, 'why ain't she being treated better?' I would do it all so different this time if there was just a chance for us to be a family. I don't want my boy growing up being illegitimate. I want him to inherit my family's fortune one day. Surely you'd want that too?" He looked at her, reaching out to graze her face with the back of his fingers.

Chloe's head was spinning. After the Lucy business, she and Shona had been getting closer again, but now, with what Kyle had seen in town, it seemed all of that was being raked up once again.

"Just another chance to make it right is all I'm asking, Chloe." Kyle backed off again. "But you don't have to tell me now. Think about it. But please, will you give the boy this?" He held out the bear once again. This time Chloe, in a state of bewilderment, took it. "I'll leave you alone now. But you really do look beautiful. Motherhood suits you. Maybe marriage will too?"

At the end of the road, out of sight of the house, Kyle stopped the car and put his hand in his pocket. As Chloe had leaned down to sort out Cooper, Kyle had swiped a pair of her panties off the hamper of dirty laundry she'd left in the hallway while she answered the door.

"Mmmm, just like I remember," he purred, pressing them to his nose.

∼

"Hey Shona, did that guy find you?" Bertie said after wandering over to the garage on her lunch break.

"What guy?" Shona replied, emerging from underneath the car she was fixing.

"Tall, black hair, thinks every lesbian in this town is gonna magically convert because of his cologne."

Shona grimaced. "No, and I ain't wanting him to find me either. He's an asshole."

"Yeah, well, Alice told him you worked here. Stupid kid. She let it slip by accident. You in trouble?"

"Hope not. He'll go soon when he realizes there's nothing for him here."

"Well, you got your girls over there, primed and ready. And I still owe you one. Just say the word if you need anything, OK?"

"Thank you, Bertie," Shona replied.

∼

"I'm home, honey. Where's my family at?" Shona bellowed down the hallway as she came through her front door. Something caught her attention. Lifting her nose into the air, the smell was unmistakable. "Chloe?" she called out, more seriously this time.

"In here," Chloe called back from the bedroom.

"Why can I smell Kyle in this house?"

Chloe turned around and almost took Shona's breath away. She was wearing a tight-fitting peach blouse and black pencil skirt with a thin black belt around her waist. It was an outfit very similar to one she'd have worn all those years ago at Ellis and Bruce. Normally, Shona would have complimented her on it, but something didn't feel right.

"Was he here?"

"Who?"

"You know who," Shona yelled. "Kyle."

"Shona, please don't raise your voice. David'll hear." She turned back to the full-length mirror to continue brushing her hair. "Yes, he was. He brought a bear for David. He's playing with it in his room now."

"Are you serious? How can you let that man anywhere near you after what he did?"

Chloe spun around to face Shona. "I'm not. But he is David's father, Shona. David has been asking questions these last few months."

"Bullshit. He's no father. He's a murdering bastard who killed my best friend and violated you. How could I ever accept him back in our lives?"

"We'll be OK, Shona. If he steps out of line, Sheriff Everett will be there to take him in. You said it yourself, the town'll be safer when he's back in charge."

"But he'll retire one day. He won't be around forever. We can't rely on anyone to protect us—it's down to us. Please, Chloe, don't trust him." Shona was leaning against the bedroom door now, relying on it to take her whole weight.

"He has rights, Shona, as David's father. We can't get around that. If I don't let him see David, he'll exercise those rights, no doubt, to the authorities. He's already threatened to tell old Miller down at the school all about us. Do you want all that to happen again? For David to be taken away from us?"

Shona groaned. "No, of course I don't. How could you even ask that? You know I love that kid as much as if I'd given birth to him myself. But that man is evil. He'll take everything away from us."

"He won't, baby, I swear. I'm stronger now. He can't scare me anymore. I've just gotta play things carefully. Otherwise we could lose everything we've fought so hard to have here."

"I'm so sorry about the letter." Shona sobbed. "This is all my fault."

"It's done now."

Shona looked at Chloe and then at her clothes. "Why are you wearing those?"

"I've spent so long stuck indoors being a mom. I just wanted to feel strong and look independent again."

"You know, you look like you did when you first appeared on that balcony."

"Yeah?"

"Yeah. I fell for you the second I saw you."

Chloe wrapped her arms around Shona's waist. "Me too, the second I looked down and saw you in that crowd. Nothing will break us, Shona. I swear it."

Chapter 41

Shona was finishing up with a customer when Kyle swaggered up to her the following morning. He leaned against the garage doors as the old man was handing over payment for the work she'd done.

"Thank you so much, Shona. You're the best mechanic this town has ever had," the old man said. He put his brown leather wallet back in the pocket of his beige slacks and, with a little help from Shona's outstretched arm, climbed into his Buick.

As soon as he'd driven away, Kyle approached her slowly clapping his hands. "You're the best mechanic this town has ever had," he mimicked. "You really have charmed everyone around here, haven't you? Men *and* women."

"Fuck off, Kyle," Shona replied without even looking at him as she turned to go back inside the garage.

"You know, you shouldn't keep a good woman like Chloe locked inside the house all day. She gets bored and..." he paused, fishing into his pocket for Chloe's panties while keeping his stare fixed on Shona, "tempted."

Shona turned around ready to fly at him but stopped dead when she saw what he was holding. "Where the hell did you get those?" Her eyes shot bolts of fire at the now-smirking Kyle.

"Hey Shona, can you take a look at my tailpipe? It's making a funny noise," a young cop shouted out from the side of the road about ten feet away from her.

"Better not make a scene in front of the law now, honey. I don't think even your magical hands will get you off an assault charge." Kyle's face was beaming with triumph.

Stepping closer to him on her way over to the cop, Shona leaned into Kyle. "It wouldn't be assault, it'd be murder." She ripped the panties out of his grasp and thrust them in her pocket. "Now get the fuck off my property, asshole."

"Go ask your girlfriend how I got those," he snarled back.

"Hi honey, good day at work?" Chloe asked, kissing Shona on the cheek as she walked through the door.

"It was OK."

"I got steak for dinner. You hungry? David's out tonight at his sleepover at Bobby's, remember? We got the house to ourselves for once." Chloe took Shona's hand and began to lead her into the kitchen, but Shona pulled her hand away.

"I have to ask you something and I need you to be honest with me." Shona took a deep breath and licked her lips. "Did you sleep with Kyle when he was here yesterday?"

Chloe recoiled in shock. "What?"

Shona pulled out the panties. "Kyle gave them to me. I know they're yours. What I can't work out is why he would have them. Unless…"

Chloe's voice abandoned her entirely. It was a moment too long before she could speak. Shona, concluding the worst, turned around and stormed out of the house.

"Can you tell me what room Mr. Chambers is in, please?"

"And you are?" the desk clerk of the dingy motel Kyle was staying at asked, looking over his horn-rimmed glasses.

"I'm the girl he ordered. I'm sure he'd appreciate a little discretion," Chloe replied.

After receiving an indifferent nod, a room number and a point, she began walking down the hallway, decorated with mismatched wallpaper and a tired green carpet. Reaching Kyle's door, she knocked on it, leaving her other hand rooted in her coat pocket holding on to a wrench she'd taken from Shona's tool belt. The door swung open, Kyle behind it wearing just a towel around his waist, clearly expecting company. "So predictable," Chloe whispered under her breath.

"Well now, I did not expect to see you here. What a lovely surprise." He noted her smart blouse and pencil skirt she'd worn again today. "You look amazing. Come in."

"We need to talk, Kyle," Chloe snapped, barging past him.

"What's the matter?"

"This." Chloe held out the panties.

"What about them?" Kyle perched on the end of his armchair, his towel opening as he parted his legs. Chloe averted her eyes and maintained a safe distance.

"Why did you take them? Then tell Shona we'd gone to bed together?"

Kyle laughed. "It was just a joke. No sense of humor, that girl."

"You told a horrible lie to her, Kyle. I need you to go and tell her that."

He stood up and walked over to her, his cologne lingering in the air between them. "You know...we could be a proper family. Surely you want our boy to grow up with a mommy and a daddy, don't you? Like normal kids?" His half-naked body was now inches away from her. "I've learned my lesson, Chloe. I've missed you so much. Just allow yourself to imagine life with me

262

for a minute. You could meet your friends for long lunches, go shopping and paint as much as you'd like. David could stay in his preschool. You wouldn't have to move him because old sourpuss Miller doesn't want the drama of all this. Oh Chloe, if you'd come back to me, I swear it'll be different this time. I wouldn't keep you locked up in that house all day, like Shona does. I'm a changed man, I swear. You're the woman I fell in love with. The woman I'm still in love with." He placed his fingers below her chin and raised it up, then moved his lips closer to hers.

"Kyle, no," she ordered, taking one even step back. Her fingers clenched around the wrench as she drew it from her pocket. "Touch me again and you'll walk funny for a week."

Kyle stepped back, shocked at her newfound assertiveness. He was smiling but his eyes were fierce. "Well, well, Chloe Bruce. Thinking she's all tough." His tone darkened. "But you're playing with fire, honey. You belong to me. You and the boy. Be smart now. You can't get away from me a second time. I own you, Chloe." He stood there smirking at her in triumph.

Chloe was unmoved. Feeling a sense of strength, the like of which she'd never felt before towards Kyle, she stepped closer to him, the wrench gripped in her bone-dry palm. Without taking her eyes off him, she pressed her face close enough for their noses to almost touch. After a huge deep breath, Chloe placed her lips against Kyle's ear.

"You don't own me," she sang in her breathiest tones.

Kyle looked at her, bewildered. Without another word, Chloe eyeballed him as she backed up towards the door, then let herself out.

Twenty minutes later, after she had stormed out of the house,

Shona was standing in the bar looking down at Bertie, Edie, Dee and Lula who were all seated at a booth.

"That favor you owe me? I'm calling it in," Shona said, her face like stone.

"Name it," Bertie replied, folding her arms.

Chapter 42

K yle smiled at Alice as he closed the bakery door behind him. "Well, good morning."

Looking up from her Wednesday morning newspaper, Alice beamed. "Hello, sir, how can I help you today?"

"Well now, that's more like it. I'd like another one of those delicious pies, please. That one the other day was just yum." He leaned an elbow on the counter.

With a sympathetic smile, Alice shook her head. "Oh, sir, I'm so sorry, but we don't have any in today."

"What? But I can smell them." Kyle looked around the bakery, confused. Alice shook her head again and returned to her newspaper. "I'll have some of that bread there then," he said, pointing at the pile on the table behind her.

Alice cast her eyes over it for a second before shaking her head again. "Nope, sorry. That's all taken, sir," she added.

"Suit yourself. I'll take my money next door." Kyle turned on his heels and left, leaving Alice grinning to herself as he slammed the door.

Minutes later, Kyle entered the grocery store.

"Packet of smokes," he ordered, slamming down a dollar bill on the counter.

"Sorry, sir, all out of smokes today," Edie replied, not looking up from her magazine.

"I can see them on the shelf behind you," Kyle said, grinding his teeth.

"Then I don't know what to tell you. *Sir,*" Edie looked up and fixed her stare on Kyle's blazing eyes. She pressed a finger on his dollar bill and swept it back across the counter to him.

"I'd like to speak to your manager. I'll have your job for this."

"Boss is away. I'm in charge and *I'd* like you to leave. Now."

Seeing two old ladies, who were browsing through the magazine rack, turn and glare at him, Kyle forced out a tight smile and turned to leave. When he returned to his car, though, his anger spilled over.

"What the fuck?" He looked at his hood and windows, which were now covered in egg stains, the words 'GET LOST, ASSHOLE' drawn in the yellow yolk smears. Over at the bar, Bertie and Dee were sniggering and pointing at him. Just about to march over there, Kyle stopped. His tires were as flat as pancakes.

"You fucking dykes," he yelled over to them. His fury only made Bertie and Dee laugh even harder.

"If only you knew a good mechanic around here?" Dee shouted back, almost doubled over.

Kyle clenched his fists and looked over to the garage. Shona was standing on the front hosing down a patch of oil. Grinning, she looked down at her foot pump just a few feet away from her, with no intention of letting him borrow it.

It was almost seven o'clock by the time Shona was locking up. She'd been so busy that she almost hadn't noticed the recovery truck from the next town's garage pull up across the street to attend to Kyle's car. Locking away her tools, she switched off the interior lights and pulled the garage doors together, then remembered she'd left her lunch box on her desk inside. Going back in to get it, she heard a voice behind her that chilled her blood.

"Think you and your dyke friends are so clever, don't you?"

Shona spun to see Kyle's leering face bearing down on her. Grabbing her by the throat, he slammed her up against the wall next to her tool chest. "Get the fuck off me, Kyle," she squeezed out, her eyes bulging.

"Ahh, this takes me back to that day. You remember? The day I was gonna fuck you, but your nigger friend got himself involved. You remember that, bitch? How the Bullen's dragged him along the dirt until his skin ripped off? You picturing that now?" Kyle's mouth was pressed up against her ear, his breath hot against her neck. "God, the thought of me being the first man to have you still makes me hard as *fuck* down there. How 'bout it, huh?"

"Never."

"What if I was to say that if you let me then I would leave town forever? You could have your little family all to yourself again."

Shona glared through blurred vision at him. His eyes were as black as night, his body pressed up against her. Reaching out her left hand, she scrabbled around the top of the tool chest until she finally managed to wrap her fingers around the thing she was praying she'd find.

"I'd rather die than have you fuck me, Kyle." She lifted her knee and aimed it between his legs, then punched him in the head. Like a felled tree, Kyle hit the deck.

"You fucking bitch! I'm gonna rip your heart out for that," Kyle groaned as he writhed on the floor.

Shona stood over him, casting a dark shadow across his prone body. In her hand, now raised above her head, she held her trusty wrench, the brown leather strap enabling it to sit perfectly in her sweaty grip.

"Last time you tried that with me, you didn't have a criminal record for assault. Now you come in here and attack me? Self-defense, they'd say it was. Sheriff Everett is my friend. You, on the other hand, are hated around here."

Kyle, in agony, could hardly breathe, let alone reply.

"So," Shona said. "I think you should do yourself a favor and leave me and my family alone. Or one word from me to Everett about what you just tried there, and he'll have your ass back in jail quicker than you can spit. Now, get the fuck outta here and don't come back."

Kyle wriggled ten feet backwards away from Shona, then stood up, using the doors to bolster him. "No one threatens me, Jackson." He turned and staggered out, leaving Shona alone in the semi-darkness. Seconds after he'd gone, she broke down in tears, the triumph of seeing Kyle at her mercy short-lived as the shock set in, rippling through her aching body.

"What the hell happened to you?" Chloe asked as Shona returned from work, an ugly red mark shining brightly on her neck, her cheek scratched.

"I had a visit. From your ex."

Chloe's face paled. "Kyle did this to you?"

"Yes."

Rushing over to her, Chloe embraced her and guided her down onto the couch. "What did he do to you?" she asked, stroking Shona's hair out of her eyes and taking a close look at her scratched cheek.

"Same as what he tried to do to me last time he threw me up against a wall." Shona swallowed and looked away.

"He didn't..."

"Don't worry, he never got close. His balls got a sharp reminder, though, not to try that on anyone again. Only wish I'd kneed him harder."

"I'm so sorry."

"Don't be.

"Do you think he's really gone?"

"I hope so," Shona replied, her voice less convincing this time.

Kyle winced as he lowered himself onto the bed in his hotel room the next morning, still feeling the force of Shona's knee. He picked up the phone on the nightstand and dialed.

"Hello? Yes, good morning. I'd like to file a complaint. There's a woman who's preying on the mother of my child. I have good reason to believe she is a homosexual leading her astray. Yes, of course I have evidence. This pervert hangs around that bar, Bertie's it's called. Everyone in this town knows what kind of a place that is and I will not have my boy exposed to that kinda depravity. Yes, I can come in. Tomorrow? It'll have to be early as I have to go away on a business trip. Yes, that's why this is of the utmost urgency that it is investigated. While I'm outta town, this woman will pounce, I'm sure of it. Thank you. Yes, my name is Kyle Chambers, and yours?" Kyle paused to write the officer's name down on the pad next to the phone. "See you tomorrow. Bye."

He lay back on the bed, grinning.

Chapter 43

Kyle walked into the opulent drawing room belonging to the person he'd returned to Alabama to visit. Within five minutes of the housekeeper showing him in, his eyes lifted up to the staircase just visible through the doorway of the drawing room. The lady of the house sashayed down the soft carpeted stairs, then walked into the drawing room, kissing Kyle on both cheeks. Pointing a cigarette holder in his direction, she rolled her heavily made up eyes as she waited for him to fish out a lighter from his jacket pocket, then released a thick plume of smoke into his face through her rouged lips. Her light brown hair was pinned high on her head in a beehive style, her pink Chanel dress matching perfectly with her designer heels.

"Good evening, ma'am. May I say how lovely you're looking this fine Saturday evening?"

Eleanor Bruce, with a look of contempt on her face, ignored his drawl. "Where's my grandson, Kyle?"

"Eleanor, please. You gotta have a little patience. I'm working on it. I won't let you down." He walked over to an armchair and sank down into it.

Eleanor raised an eyebrow. "You mean like the last time? When you let my daughter dump you and run off with that..."

Eleanor paused and sucked in her cheeks as if a bad taste had crept into her mouth. "And it's Mrs. Bruce to you. Don't forget your manners, Kyle."

Kyle held his hands up in defense. "My apologies. As I said, it's just a matter of time before Chloe comes around to my way of thinking. That busybody principal at your grandson's school is already asking questions about her and Jackson."

"OK then. That's a good start." Eleanor sat down in the chair opposite and rested the frown creasing her face. "So you've told my daughter that she is to come home immediately with the boy?"

Kyle shifted in his chair. "Well, not exactly in those words. Wheels are in motion, though."

"And the lesbian?"

"I visited her a couple of days ago. Let her know not to mess with me. She thinks she's got the upper hand because of her friends at the police station, but I got a good man on my side. He's still got some influence over there, with the officers who want that town clear of perverts."

"Then you need to work harder on getting him back here, don't you?" Eleanor pursed her lips. "What's your plan?"

"Simple. You write a letter to the authorities telling them I want custody of David, to raise him properly, with your support, of course. I've already filed a report making a complaint, so your letter will reinforce that."

"Yes. It will."

"I'm just sorry I've already missed six years of his life. If my mother hadn't paid that judge to oversee my parole hearing, then I wouldn't have even known about him." Kyle leaned forward in his seat. "He's gorgeous, Mrs. Bruce. Looks exactly like me."

"And my daughter? How was she?" Eleanor's icy demeanor cracked ever so slightly.

"Still as beautiful as ever. I'd still want to marry her if you'll permit me to?"

"Well, her father isn't around anymore so I guess my permission will have to be enough."

Kyle sipped his scotch. "Have you heard from Larry?"

"Not for a while now. After the first five years of his sentence, he stopped writing me every week. He must have got the message that I didn't want him in my life anymore. He left me with nothing after he was arrested. If it wasn't for the kindness of Jeffrey Ellis in my hour of need, I'd be on the streets by now. I guess he had his uses after all." She looked over to the mantelpiece where a picture frame containing a photograph of David that Chloe had sent when he was only a year old sat proudly. Turning back to Kyle, Eleanor sat upright. "So. What should I write in this letter, then?"

Chloe took the mail out of the box outside the beach house and sifted through it that sunny Monday morning. It had been almost two weeks since Shona's altercation with Kyle and he hadn't been seen in town since. Both Chloe and Shona were starting to regain a sense of normality over their lives. Until now.

"Shona," Chloe yelled, clutching the letter in her fist. She ran back up the porch steps trying unsuccessfully to keep calm. "Shona."

"What?" Shona yelled back, drying her hands on a dish towel.

"Look." She held out the letter and the crumpled envelope it came in. "It's from the Children's Bureau. Says there's been an allegation, from several people this time, that we are living together in sin and David is at risk."

Shona snatched the letter from Chloe, then recoiled in

disgust. "And I drink every night? Where the hell did they get that from? The odd beer is hardly *every* night."

"And who's 'several people'?" Chloe replied, folding her arms across her chest. "I was so shocked I didn't read it all."

Shona skim-read to the bottom of the letter. "Says there have been four separate allegations. They're listed here. Apparently Kyle filed the report, then Deputy Lawrence added his dime to the pot mentioning my 'involvement in the riots' the other year. The third mentions 'neglect.' That must be Miller, after you forgetting to pick him up that time."

"We can't fight that. They're all true." She wiped her tears away. "Oh Shona, what are we gonna do?"

"It says here that if I move out, you can keep David, but if I stay then they'll investigate further. Wait a minute... It mentioned four allegations, didn't it?"

"Who made the fourth allegation?"

Shona swallowed hard. "Your mother."

Chloe had been sitting on the porch swing for the last hour in shock. Holding the crumpled letter, she took another sip of her bourbon and watched as the sun began to set.

"Hey," Shona whispered. She walked over and wrapped a blanket around Chloe's shoulders. "You OK?"

"No, not really. I've been sitting here trying to work out what to do. I can't believe after all these years my own mother is *still* trying to control me. And to side with Kyle again, after what he did to me?"

"I know, baby, I'm so sorry. It's all my fault. That damn letter."

"Don't, Shona, we've already been through this. What's done is done."

"Do you think your father is involved too?"

273

"It doesn't mention him. And after he went to jail, Mother washed her hands of him, so I doubt it."

Shona stared out into the distance, the sun almost disappearing into darkness now. "Should I move out?"

Chloe stared at her open-mouthed. "Of course not. I'm not losing you."

"But to keep David, you might not have a choice."

They sat staring at each other in silence before Chloe took Shona's hand in her own. "We've fought the odds before. We'll find a way to sort this out. Hey, why don't we speak to Minnie? Maybe Judge Barker could help us work through the legalities?"

Shona's face lit up. "Of course. Minnie will know what to do. We can go over there first thing in the morning."

"Minnie, please come in. Can I get you a glass of tea?" Chloe said as the old lady appeared on their doorstep that sunny morning.

It was the day after they'd visited her when Minnie came over to the beach house with news. She thanked Chloe and sat down in the armchair nearest to the living room door. "Is Shona here? I should relay what William has said to both of you."

After calling Shona in from the yard, they both sat on the couch opposite Minnie as she took a huge deep breath in and began. "Well, it's worse than we first thought. Turns out these four allegations were just the start."

Chloe and Shona looked at each other in shock, then back at Minnie.

"Apparently there's been two more. One from Marion Lawrence, wife of the deputy. The other was from Mr. and Mrs. Chambers, Kyle's parents."

"Are you serious? His parents hate him," Chloe spat out. "He told me years ago that they wouldn't help him anymore, that he was on his own."

"Well, now things have changed. They have a grandson now. An heir to their steel business back in Pittsburgh. And for David to inherit, Kyle must make him legitimate by marrying you. Kyle's promised them he'll be a good husband and father, and that it's helped him change his ways."

"And they bought that load of crap?" Shona retorted.

"It would seem so."

Chloe exhaled at length.

"But there is some good news," Minnie said with a glint in her eye.

"What?" Chloe and Shona replied in unison.

"Well, William has concluded that there simply isn't any hard evidence. You both sleep in separate rooms," she winked, "and David is thriving at school now. Oh yes, that one time he was picked up late was an issue, but he was safe at school with that young teacher, Lucy, and Shona did the right thing by fully registering herself as his secondary caregiver before David left the building. Legally on that one, they have nothing. The girls at the bar will testify that all you drink is Coca Cola when you go in there, and there is no evidence that you've ever been drunk in public or caused any fuss. And yes, you were at the riots back then, but you were responsible for three police officers ending up safe at the hospital, including Bill Everett's own son. And you don't need me to tell you he's more than willing to speak up for you. Then there's the issue of Kyle wanting custody."

Shona and Chloe lowered their eyes to their laps until Minnie tutted.

"Hey, you two, now don't you worry none. No court in the land is gonna grant custody of a minor to a man like that. Not with his record, even if your mother is standing by him. She isn't as highly thought of as she seems to think she is. The Bruce surname is toxic in business circles now, not to mention in high society. It's gonna be fine, girls. William will talk to his friend in the Children's Bureau tomorrow and get these allegations thrown out once and for all."

Chapter 44

Shona returned home that Friday night with a glint in her eye after having arranged for Minnie to have David overnight. She stepped out of the shower and slipped on a clean white undershirt and loose khaki pants just as the doorbell rang.

"I'll get it," Chloe called from the hallway, already halfway there. She opened the door to see Minnie beaming at her.

"The little guy all ready?" Minnie asked, clasping her hands to her chest. "I'm really looking forward to having him tonight."

"What?" Chloe replied, perplexed.

Shona came bounding out of the bedroom a little red-faced. Holding a towel to her wet hair as she ruffled it dry, she flashed a lopsided grin at Chloe. "I thought we could have the night to ourselves." She passed David's overnight bag to the old lady. "I really appreciate this, Minnie. David?" she called backwards over her shoulder.

"Can we have cake?" David asked, wiping his hand against his nose as he traipsed down the hallway towards Minnie who rolled her eyes and nodded.

"Of course. You like chocolate cake?"

David's face spread into a huge grin. "Yes ma'am."

Chloe smiled through her confusion. "OK then, well, I guess that's settled. Have fun."

"You too," Minnie replied, winking at Shona, who blushed.

After closing the door to them, Chloe swayed over to Shona and wrapped her arms around her. "So, what have you got in mind for tonight then?"

"You'll see. While I was in the bathroom, I drew you a bath. Thought you could go for a long soak to relax. Make the most of the peace and quiet," Shona said, kissing her earlobe. "But don't be too long, OK?"

Chloe padded into the bathroom and gasped when she saw the effort that Shona had gone to. All around the edge of the tub were little candles, their light bathing the room in a soft amber glow. In the water were little rose petals sitting proudly on top of thick luscious bubbles created by her favorite bath soak. Everything was just perfect. Stripping off, Chloe dipped a toe in the water. The temperature was exactly right for her and, sinking below the water line, she breathed out at length, enjoying the pleasure of the water enveloping every part of her. After thirty long minutes making sure every part of herself was attended to, Chloe dried off, slipped on her robe and headed back into the bedroom. Shona was nowhere to be seen. Confused, Chloe walked towards the living room.

"Are you coming in?" she began, then stopped and stood open-mouthed at the sight before her. Shona had lit candles all around the room and pushed the furniture back so it left a huge space. She had arranged blankets and pillows, making a floor bed. There she lay until she saw Chloe appear at the door. She jumped up and walked over to her.

"Come with me," Shona said, taking Chloe's hand and slowly leading her to the floor bed. Untying Chloe's robe, she pulled the silk cord out from it, throwing it on the ground. Without a word, Shona slipped her hands underneath the shoulders of the robe and let it fall away from Chloe's baby soft skin.

"Lay down," Shona commanded, her voice barely above a whisper. Chloe obeyed, her whole body tingling with anticipation. She lay on her back completely naked, looking up at Shona whose movements were almost ethereal. Shona kneeled down and spread her body over Chloe, who lifted her face to reach Shona's lips, but Shona pulled away. The look on her face was pure seduction as she reached over for the silk cord she'd taken from the robe and instructed Chloe to put her arms above her head, which she did without question. Shona wrapped Chloe's wrists with the cord, not too tight but enough to keep them where she wanted them, threading one end through the leg of the armchair behind Chloe's prone body to anchor her. Chloe murmured, the pulsing between her legs growing.

"I want you to lie still, understand?" Shona breathed in Chloe's ear, then kissed her on the neck.

"I understand," Chloe replied. The ache was pounding now.

"Chloe, do you trust me?"

Biting her lip, Chloe nodded.

"Completely?" Shona added, her blue eyes mesmerizing.

"Yes."

Shona then sat back on her heels after gently pushing Chloe's head back so it was resting on the blankets. She took a thin silk scarf out of her back pocket and laid it carefully over Chloe's eyes, tucking the ends underneath her head.

"Can you see me?"

"No."

Leaving it a second, Shona stood up. "Promise?"

"I promise."

Seconds ticked by. Long, agonizing seconds.

"Shona? Are you there?"

"Yes."

Crouching down, Shona began tracing the back of her finger down Chloe's side, reaching one naked hip, then circled around the bone. Chloe gasped at Shona's light touch, lifting her body to try and catch a firmer contact, but Shona pulled her fingers away.

"Stay still," she commanded, then lowered her face to Chloe's hip bones. Moving across from right to left, Shona kissed every inch of Chloe's lower body, apart from where she knew Chloe craved to feel her mouth the most. With her long, wet tongue, Shona travelled the length of Chloe's inside leg all the way down to her ankle bone, then, picking up the other silk scarf she'd brought in and choosing her spot, she took her time to run it delicately over Chloe's breasts, circling the rougher part of the tassel around her nipples, generating more gasps from Chloe who was struggling to take any more. Pressing her mouth against Chloe's breasts, she took in each nipple, one after the other, feeling them harden almost in an instant against her tongue. She then drew back and blew very lightly on one, then the other.

"Oh my God, Shona. I can't..."

Ignoring Chloe's please for mercy, Shona picked out an ice cube from her glass of tea and ran it along the same path her fingers had traced only moments earlier. Squeezing the ice in her hand, Shona let her body heat slowly melt it onto Chloe's skin. Smiling, she watched the droplets dribble between Chloe's breasts and stomach, until they eventually rolled down over her hip bones. The ice water now mixing with the throbbing heat between Chloe's legs, Shona's hungry mouth followed, catching every drop. Then, gently pulling apart Chloe's delicate lips, Shona blew on her most sensitive spot, softly at first, then harder, each breath longer than the last. The sheer cold of the ice water running over her skin simultaneously made the sensation even more intense. All Chloe could do was groan, waiting, hoping, that soon Shona would put her out of her delicious misery.

"Shona, please," Chloe's strained voice begged.

Shona lifted off her undershirt and laid her naked torso on top of Chloe, kissing her hard and wrapping her hands around Chloe's still-bound wrists as she did so. Chloe could just about make out Shona's shadow through the blindfold. Their bodies moved together as one, then, letting go of Chloe's wrists, Shona kissed her way down her body again, revisiting the parts she'd tormented earlier, finishing up where the droplets from the ice cube had come to pool between her legs. This time, without hesitation, Shona allowed her mouth to explore there, slowly at first, her tongue finding all the places Chloe had been aching for it to find. With a hunger she could barely control, Shona buried her tongue deep inside Chloe, her hands gripping on tightly to Chloe's writhing thighs.

"Oh God, Shona. Just there, yes."

Shona needed no encouragement. All her attention was now on that one spot, her tongue working hard and slow, then speeding up to encourage the inevitable conclusion. Feeling Chloe's body about to give way, Shona suddenly stopped what she was doing and lifted her head up, licking every delicious drop of Chloe from her own lips.

"No, please Shona, don't stop…"

"Shhh… All in good time. I'm not finished with you yet," Shona replied with a devilish grin, the menace oozing out of her. She waited another few seconds, then sank her face back to the same spot as before. As if a switch had been flicked, Shona felt Chloe's wetness increase in an instant as she worked her tongue against Chloe's spot over and over again. Then stopping again. Seconds later, with the loudest groan Shona had ever heard from her, Chloe raised her back off the blankets, her whole body convulsing with ecstasy as her orgasm thundered through her.

Panting now herself, Shona wiped her wet mouth and looked up to see the silk scarf still draped over Chloe's face. Then a panic appeared to set in with Chloe, startling Shona into action.

"What? What is it?" Shona asked, climbing back up her body to rip the scarf off. Chloe's sweaty face was bright red, strands of hair matted to her forehead.

"Get me out of this," Chloe demanded, yanking her wrists against the legs of the armchair.

Untying the cord as quickly as she could, Shona threw it away and clamped her palm around Chloe's face. "What's the matter?"

"Nothing. I just need to fuck you. Now."

Chloe's eyes were filled with pure lust as she rolled over the top of Shona and ripped down her pants. Pinning Shona's wrists above her head with one hand, Chloe used her knees to spread wide Shona's legs, then positioned her free hand between them. Carefully, she slipped in her long fingers, letting them travel deeper and deeper until her fingertips hit the ridges inside of Shona, who groaned as she felt Chloe rub against them, then pull out. Chloe slid her fingers back inside Shona again, pressing harder this time against her inner walls.

"Oh, Chloe. That feels... Oh my god..." Shona could hardly catch her breath, let alone form words.

Rubbing herself against Shona's thigh, Chloe felt the sensations inside herself build again. With Shona's inner muscles tightening around her fingers, Chloe could tell she was almost there too and, after a few more seconds, they cried out together. Collapsing into the blankets of the floor bed, they lay in each other's arms completely exhausted.

"Oh my God, Shona, I've never felt our bodies do that before," Chloe panted, then laughed, her mouth pressed to Shona's ear.

"I know," Shona replied with her eyes closed. "It's a good

thing we live far away. The whole town would have heard you scream just then."

"We should get a sitter more often."

Together, locked in each other's arms, they lay there watching the candles flicker, feeling closer than ever.

Chapter 45

Shona woke up with Chloe still in her arms. She hadn't moved an inch, as if a minute hadn't passed since they had fallen asleep together. Slipping out from underneath Chloe's arm, she rose up, put on her undershirt and pants, and headed into the kitchen. As she poured the second cup of coffee, she felt Chloe's arms wrap around her.

"Well, good morning," Shona said, smiling and turning around to hand Chloe her coffee cup. "You sleep well?"

"I sure did. I woke up at one point to find a gorgeous blonde lying naked next to me."

At that moment, a loud knock at the front door made them both jump. Cooper sat up in his basket, the faintest growl coming from him.

"Cooper, lie down," Shona commanded, to which he obeyed. "I'll go see who it is." She kissed Chloe on the cheek and hopped down the hallway. After opening the door, her blood ran cold.

"Hello, Shona."

Shona stood motionless, hardly able to breathe. Every punch and kick of the beating she'd received back in Alabama came flooding back to her. Feeling her legs start to wobble, she leaned against the door frame.

"What the hell are you doing here?"

"I don't want any trouble. Is Chloe here?"

Leaving their visitor on the doorstep, Shona padded, slower this time, back to the kitchen. The second Chloe looked at her pale face, her heart began to race.

"Who is it?" Chloe strode over to her. "Who's at the door, Shona?"

Shona raised her eyes to meet Chloe's.

"It's your father."

The coffee cup in Chloe's hands slipped to the floor, smashing into pieces.

After dressing as quickly as she could, Chloe approached the door, her face like stone. "What the hell are you doing here?"

Larry Bruce had stepped down from the porch by this time and was now stroking his moustache and looking out to the ocean. His formerly rotund figure was now noticeably thinner, his face much grayer. "I needed to see you. To talk to you."

"I thought they'd lock you up for life for what you did," Shona shot back from the hallway.

"They let me out early," he replied over Chloe's shoulder. He looked back at his daughter. "I'm dying."

"Of what? Shame? The devil finally caught up with you, huh?" Shona blasted.

"I guess so," Larry replied. "I've got weeks, if I'm lucky."

Shona laughed. "Please tell me it's painful what you've got? Tell me it hurts every fucking day just to breathe?"

Larry cleared his throat "Yes, actually. It does. I got cancer. My lungs are riddled. Can't hardly breathe most days. Fifty years of cigar smoke has finished me off." He paused to sniff the cool sea air. "Your mother told me you were here. I can see why you chose this place now."

"Yeah, well, now that you've seen it, you can fuck off again." Shona spat on the ground next to him.

"I'd like a minute with my daughter. Alone. Please?" Larry motioned for Shona to go back in the house, but she stayed put. "Look, I promise I won't hurt her."

Chloe looked at Shona and nodded. "I'll be OK. You go inside."

"Are you sure?"

"Yes. Honestly, go on."

"I'll be right inside the door. OK?" Shona traipsed back inside the house, leaving the door open.

Chloe stepped down from the porch and joined her father at the edge of the yard leading down to the beach. "So, what do you want to talk to me about, Larry?" Chloe still, from the day she'd found out about what kind of a man her father was, and what he'd had arranged to be done to Shona back in Alabama, couldn't bring herself to call him "father."

"I wanted to try and put things right between you and me. You're my only child now, Chloe. A man should go to his grave knowing his affairs are all in order."

"Shame you couldn't have afforded the same consideration to all those guys you had murdered. Poor Cuban. You remember him? He was Shona's best friend. He didn't deserve what you did to him."

Larry shook his head. "You're right, he didn't deserve that. If I could take it back, I would. As God is my witness, Chloe, I swear I would."

Chloe stared in disbelief at her father. Was he really the same man? He seemed so different, a shadow of his former intimidating self. He'd lost at least fifty pounds and the gray sack suit he was wearing was nowhere near the quality of the expensive tailored ones he used to wear.

"While I was in prison, I met a couple of nig...um, negro men. At first I was wary, I was disgusted, but the more I got to know them they seemed like decent enough fellas. One helped me out when I wasn't well. Made sure I saw the doctor. If he hadn't have insisted on it, I would be dead by now and not have this chance to speak to my daughter for the last time." He turned to Chloe and exhaled at length, his breath crackly. "What you told me the day I was arrested. About Moses and how he helped on the day your brother died? It hit me hard, Chloe. I couldn't stop thinking about how wrong I'd got it all those years. And after that, all those men that died because of me and my actions. I am truly sorry for that. I've found God, Chloe. Done a lot of work on myself, a lot of thinking. Tried to do some paying back when I can. That's why they let me out early. They knew I was dying and my lawyer got a deal with the D.A. back in Alabama."

"How's Mother? Have you seen her since you've been out?"

"Not really, just told me you were here and shut the door in my face. Can't say I blame her." Larry replied. "Apparently Ellis gave her some money to help her to keep the house, but on the agreement that she'd never have anything to do with me again and that I never came back to Daynes after that."

"Yeah, that's Mother all over really. All about the wealth and status."

"She did ask me to get you away from here if I could. She never did get over you dumping Kyle, and his money, for Shona."

"And what about you, Larry? After what I told you about what he did to me, you still think I should be with him?" Chloe glared at her father.

"Of course not. If I ever see him again, I'll kill him." He paused. "You seem happy now...living here. It's beautiful. And if Shona is the reason for that then you both have my blessing."

Chloe was stunned.

But, after everything that had happened, and the news he'd brought with him, it was just too late now.

Larry coughed and wiped his mouth. "I've made so many mistakes, Chloe. I just wanna put them right now. I brought a few gifts for the boy. Will you allow me to give them to him?"

"He's not back from his sleepover yet. I need to think about all this before I agree to that," Chloe replied, shaking confusion from her head.

"I understand. I'll come back tomorrow morning if that's OK? I'd leave it longer but..." He coughed again, leaving his sentence rhetorical.

"OK. Say around ten?"

"OK. I'll be here. Here's my number at the hotel, in case you need it." He handed her a business card. Chloe noticed it was the same place Kyle had stayed at.

Larry reached out his arms for a hug, but Chloe recoiled.

"I understand. Not yet," Larry said, nodding.

"I'll see you tomorrow." She waved goodbye as Larry drove slowly back up the drive to the highway.

"Did he tell you he's changed? That he's seen the light finally?" Shona scoffed as Chloe walked back inside the house.

"Yes. And you know what? I actually believe him."

Sunday morning, ten o'clock on the dot, Larry Bruce's battered old Chevy parked outside the beach house. He got out and walked up to the door. It opened before he had chance to knock.

"Larry," Shona said, her tone emotionless.

"Shona. Chloe said it was OK to come back today. I brought this for the boy." He held out a small box of painted wooden toys he'd clearly bought from a thrift sale.

"Good morning, Larry," Chloe said after appearing in the hallway seconds later. "Come in."

"Thank you," Larry replied. He took a seat at the kitchen table next to Shona as Chloe went to fetch David.

"What are you playing at, Larry? You think I believe your act? We got nothing now other than each other. We're a family, which is more than you offered Chloe."

Larry, wearing the same creased gray suit as yesterday, looked defeated. "I know. Look, I said this to Chloe and I promised I'd say it to you too. I'm sorry for everything I did. I know you won't believe me, and I don't blame you, but I'm dying. I've got nothing left to lose now by admitting my mistakes."

Chloe appeared at the kitchen door. Behind her was a wide-eyed David, looking around her to see who the strange man in the kitchen was.

"David, go say hello. This is your grandfather. His name is Larry." Chloe brought him out from behind her and pushed him forward. "Go on, don't be shy now."

David stepped forward. Larry bit back his tears, then looked at Chloe. "He's the image of his..."

"I know," Chloe whispered, her expression broadcasting her regret at that fact.

"Well, he's grown up around you both, so I know he's been well loved. He'll be OK," Larry said to Shona, who raised an eyebrow. "Come here, boy. See what I got you."

David edged closer and looked into the box. "Can I play with the red one?" he said, pointing at a wagon near the top.

"Why, sure you can. Here." Larry fished into the box and handed his grandson the wagon. David beamed and began rolling it up the back of the wooden chair Larry was sitting in.

"David, no. On the ground," Chloe said.

Laughing, then coughing, Larry reached down and picked him up, seating him on his knee. David began to roll the wagon gently up Larry's arm and up to his shoulder. "I'm gonna drive wagons when I'm older."

"Is that a fact?" Larry replied, hugging him in close. "He's beautiful, Chloe. You've both done an amazing job." His eyes filled with tears.

"Grandpa, why are you sad?" David asked, looking up at him.

"I'm just sad I missed out on this, that's all. But, um, they're happy tears. Yeah, happy tears."

"Hey, why don't we take a picnic down to the beach? You can show off your new ball, David. Would you like that?" Shona's suggestion surprised and delighted Chloe in equal measure.

"You mean...?" Larry began.

"Yeah. All of us."

Shona left the kitchen to go into the bedroom to get David's sun hat, closely followed by Chloe.

"Are you sure? I mean. I'd understand if you..."

"Look," Shona replied, "as much as I wanna hate him, and I do, he's your father, and David's grandfather and he's dying. And you're right, he does seem different somehow. Maybe, in the time you guys have left, you can make peace. Perhaps he can even be a father for once."

"When I was in my first week in jail, they paired me up in a cell with a black man. Oscar, his name was. Oscar Jefferson the Third." Larry let out a chuckle. "At first I was surprised they'd put a man with my reputation in with a negro. I think they thought it'd be funny." He sat forward and clasped his hands around his knees as he looked out onto the ocean. Up ahead on the shoreline, David and Shona were kicking a soccer ball to each other. "Oscar looked after me that week, when the others had an axe to grind with me. I'll always be grateful for that."

"Is he still in there?" Chloe asked, handing him another bottle of soda.

"Yeah. They had him on a charge for every crime in the area the local police couldn't solve. I doubt he'll ever get out. But he helped me when I got sick and brought me food when I couldn't make the journey down to the food hall. He was a good man." He took a long sip of his soda, then coughed.

"Have you seen a doctor recently?"

"Nothing they can do. It's in my lungs. They'll give out soon, so I gotta make every day count." He looked at his daughter.

"What was that?" Shona breathed, rushing up to them, closely followed by Cooper and David.

"I was telling Chloe here that I'm a changed man. I don't wanna fight anymore. I just wanna see out my days around the people I love."

"You should stay here," Shona said.

"Really?" Larry's grey eyes beamed.

"Yeah. We got a spare room you can have until..." She paused. "If anyone in town wants to make an issue out of it, I'll say I'm sleeping on the couch."

"Thank you, Shona. I don't deserve your generosity. But I'm very grateful for it." Larry reached out his hand for Shona to shake.

"Everyone deserves a second chance at a family." Shona's eyes misted over for a moment. "We should go back in, it's getting late. David will want food."

They arrived back at the house. Shona's grin slid off her face. Chloe pulled her arm. "What's the matter?"

Shona stood frozen on the spot, her nose high in the air. "You smell that?"

Chloe sniffed and stared back in panic at Shona.

"Gasoline?"

Noticing the front door at the end of the hallway was ajar, Larry walked ahead of them, looking from side to side trying to find the cause of the smell. Reaching the door, he looked to his left and recoiled. "What the hell are you doing here?"

Chloe and Shona ran up behind him and looked into the room. There, sitting in an armchair in the farthest corner of the room, shrouded in the darkness created by the closed drapes, sat Kyle.

"Well now, isn't this a cozy little reunion," he drawled. "I must admit Larry is a bit of bonus. Must be my lucky day." As he spoke, his eyes moved to the armrest of the chair on which he sat. There stood a tiny silver object.

A lighter.

~

"Chloe, you and Shona take the boy and go. Get in your truck, now," Larry ordered, his breath almost abandoning him as he spoke.

"No," Kyle barked. "Oh no you don't." He flicked open the top of his lighter. "One strike and boom. This whole room will light up."

"What the hell do you want, Kyle?" Larry said, trying to keep calm for the sake of David, who was looking over at his father.

"Well, first I wanna know why I had to get my parents to pay thousands of dollars to get me out yet you, without a penny to your name anymore, and who did much worse than me, are standing as free as a bird right now."

"You should have gone away for the rest of your life, Kyle. My evidence should have made that happen. Always were a spoiled little rich boy, weren't you?" Larry stepped forward into the living room. Chloe and Shona didn't dare move, with Kyle's beady eyes darting between Larry and them. "Let the girls go. Your argument is with me, not them."

"Oh, father of the year now, are we? From what Eleanor said last week, you'll be dead soon anyway."

"What? You've been to see my mother?" Chloe gasped, then rolled her eyes. "Of course you have. It all makes sense now." She turned to Shona. "The allegations."

"What I don't understand is why he gets to see my son, but I don't." Kyle pointed his lighter precariously at them, his thumb grazing against the flint.

Chloe tried to keep her voice as even as possible. "Kyle. Please put down the lighter and we can ta—"

Shona, her mouth clenched, threw herself towards Kyle, but Larry held her back. Pressing his face into hers, he held her arms tight. "No, Shona. That's exactly what he wants."

"I'm gonna kill him, Larry. Get out of my way!" Shona shrieked, but stopped dead when she saw Kyle strike the flint.

"Let's all calm down, shall we?" Kyle said, the lighter now glowing with a bright yellow flame.

"Momma, what's that man doing with the fire?" David whispered up to Chloe.

"Nothing, baby, he's just leaving."

Kyle glared at her. "Hey David. Has your momma told you I'm your father?"

Chloe froze. Shona groaned and leaned against the doorframe. David tugged on Chloe's arm again. "Momma?"

"I think it's time we told him how the world works." Kyle shifted his dark stare from Chloe and softened it towards his son as he leaned forward in his armchair. "You see, kids have a mommy *and* a daddy. Would you like that? Would you like a daddy?" Kyle clicked the lighter shut and kneeled in front of David, holding his forearms.

"I like Shona," David replied. He wriggled out of Kyle's grasp and snuggled into Shona's open arms.

"You need to go, Kyle. Now. Your allegations didn't work, and neither will this. It's over," Shona snarled.

Chloe, Shona and Larry formed a wall between Kyle and David, their faces stern and unwavering.

A grin spread across Kyle's face. "I've poured gasoline where you're *all* standing." He clicked open the lighter. "If I can't have my son, then none of you can and yes, I will do it."

As if in slow motion, he ran his thumb over the flint wheel and threw the lighter on the ground. In an instant, a searing blue flame had engulfed the floorboards between them, the drapes now completely ablaze. Everybody jumped back in complete shock to avoid the fireball that had now brought the drapes, and the pole, crashing down.

Chapter 46

"Get out of here, now!" Larry yelled as the flames caught the bottom of the armchair nearest to the door.

"I can't see anything," Chloe spluttered, choking on the acrid black smoke. Blinded by the heat, she reached out to try and find Shona and David, but Larry grabbed her first and threw her towards the front door. "No, Larry, I need to find Shona."

"I'm here," Shona yelled back. Through the flames Chloe could just about make out Shona and David huddling together in the far corner of the room, their hands shielding their faces from the unbearable heat. "I'll get David out, baby, you just go. Now."

"I'm not leaving you," Chloe bellowed back from the hallway, just as the first of the ceiling tiles melted and crashed to the ground, blocking the living room doorway between them.

"Go," Shona ordered, then crouched to shield David from another tile falling on his head. "I'll pass David through the window."

"We gotta go, Chloe." Larry yanked his daughter's arm and threw her onto the veranda outside the front door.

"Shona! Where are you? I can't see you!" Chloe screamed,

but the flames licked without mercy around the door, stopping her from getting back in. Seconds later, the door frame collapsed. In sheer desperation, Chloe banged her hands against the front window even though the glass was red hot and burning her palms. Tears streaming with utter panic for Shona and David, she looked around the veranda for something to smash the glass with, but Larry pulled her aside. He was struggling to breathe through the thick black smoke.

"Look out!" he roared.

The windows blew out above them and flames cascaded all around the peeling blue wooden frames. As the smoke cleared, Chloe looked through to see Shona huddled in the corner waiting for her opportunity to make a run for the window. David was wrapped tightly in her arms.

"Shona, now," Chloe ordered, seeing a break in the flames.

Shona leaped over in one bound. "Quick, grab the boy." She lifted David through the shattered window, avoiding the shards of melting glass.

"Momma," David coughed, his little face black with soot.

"I got you, baby." Chloe clutched on to David with one arm, her other not letting go of Shona's forearm. Turning to her father, she passed David over to him, then looked back at Shona. "Now you, come on."

As Shona lifted her foot onto the window frame, a pair of strong hands pulled her back.

"Not so fast there," Kyle growled, grabbing on to the bottom of Shona's shirt.

"Get the fuck off me, you fucking animal!"

"Kyle, no. Shona!" Chloe tried to hold on to Shona's hands, but the heat had made both hands too slick with sweat. "Oh God, Shona, no!" Chloe wailed as their fingertips slipped away from each other. "I'm so sorry."

Shona was gone. The last glimpse Chloe had of her was her

disappearing back into the living room, with Kyle's forearm wrapped around her neck.

～

"No, Chloe, I forbid it. You are not going back in there—it's too dangerous. Think about your son!" Larry bellowed over the noise of another batch of tiles melting away from the ceiling and smashing on the floor inside the house. Moments later, the gutter on one side of the roof crashed to the decking inches away from him and Chloe. David was now safely sitting in the truck parked twenty feet away from the house.

"I will not leave her to burn alive in there. I will never leave her!" Chloe screamed back, her soot-covered face a sweaty mess. Using her shirt to shield her eyes, she looked through the window and through the flames, which had eased off a little now that the direction of the breeze had changed. Squinting, she could just about make out the figure of Kyle lying on the floor with blood seeping from his forehead, a desk lamp smashed into pieces by his side. Three feet away in the corner, with smashed tiles burning at her feet, Shona lay slumped next to the couch.

"Shona, get up, goddamn it. Come on, baby, please hear me."

Shona jerked her head and opened her eyes. She held her hand to her brow, the sight of Chloe reinvigorating her enough to drag herself to her feet using the armrest of the couch for leverage. She launched towards the window but was beaten back by another wave of flames reignited by a gust of ocean air.

Kyle started stirring on the ground by Shona's feet as she tried to see a way she could get out. Encouraged by Chloe's shouts, Shona staggered for the window.

"Shona, give me your arms," Larry ordered, reaching out for her. But just as she did so, the towering figure of Kyle appeared

297

behind her. He stood motionless, like he had risen from the dead, his bloodshot eyes murderous in his soot-covered face.

"Shona, quick!" Chloe screamed.

As Shona launched her body through the window towards Larry's outstretched arms, Kyle shot out his hand and clamped it around her shoulder.

"You're coming to hell with me, bitch," he growled in her ear as Shona grabbed desperately for anything to stop her from being dragged backwards again.

Struggling to breathe through smoke and through the struggle that ensued, Larry held on to her hands as long as his depleting strength could manage it, but he lost his grip and she disappeared into the dark smoke again.

"No," Chloe sobbed uncontrollably. She would have thrown herself through the window into the fire if Larry hadn't wrapped his arms around her.

"No, Chloe. Go sit with the boy, comfort him. I'm going around the back to find a way in."

Wiping the blood he'd coughed up on his shirt sleeve, Larry staggered off along the veranda and around the back of the house. There, he found Kyle lying on the ground. Shona was nowhere to be seen.

"Where is she, you bastard?" Larry growled, crouching down next to him and grabbing him by his jacket lapels. Shaking him until he came to, Larry repeated his question.

Kyle raised a limp arm. "In there. The bitch can burn."

Larry threw him back down to the ground after punching him square in the face. He took in the biggest breath his failing lungs could manage and raced into the house, seconds later recoiling as a huge wall of flames pinned him back against the bannisters. While he waited for it to clear, he looked through the destroyed front door frame at Chloe outside, his heart breaking with regret at all the things he hadn't had the chance to say.

"I'll get her back for you. I promise," he whispered to himself, then disappeared into the smoke.

~

An almighty crunch echoed through the air. Chloe watched in horror as the roof of their beautiful beach house completely gave way. She ran around to the back of the house, most of which still stood intact.

"Please. Please. Just a few seconds more," she begged.

As she heard a splintering sound, Chloe's eyes were drawn up to the center of the roof where she saw it had started to sag. Time seemed to stand still, all sounds around her muffled, but the inevitable happened moments later. As the roof collapsed inward, a huge plume of fire, smoke and dust flew up. It was hopeless. Sinking to the ground in agony, Chloe screamed Shona's name over and over again.

"Momma, Momma!" David appeared by her side, pulling on her arm to get her off the ground. Cooper barked and nudged her until she came to her senses.

"Baby, why are you out of the truck? I told you to stay in the truck," Chloe barked at David.

"I wanted to help. Where's Shona?" David's question made Chloe break out into fresh sobs. She grabbed hold of him and hugged him tight.

"Baby, I'm so sorry. Shona's gone. I couldn't save her."

David looked over her shoulder and pointed. "No, but Grandpa did."

Chloe turned around to see the back door wide open and her father staggering towards them carrying Shona's motionless body.

"Shona!" Chloe cried, running over to catch her father before he slumped to the ground, his energy all but gone. He dropped to his knees and laid Shona as gently as he could on the ground. She wasn't breathing.

"Come on, baby, please. Wake up." Chloe shook her and breathed into her mouth over and over again until finally Shona coughed and rolled into her arms. She opened her eyes, the blueness of them contrasted starkly with the red rawness of the whites.

"David. Where's...?" Shona croaked.

"Shhhh... It's OK, it's OK. Don't try to talk. David's safe, thanks to you. You saved him." Chloe stroked her hair to fully rouse her. Shona lifted her head to see David sitting with Cooper at the far end of the yard next to the little fishing boat.

"Thank God," Shona breathed before sitting up and wrapping herself in the safety of Chloe's arms.

"Get down," Larry cried out and pushed them both back down to the ground. Before Shona and Chloe realized what was happening, a bullet had whizzed through the air and struck Larry on the right side of his chest, sending him crashing to the ground next to them with blood seeping out onto his blue shirt. Chloe looked over to where the shot had come from and saw Kyle drop the gun, almost dead himself. She watched as he staggered forward a few steps and collapsed. His usually neat hair was a matted mess, his handsome face grimy from the smoke.

"You bastard, Kyle!" Chloe screamed, jumping up and running over to him. She kicked the gun he had just fired out of his hand. It landed with a thud in the grass five feet away. He grabbed her ankle as she leaped to retrieve the gun.

"Oh no you don't. Come here," Kyle growled.

Crawling her way along towards them, inch by inch, Shona kept her eyes fixed on Chloe and Kyle wrestling on the ground. Chloe's fingertips were agonizingly close to reaching the gun and with one swift kick to his groin she managed to free her ankle from his cloying grip. Standing tall, gun in hand, Chloe aimed it down to him.

"No, Chloe, don't. He's not worth it, he's not worth it," Shona spluttered before coughing up a globule of blood.

"You won't shoot that thing. You don't know how to," Kyle mocked, his stare piercing.

Looking once at Shona out of the corner of her eye, then at her father who wasn't moving, Chloe returned her attention to Kyle.

Without flinching, Chloe cocked the gun and fired into his ankle. He let out a screech of agony, then smirked. "Go on then, do it. Finish me off. And when they prove *you* killed me, you'll go away for a long, long time. David won't have a mother or a father, and Shona won't have you either. I win. Do it. Go on, I dare you to fucking do it." He rolled over, his resolve melting into blistering pain as he clutched his shattered ankle.

Still aiming the gun at Kyle, Chloe paced backwards over to her father. After kneeling down next to him, she began to sob, her free hand trying to staunch the flow of blood from his chest. "Don't leave me now. Please. We've got so much to still talk over." Chloe's face screwed up with the agony of losing her father right in front of her.

Larry opened his weary eyes and looked up at his daughter, a sad smile on his ashen face. Out of the corner of his eye, he saw a movement that made him push Chloe back. Kyle had reached into his inside pocket and taken out a knife. He rolled on to his other side, and aimed towards Shona instead, who was almost lifeless and only feet away, but it was too far for Chloe to reach her in time.

"Time to die, bitch." Kyle brought his arm back to launch the knife at Shona.

"No!" Chloe yelled, and squeezed the trigger with all her might.

Kyle's body slammed back into the ground, the bullet

lodged in his forehead. The knife in his hand dropped like a stone in the grass beside him.

The air fell silent, the flames continuing to consume the house. Shona had dragged herself off the grass and on all fours over to David to check him over. Returning to her father's side, Chloe heaved him up into her arms.

"You're all safe now, Chloe," Larry whispered into her ear. "That bastard's gone for good now." He licked his dry lips. "Listen to me carefully. Put the gun in my hand, now. Do it."

"Why?" Chloe face puzzled.

"Just do it. We don't have time. Let me do this one thing for you."

Chloe placed the gun in Larry's limp hand. He lifted his arms, aiming the gun at the Kyle's corpse. He pulled the trigger, the bullet thudding into the body. They sat quiet for a second in shock. Chloe looked at her father.

"They'll think it was me, they'll match it to me." Larry was whispering now. "Just tell the sheriff I shot Kyle. No one will question you." Larry gently pinched Chloe's chin and pulled her face close to his own. "Go be with Shona. Be happy together, always. You're a beautiful family. I love you, Chloe. I'm so sorry. I shoulda been a better father. You deserved it... I'm sorry...for...everything."

He fell limp in her arms, his bloodied chest no longer moving.

"Daddy, no," Chloe sobbed, her face buried into his neck.

Chapter 47

The house was an unrecognizable lump of charcoal against the setting sun when the fire service finally arrived. Sheriff Everett sat down next to Chloe on the end of the upturned rowboat at the far end of the yard as they watched the coroner place two black body bags into the back of his truck. At the other side of the yard, Minnie was sitting with David who she'd wrapped up in the blanket the medics had given her. In the back of the ambulance Shona was also wrapped in a blanket, her burned hands bandaged.

"Sheriff, I need to tell you what happened," Chloe began. Everett shushed her and shook his head.

"It's pretty clear to me, ma'am. That asshole Chambers tried to kill you in your own home and your father got there first to try to protect you. Chambers then attacked your father. As clear a case of self-defense as I ever saw. That's the way of it, right?"

"What?" Chloe whispered. Fresh tears of shock and exhaustion trailed down her face.

Everett let out a long breath and set his lips. "You're probably still in shock, so I'll assume you agree. Chambers was a piece of work, wasn't he? Pissed off a lot of people. Creepy son of a bitch too. If you ask me, it's good riddance to bad rubbish.

Your father's a goddamn hero!" He stood up and offered his hand to help Chloe. "Alright, well, let's get you all to a hotel for the night." He left her to attend to Shona and walked over to the two officers who were finishing up their notes on the scene.

"Boss, there's something here that doesn't add up. This guy, Kyle Chambers, was shot three times. One in the head, one in the ankle and a third in the torso."

"And?" Everett said, his hands on his hips.

"Well, sir, it would appear that the bullets came from different angles at different times, so maybe it wasn't self-defense? The old guy, the one you said shot Mr. Chambers, wasn't able to move, not with his injuries, and where they said he was when the first shot happened doesn't make sense with the bullet trajectory, so what does that mean?" The young officer looked perplexed as he scratched his head with the eraser end of his pencil.

"Listen," Everett said sternly. "It all makes perfect sense to me. We found the gun in the hands of the old guy, right? Write the report how I say to write it, OK?" He fixed his stare intently at the young cop who nodded with obedience.

Chloe walked over to Shona who had climbed out of the back of the ambulance and was talking to Minnie. "Sheriff Everett says he'll drive us to a hotel for the night," she announced, wrapping her arms around Shona, who winced.

"Nonsense," Minnie replied. "You will all stay with me tonight and for as long as you need to."

"Thank you, Minnie," Shona said, her voice still croaky from the smoke damage.

Shona took one last look at the smoldering house, then at the body bags in the truck. "Our beautiful home, Chloe. It's all gone."

"I know," Chloe whispered back. "But we have each other. And now, we're safe."

Chapter 48

Sitting on the beach the next morning, looking up at the blackened and twisted remains of their once-beautiful beach house, Shona wiped a tear from her eye. Moments later, Chloe sank down next to her with David on her lap.

"Maybe this wasn't the place for us after all? The town will never accept us now that our secret's out. Kyle couldn't keep his mouth shut. We should just finally understand that and go."

"Go where?" Shona replied, her wet eyelashes intensifying her deep blue-eyed stare.

"San Francisco, maybe? Or Illinois, now they've passed that new law."

"I can't fight anymore, Chloe. I'm done," Shona said, burying her head in her hands. "They've beaten me."

"Um...I'm not so sure about that. Look." Chloe clasped Shona's hand and pointed to the driveway, where several cars were now pulling up, led by Minnie's Toyota.

Clamoring off the sand, Chloe, with Shona trudging behind, ran towards Minnie, who had stepped out of her car.

"Minnie? What's going on? Who are all these people?"

"Well, I got to talking, and well, it turns out that quite a few folks around town were none too happy about two of their own suffering such a tragedy, especially after everything Shona has done for people, with the garage, so..." Minnie smiled and turned to face the men and women walking over towards them. "John here's gonna oversee the rebuild—"

"The *what*?" Shona piped up, confused as she looked at a man she recognized from the diner, tipping his cap to them as he walked past and over to the wreckage.

"Hey girl," Bertie's familiar drawl sounded behind John. "The old gal mentioned you might need a little bit of help over here, so we all decided to pitch in. Figure you guys needed some muscle, so I brought the others." She flicked her head towards Dee, Lula, Edie and Alice, who were standing by, armed to the teeth with hammers and nail boxes sticking out of brand new-looking tool belts. They waved, with Dee blowing a kiss towards Bertie. Shona raised her eyebrows.

"Oh yeah. We're kinda seeing each other now. She's helping me write letters to the authorities, encouraging me to use my words, not my fists this time, to get people to acknowledge our rights. Never thought I'd ever again find someone to..." She broke off and swallowed.

Sensing her discomfort at showing her feelings, Shona thumped her on the arm. "Put up with your shit?" she said, then grinned.

"Watch it, blondie," Bertie replied, then grinned also.

"Are they serious? They're gonna help us rebuild?" Chloe asked, her eyes wide.

"Yes, Chloe," Minnie replied. "Looks like you're all gonna have to stick around here a little bit longer."

EPILOGUE

C hloe sat on the newly fitted porch swing and breathed in a huge lungful of spring ocean air. Inside the beautiful new house, David was with Shona. He'd been washed, his hair neatly combed, and he was wearing smart blue shorts and a white shirt. Shona was kneeling in front of him, straightening his tie.

"So, how's your new preschool teacher? I heard she's real nice," she asked, looking up at him.

"She's alright. Not as pretty as Miss Adamson, though. And we don't have a cookie jar anymore, but I guess Mrs. Bradshaw is OK."

Shona stroked David's cheek, sweeping off a little cookie crumb. "All for the best, then," she said with a smile. She stood up and inspected David. "So, you know what you have to say when you get outside, don't you?"

"Yeah. You told me already."

"OK. I'll give you a minute or so, then I'll come out. Here's the tray. Don't drop it." Shona pointed at David.

"I won't," David called back, heading out of the door. Three seconds later, there was a crash.

"Every time," Shona whispered to herself, then smiled.

She found David outside on the freshly painted white veranda staring down at spilled coffee and toast strewn around the planks.

"Uh-oh," he said, looking up red-faced at Shona.

"What on earth was that noise?" Chloe shouted out from around the corner.

David and Shona looked at each other, their eyes wide. "Go on, go say your line," Shona prompted as she set about picking up the broken crockery.

David walked up to Chloe, his brow furrowed as, in all the commotion, he'd forgotten the line Shona had given him. After heading back around the corner to Shona, he reappeared in front of Chloe looking a bit more confident this time.

"Can I help you, sir?" Chloe joked, seeing him dressed in his smartest clothes.

"I have an important question to ask you, Momma." He cleared his throat and opened his mouth to speak. "Um... Oh no." He turned back to the corner. "What was it I had to say again, Shona?"

Closing her eyes and sighing, Shona appeared from around the corner and ruffled David's hair. "You want something done properly, do it yourself," she said, acting weary.

Chloe laughed at the little double act playing out in front of her. She noticed Shona was also wearing her best white pants and royal blue shirt, both ironed. Her hair was freshly washed and combed, her skin glowing. "What's going on with you two stunners?"

"I remember now. Shona's got something to show you. I had to ask you to come down to the beach, where she was gonna meet you, but I messed it up." David looked downcast until Shona scooped him up in her arms and threw him on her back. Clinging on to her like a spider monkey, David giggled.

"What have you got to show me?" Chloe's eyes were full of curiosity.

"Come with me." Shona took Chloe by the hand and led her down to the beach. In the distance Chloe could just about make out a towel lying on the sand, with a picnic basket and a parasol. As they got closer, she saw Cooper lying on the towel with a red ribbon around his yellow fluffy neck. He stood up and then sat down, his long wet tongue hanging out.

"I wanted to bring you here because it was the place I'd always dreamed that one day I would do this." She reached down and removed something dangling from Cooper's silk ribbon.

Chloe gasped as Shona took in a deep breath, then bent down on one knee before her.

"I love you, Chloe. More than I ever thought I'd love anyone. You are my soulmate. My everything. I wanna wake up with you every morning for the rest of my life. And I know we can't legally do this, but..." She held out a small red velvet box and opened it. Inside was a silver ring. At the center of it was a tiny, perfectly cut pink rose quartz pebble.

Chloe's eyes brimmed with tears as Shona looked up at her.

"If we could dream for a moment, pretend that it's possible." Shona paused, a lump forming in her throat. "Chloe, will you marry me?"

"Yes... Yes." Chloe sank to her knees and embraced Shona, kissing her with abandon. David squealed and clapped.

They both reached out to grab Cooper and David and sat back on the white sand, listening to the clear Californian ocean lapping against the shore with tears of complete love. Looking up behind them at the bright white beach house glistening in the morning sunlight, they knew in their hearts they were both finally free.

They were finally home.

JOIN IN!

We'd love to invite you to join in with our ongoing adventures. In our newsletter, you will receive regular behind-the-scenes updates, beta reading opportunities, giveaways and much, much more!

Simply visit the site below and enter your email address so we know where to send your newsletter:

www.hackneyandjones.com

Don't forget to leave your feedback on Amazon for the books.

ALSO BY VICKY JONES AND CLAIRE HACKNEY

Shona: Book 1

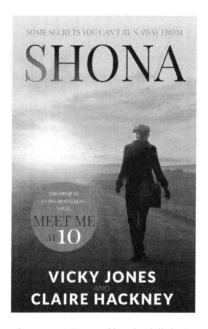

Everyone has a secret. Hers could get her killed... Mississippi, 1956. Shona Jackson knows two things—how to repair car engines and that her dark childhood secret must stay buried. On the run from Louisiana, she finds shelter in the home of a kindly old lady and a job as a mechanic. But a woman working a man's job can't avoid notice in a small town. And attention is dangerous, especially when it comes from one woman in particular...

Meet Me At 10: Book 2

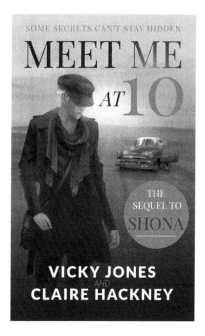

Four lives inextricably linked. Will tragic events part them forever? Shona Jackson is on the run again, forced to flee Mississippi and the town she'd called home. Arriving in Alabama, to continue her journey to safety, she convinces Jeffrey Ellis, the wealthy co-owner of a machinery plant, to give her a job. But when Chloe Bruce returns from college and is introduced to the workforce, there are devastating consequences for all those involved.

ALSO BY VICKY JONES AND CLAIRE HACKNEY

The Burying Place: Book 1

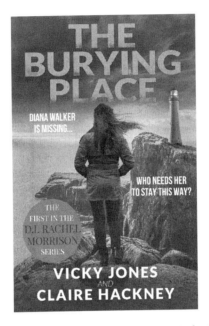

One high-profile case. No leads. No witnesses... And no body.
Amanda Walker's mother is missing. Detective Inspector
Rachel Morrison has no leads on the case and time is running
out. Amanda appeals to the public, but when no one comes
forward, she chooses to immerse herself within a murderous
underground group she believes is responsible for her mother's
disappearance. But will the group believe Amanda's cover
story? Or is time running out for her as well?

ALSO BY VICKY JONES

Bucket List Book I: Project Me, Project You

"Writing this book changed my life. Reading it could change yours." Back in 2011, suffering depression after leaving the Royal Navy, author and songwriter Vicky Jones embarked upon a life-changing bucket list, including 300 things to tick off over the course of the next decade of her life. This is the story of how this list came about, how it has helped her combat her depression, and how it can help you too.

ACKNOWLEDGMENTS

This book has been a passion project, but we couldn't have done it without all our friends and family supporting and believing in us every step of the way.

Special mention to Sharon Atkinson for being so supportive in the writing group where it all started.

Many thanks to all of our beta readers, and for all the amazing support we've received from our **Hackney and Jones** Facebook group.

OUR TEAM

Virtual Assistant:
   Erin Hodgson
   writehandwomannz@gmail.com

Book Covers by:
   WooTKdesign
   wootkdesign@gmail.com

Edited by:
   Gary Smailes
   Bubblecow.com

Proofread by:
   Melanie Bell
   inspire.envisioning@gmail.com

Printed in Great Britain
by Amazon

38876943R00206